The Baby Group

THE BABY GROUP

JADE LEE WRIGHT

JOFFE BOOKS

Joffe Books, London
www.joffebooks.com

First published in Great Britain in 2025

© Jade Lee Wright 2025

This book is a work of fiction. Names, characters, businesses, organizations, places and events are either the product of the author's imagination or are used fictitiously. Any resemblance to actual persons, living or dead, events or locales is entirely coincidental. The spelling used is British English except where fidelity to the author's rendering of accent or dialect supersedes this. The right of Jade Lee Wright to be identified as author of this work has been asserted in accordance with the Copyright, Designs and Patents Act 1988.

No part of this book may be used or reproduced in any manner for the purpose of training artificial intelligence technologies or systems. In accordance with Article 4(3) of the Digital Single Market Directive 2019/790, Joffe Books expressly reserves this work from the text and data mining exception.

Cover art by Nebojša Zorić

ISBN: 978-1-80573-139-9

For Dad, Stephen James Wright,
Who always believed in me more than anyone else. I did it,
Dad — wish you were here to see that. This is for you.

PROLOGUE

'My baby's been taken,' I weep into the phone. 'Please hurry.'

My fiancé, Alex, is keeled over the birthing pool, the water tinged pink. He's rocking back and forth, his jaw slack. His shoulders are heaving, blood from the deep gash on the side of his head coagulating, baking onto his skin in the summer heat. I can't bring myself to crawl over to him. My trembling body is weak, in shock. The weight of what has happened is smothering me. I've lost a lot of blood. Outside, the world is oddly still, as though someone hasn't just come in and upturned our entire lives.

I stare out of the living room window, searching for someone long gone. The sandy bay is bathed in a golden glow, the sun beginning to set over the water. An overpowering scent of sweet peas wafts in with the breeze, and an angry gull squawks, snapping me from my daze. I move my bloodied fingers up to my rounded stomach, holding the bump still very much there, even though the baby is not.

In the distance, a cry of sirens gets louder as the police hurtle towards our house. Alex casts his gaze to me, his eyes rimmed red. *They're on their way. They'll help us get our baby girl back*, I want to say, but I have no voice. Instead, I sit cradling my empty arms.

The police pull up outside, gravel crunching beneath tyres. Their heavy boots pound up the front steps. Before they get to the door, hanging open on its hinges, Alex snaps his head back in my direction.

'I never wanted to do antenatal classes.' He pauses, his eyes boring into mine. 'I told you that, Darcy,' he says, his voice heavy with resentment.

My heart plummets as realization dawns. Even now, he blames me.

My eyes swivel to the two police officers padded out in bulletproof vests, handcuffs dangling from their belts. That's when reality hits me. It takes a moment for my lower lip to tremble before I let out a blood-curdling, guttural wail.

**PART I
APRIL**

CHAPTER 1

Before

'Darcy, look. I've been working on this for two days now,' Debbie says, thrusting a ghastly yellow piece of knitwear at me.

'Looks great,' I say, forcing a tight smile. Placing down the book I was about to start, I rest my swollen ankles up on the coffee table.

Silence stretches, and I wait for her to fill it. The large skeleton wall clock is tick, tick, ticking the time away, the hand jolting at every roman numeral it passes by. I almost hadn't answered when I'd seen Alex's mum's face on the screen as my phone trilled. My thumb hovered over the decline button, but I must have been desperate for company, because eventually I'd swiped to answer.

'How're things going in Rock?' she asks, her expression flat.

'Well, it's not London.' I sigh, looking out at an impenetrable mist starting to settle. Heavy rainclouds are quickly rolling in, trapping me indoors for the remainder of the day.

'I could've told you that before you up and left,' she says, touching her shock of bleach-blonde hair. It's tattered and unkempt, and the whites of her eyes are yellowed as though she has jaundice. She's leaning in so close to the camera I can almost smell the permanent tang of whiskey and cigarette smoke emanating from her.

'It's just a bit of a shock to the system,' I mumble, my heart aching for the restlessness and immensity of the city. Our new home on the north coast of Cornwall is so different from our rented skyscraper apartment. This huge beach house with its delicate, calming hues and large windows framing the landscape is beautiful, but it echoes with loneliness at my every breath.

'I think you should both just admit you've made a mistake and come back,' she says. 'Clearly this new life and fresh start you were after hasn't worked out.'

I grit my teeth, glaring at her. Her words are dripping with amusement. She's enjoying this a little too much for my liking.

'It's not that simple, you know it isn't,' I say, and she rolls her eyes in response. Debbie doesn't know the real reason we left, and hopefully she never will.

Our cat, Henry, saunters in and wedges himself into a snug ball beneath my stomach. For the last few months he's clung to me, rarely leaving my side.

Alex hadn't wanted a cat. He'd said no to adopting one at first. It'd taken a lot of convincing, and he's still not entirely warmed to him. But Henry and me? We have a special bond. I tickle behind his soft ginger ears as the baby growing inside me stretches, limbs poking in every direction.

'Where's Alex? Not working again, is he?' she asks.

'Cooped up behind his desk as always,' I say, trying to sound light-hearted but failing dismally.

'You really should think about joining a local antenatal class, you know. I made some of my closest friends when I was pregnant with Alex through those classes.' There's a wistful nostalgia to her voice, making me wonder if she still has those close friends today. I've certainly never seen her anywhere else other than in her musty little lounge, alone and sipping on an Old Fashioned.

I consider her words, doubt creeping in as my eyes drift to the ebbing of the tide. The wind twirls up sand from the dunes, a storm darkening the horizon.

'I'm not sure it's Alex's thing,' I say.

'Rubbish. He'll finally make some friends of his own again. The two of you need lives separate from each other as well, you know,' she says.

Usually, I take no notice of anything Debbie says, knowing it's the alcohol talking, but now her words sting with a truth I can't ignore. We do need our own lives, our own friends. We do need to stop depending on each other so much. Antenatal classes might just be exactly what we need to kickstart our lives here.

'Harriet never pandered to him the way you do.'

I can hear her smile, and it makes me bristle. She must know bringing up his ex-wife, the one he'd married in his early twenties, is forbidden territory. Their marriage hadn't lasted long. Less than two years, Alex had said. But her presence somehow still lingered. Swallowing the words threatening to spill from my lips, I bite my cheek until I draw blood, the metallic taste a welcome distraction.

As she drones on, her words blur. I toss in a grunt here and there, just enough to feign attention. Five minutes in, I push out of the armchair and pad down the cold tiles into the kitchen. On my way I glance up the stairs to where Alex is still hammering away at his keyboard. The missing Nescafé pods by the coffee machine tell me he's already on his fourth cup of the day.

Propping the phone up against some old cookbooks, I lean against the cold granite countertops. The surface is sticky, scattered with sugar and breadcrumbs. I grab a damp cloth and mop up the mess Alex left behind.

'I should really get going. There's still a lot of unpacking to do,' I say to Debbie, rinsing the cloth under the hot tap.

'Don't know why you're bothering,' she says. 'Think about the classes though, please. You might find yourself really enjoying them.'

'I'll look into it,' I say, my shoulders sagging as I disconnect the call.

I wander around the room, searching for things to tidy up as I mull the idea of antenatal classes around in my head. Tacked up to the fridge, I read a scribbled message Alex has left for me to find.

I love you. You're beautiful, I'm so lucky ☺

My eyes soften as I soak up his familiar handwriting, his words flooding me with warmth. Caressing the swell of my stomach, I touch the dry ink on the curling paper.

Small traces of Alex are scattered throughout the house, the rim of his coffee cup marring the countertops in the kitchen, specks of toothpaste splattered up the bathroom mirror, his holey Calvin Klein trunks discarded on the bedroom floor. These things should annoy me, but instead I find the corners of my mouth tugging up. They're little reminders that he's here.

* * *

By eleven o'clock, the day has slipped through my fingers. Alex is still in the office, the glow from the monitor bleeding out onto the landing.

I try telling myself he's still the same man I'd met in London. The guy who'd sat down next to me on the Northern Line, striking up a conversation about what I was reading.

'Love that book,' he'd said, making me look up from my battered Jojo Moyes novel.

'Really?' I'd tilted my head at him, smirking.

He'd looked down at the garish cover, and his face had fallen.

'Uh — yes,' he'd said, faltering. 'What can I say? I'm a romantic.'

'I'm sure you are.' I'd laughed.

'Sorry. I'm not good at this,' he'd said, grimacing.

'Not good at coming up to random people on the tube?'

It had been his turn to laugh, then. 'It's not something I'm in the habit of doing, no.'

I'd waited, my fingertips fanning the pages of my book.

'I'm usually incredibly shy,' he'd admitted. 'But I couldn't not say hello to you.'

He'd made me giggle, and I was already certain my life was heading in an exciting, unexpected direction.

Thinking of the day we met calms me, and I feel every painful bite my anxiety takes from me. He is still the same guy, I tell myself. He still goes out of his way to make me feel special; he's just been so busy with work since we moved here.

When he'd told me he was a senior UX advisor, I had no idea what that meant, and even as he'd tried explaining how he creates user-friendly interfaces for apps and websites, I didn't get it. It was, and still is, a world I know nothing about. Even after all these months, I'm not entirely certain what his job entails. All I know is it keeps him very, very busy.

I'd been more than happy to change the subject to slightly less complicated things, like what I did for a living back then.

'A bit of this and that,' I'd said, enjoying the air of mystery it gave me. 'I've never really had a career. It's easier to move around that way.'

'Think you'll ever settle down?' he'd asked, and just that was enough to give me heart palpitations.

'Who knows. They'd have to be pretty special to tie me down.'

'So, that means you don't have a boyfriend?' he'd asked with a glint in his eyes as the tube had hurtled towards Camden Town.

'No, I don't,' I'd said, shaking my head. I was already laughing at our exchange, flutters beginning to build inside me.

'Excellent, then I propose I take you out.' He'd smiled at me.

'And what would we do on this date?'

'Oh, I don't know. Go to a bookshop? I could show you some books I actually *do* love.'

I'd tucked my paperback away in my Kate Spade bag and given him a once-over.

'You free now?' I'd asked him after a beat.

We'd never wound up at a bookshop. First, we'd walked through Camden Lock Market together, then we'd been lured into The Hawley Arms, where we'd had far too much to drink. The walk to my narrowboat mooring on Regent's Canal had only intoxicated me more.

'Wow, you really don't like being tied down,' he'd noted, raising an eyebrow.

'Have to move every two weeks.' I'd grinned, inviting him inside, where he'd spent the night.

Back then, just a few months ago, he'd spend every evening with me. His job had taken a backseat. A lot has changed in such a short space of time.

Sometimes it makes me wonder what things would be like if that condom hadn't split. When I'd first noticed something warm dripping down my inner thighs, I'd panicked. I'd been scared to tell him, but I shouldn't have been. Alex hadn't even flinched. He'd taken my hands in his, promising me we'd get through everything together, and he'd kept to his word. The guy from the London Underground had become my rock and, very quickly, my family.

* * *

I dog-ear the page of the book I've all but inhaled and start thinking about Debbie's suggestion.

Could I really make lifelong friends from an antenatal group? The idea of practising how to put a nappy on a teddy bear (like that has any similarity to wrestling a wriggling baby) makes me laugh. My curiosity wins though, and I find myself googling classes in the area.

I blink in surprise as a class starting next week appears on my screen, and then again at the price. I can't afford this. It's something I'd need to ask Alex to help pay for. I'm about to exit the page in defeat when he drags his feet through the bedroom door. He's fresh from the bathroom, face washed and teeth brushed, ready for bed. I drop the phone to my lap, smiling up at him.

Deep grooves hang beneath his eyes, becoming a permanent feature. His beard is unruly, his coffee-stained shirt crumpled, begging for a wash.

'Hey,' he says softly, leaning over to kiss me on the forehead. His minty breath prickles the skin on my neck as his lips venture to my collarbone.

'Hey,' I say. 'Thanks for the note in the kitchen today.'

'You're even more beautiful without makeup.' He smiles, his hand grazing over my freshly washed face.

'I missed you today,' I admit, a blush working its way onto my cheeks.

'How much?'

A grin plays at the corner of his mouth as he eases his way on top of me. My legs wrap around his skinny waist, and I pull him closer, connecting us like two puzzle pieces. Instead of answering, I let my body show him just how much I've missed him. Our need for each other is all consuming.

***

'Alex,' I whisper, my fingers lacing through his chest hair, re-familiarizing myself with the body I've neglected for months.

'Mm?'

'I want to ask you something and I need you to know I wouldn't ask if I didn't think it'd be really good for us.' I lick my lips, swollen from his kisses.

My whole body aches, raw from sex. He feels strong, sturdy beneath my touch, and I find myself wondering why it's been such a long time since we've done this.

His hand stops stroking my hair as he repositions himself, eyeing me seriously.

'What is it?'

'I think we should sign up for antenatal classes. I know it might be a bit weird, but it could be a great way to finally meet some people here. Your mum said it's how she made some of her closest friends,' I say. 'I looked into it already. It's just a bit pricey and I'm running out of savings. I was wondering if it's something you'd consider doing and helping me pay—' Alex silences me with a kiss.

'Darcy, slow down. Of course I'll pay for it if that's what you want to do.' He beams, pulling me back into his chest. Relief washes through me. If anyone knows how hard it is for me to ask someone for help, it's him.

'You'll really do this for me?'

'Yes. I'll admit, it isn't really my thing,' he says. 'I don't *want* to do it. I can't promise I'm going to enjoy it or that I won't take the piss, but I'll do it for you if it'll make you happy.'

'It will!' I laugh, lunging into him.

'God, I thought you were going to ask something way more serious,' he says. 'I overheard my mum trying to talk you out of living here earlier.'

I shake my head at him. 'She couldn't do that. This is home now,' I say. 'We're going to make it work here.'

I'm so convincing I almost believe it myself.

CHAPTER 2

On Wednesday morning Alex's priority is cleaning the car, removing the layer of salt dust coating its surface. I'm in the kitchen trying to keep myself busy brewing a cup of tea when a notification lights up my phone. I stop what I'm doing and unlock the screen.

It's an email about our antenatal classes. I stray from the kitchen out onto the veranda, reading the message eagerly.

A Warm Welcome to Our Antenatal Classes!
Firstly, congratulations on your pregnancy. It is our pleasure
to confirm your place in our upcoming classes.

WHEN:
Beginning this coming Wednesday, 17th April.
Henceforth, classes will be every Wednesday
evening from 19:00 to 20:30.

WHERE:
Rock Village Hall, Seashell Lane, Rock,
Cornwall, PL27 9FC

CLASS SCHEDULE:
Week 1: Feeding Your Baby (from breastfeeding to formula)
Week 2: Labour and Delivery (pain management and birth plans)
Week 3: Nappy Changing Workshop
Week 4: First Aid
Week 5: Bonding with Baby and Newborn Care (sleep, routines, bathing)
Week 6: Emotional Wellbeing

As you can see, Week 1 is our breastfeeding class. PLEASE NOTE THIS CLASS IS JUST FOR THE MOTHERS TO ATTEND. We intentionally structure it this way as we are well aware that many, if not all of you, hope to form friendships from this group. This is a chance for the mothers to get to know each other away from their partners. PARTNERS: don't think you're getting off lightly! You'll see attached some light reading to keep you busy during this time.

Your assigned teacher will be the experienced and lovely Emma Bonsu. Her aim is to support you and your partner throughout this special journey to parenthood, offering valuable insights and practical advice along the way.

Please click the link at the bottom of this email to join an instant messaging group chat set up for your class.

Emma looks forward to meeting you all soon.
Best Wishes,
Ashley Parker
Antenatal Class Administrator
Rock Village Hall

The email should excite me, but instead a flutter of nerves courses through me. Attending the first class by myself isn't what I'd expected. Of course I want to make friends, but this is like kicking a bird from a nest too soon.

The thought of Alex not being there daunts me, making my heart race rapidly. I consider cancelling the classes, demanding a refund. I'd assumed they would be a way to get some much-needed quality time with Alex, not more time without him.

Dispirited, I read through the weekly schedule once more, trying to collect myself. It's just one class; I can get through it alone, I tell myself.

Clicking the link at the end of the email, I accept an invitation to a private group chat. A few others have already joined, so I spend the next few minutes peering at their profile pictures. It's riveting getting a glimpse into who our potential new friends could be, but unease settles in as I compare us.

* * *

'They're all going to be married, Alex,' I say, blending bronze powder into my cheekbones.

'You're overthinking.' Alex chuckles. He's leaning against the doorframe, watching me get ready for the first class.

'Everyone's going to have questions about us though,' I say, holding my stomach protectively. 'I'm tired of people judging us wherever we go.'

'They really don't, Darcy. It's all in your head,' he says.

'Don't say that,' I snap, narrowing my eyes at him.

'People start a family without being married all the time, my love,' he whispers.

'After dating for less than a year?' I ask, my eyebrows knitting together. I glance down at my ring finger, the missing wedding ring a constant chasm between us.

'No one will notice, or care for that matter,' he says, his voice clipped. He's losing his patience, and I don't blame him. We've had this same argument on multiple occasions, but I just can't seem to help myself.

I gather up my makeup brushes, turning with a huff from the dressing table to face him. I'm ready for a fight, but the sight of him makes me groan. His joggers hang low on his hips, and without a shirt on, his chiselled frame is tantalizing. He walks up to me slowly, exhaling. I breathe out too, trying to let the worry and tension fade.

'You're just nervous,' he says softly. 'When you get there it'll all be fine, you'll see.'

He closes the space between us, touching the bun I'd scooped my hair into. I lean into him, softening.

'We *are* getting married. They'll see that.' His thumb twists the engagement ring around my finger.

'What if they ask why we left the city?'

'Lie,' he says, without hesitation. 'The past is the past. It's not going to get in the way of things here.' The smile on his face fades as he searches my eyes.

I nod slowly, unsure what else to say.

'Now go, have fun. Make some friends.' He kisses me, his hand drifting down the small of my back. 'This is what you wanted, remember?'

* * *

As I get into the car, I start to sweat, my anxiety building again. This is my chance at starting a normal life here in our home by the sea, a life with real friends. What if I mess it up? The knot in my stomach tightens at the thought of the other mothers not liking me. Will they sense I'm not normally a social creature, that I'm someone who has been living a life of solitude for what feels like the longest time?

My clammy hands tug at the outfit which took me hours to choose. I crank the air conditioning up despite the frostiness of the evening. If Alex were here, he'd put a steady hand on mine and tell me to breathe. I try to do just that, inhaling through my nose and out through my mouth for the remainder of the drive.

'You have arrived,' the satnav tells me in her singsong voice. The car park is lined with boastful wagons and SUVs, all rivalling each other for space and luxury. The black enamel of our car, sandwiched between the other vehicles like a sardine, glistens in the moonlight. I make a mental note to thank Alex for cleaning it later.

Walking up to the hall, I fight the urge to go straight back home and avoid the humiliation beyond that big timber door. A woman reaches the door before me. She's carrying a purple yoga ball under her arm and struggles as she yanks the door open. She's strawberry blonde with huge clear-rimmed glasses and a face full of sun-kissed freckles. She looks *nice*. Not the type of person I'd have expected from Rock with her mandala-print harem pants and stretchy black vest. She isn't as glamourous, as 'Chelsea-on-the-Sea', as I'd anticipated. I watch as she waddles inside.

I'm about to follow her when my attention is stolen by another woman striding confidently towards the hall. She's pushing a ginormous pair of sunglasses up her long nose, a Costa coffee cup in hand. She's so tanned she's almost orange and I notice a very expensive handbag getting swung carelessly about as she steps inside. Not wanting to be the last to arrive, I quickly scurry after them.

It's cold and dark inside, void of any kind of character. The oppressiveness of the space makes my anxiety soar. There's an older lady, who I presume to be Emma Bonsu, the teacher, setting up a bunch of chairs in the centre of the room. She bounds towards me on stumpy legs, her wiry red hair swishing against what little jawline she has. Smiling shyly, I give her my name, which she finds on her list.

'Lovely to have you. Bathrooms are down there and there's a kitchenette with some tea, coffee and biscuits if you'd like anything.' She goes back to setting up chairs.

To avoid hovering, I make my way to the kitchenette. The woman with the clear-rimmed glasses beams at me warmly when I enter the room.

'Hi, I'm Cora,' she says.

'Darcy,' I say, instantly pouring myself a mug of percolated coffee to keep myself busy.

'You struggling to stay awake too?' she asks, gesturing to my drink. Admittedly an odd choice for this hour.

'Oh, yeah. Been up since about four this morning. Baby decided that was the time for a womb party.'

Cora laughs at my joke, making me flush. Her baby bump is proudly on display, a hand resting over it as she takes a sip of the strong, bitter coffee. We meander back to the main room where another woman with a pixie cut has arrived, looking as nervous as I feel.

'We're still waiting for two more to join us, but if you wouldn't mind all taking a seat in the meantime,' Emma says, gesturing towards the chairs.

I sit next to Cora, perched on her yoga ball. She starts a slow, rhythmic bounce.

'Hi, I'm Rachel,' the woman with the fake tan says, having materialized from the bathroom. She sits down on my other side.

'Darcy. Nice bag.'

'Oh, thanks. Hubby did good. Wedding present.' She waggles her ring finger at me. It's dripping with diamonds. I discreetly tuck my vastly less impressive engagement ring out of sight.

Emma glances down at her smartwatch. The other two still haven't arrived. 'It's past seven o'clock now, so we best get started,' she says.

At that moment the door to the hall bursts open. A lanky blonde with abnormally large dove-grey eyes and a mousy brunette with no makeup scuttle in. The blonde has a waxen face, and everything about her is plain and reserved besides a pair of leather sandals, shimmering with cut crystals. Her heels clack on the floorboards as she makes her way over to us. They're the only sign she's undoubtedly a Rock local. The brunette is hunched over herself and has droopy eyes that scan the room.

One of her slender manicured hands pulls out a chair directly opposite me. She doesn't make eye contact as she takes a seat.

'Sorry we're late,' the blonde says.

'That's alright. You two know each other?' Emma asks.

'Oh, no. We just met outside.'

'Okay then. So, I'm Emma and I'll be hosting these antenatal classes every Wednesday evening for the next six weeks,' she says. 'I thought to get everyone acquainted we could start by going around the circle introducing ourselves and share what we're most excited for with this pregnancy before I put you in pairs for a fun activity.'

'Oh joy,' Rachel mutters under her breath, just loud enough for me to hear. I stifle a giggle, stealing a glance in her direction. She sips at her cup of coffee to hide the smile spreading across her face.

The brunette goes first, introducing herself as Carmen. Her baby bump is hardly visible beneath the oversized cotton maxi dress she's wearing. She makes a joke about how she's looking forward to not being pregnant anymore. Her words are met with a peal of laughter. We all nod in unison, a shared unanimity binding us together.

'I'm Violet.' The woman with the pixie cut introduces herself next, a posh twang to her accent. She's radiating a nervous energy, her hand persistently stroking at her stomach. 'Like Carmen, just not being pregnant anymore would be great. I want to sleep on my back again and have some sushi.'

I zone out while Cora and Rachel introduce themselves, my eyes travelling over the women I've been paired with. Out of everyone currently pregnant in Rock, these are the women I'll be experiencing the journey to motherhood with.

My defensiveness spikes at their weighed-down ring fingers, perfect highlights and extortionately priced clothing and accessories. I'm judging them before I've even got to know them because of my own insecurities, and I'm not proud of it. Guilt bubbles to the surface of my skin, seeping from every pore. I duck my head in an attempt to hide the envy. This isn't what I'd have been like years ago, before everything that happened to me.

When Emma turns her attention to me, it takes me a second to realize it's my turn. Blood rushes to my cheeks. All eyes are on me. I lick my lips and clear my throat, hoping I don't trip over my words.

'Hi, everyone, I'm Darcy,' I say, like I'm at some sort of AA meeting. 'I guess I'm just excited to have a family. I don't have parents or siblings, so starting a family of my own is really special for me.'

I'm not expecting the emotions that skitter up my back the way they do. I haven't spoken about myself or my past in so long that it feels almost like a release. I blink furiously, trying not to cry.

When I look up, sympathy is written across everyone's faces. I clench my jaw, holding back the urge to scream. I didn't say it to make anyone feel sorry for me. I didn't even really know I was going to say what I'd said until the words tumbled out.

'I'm Lucy.' The lanky blonde's voice slices through the silence. 'Thanks, Darcy, for sharing that. It had me tearing up.' She dabs at those ginormous grey eyes.

'Blame the pregnancy hormones!' Violet chimes in.

'My husband and I are just excited about becoming—' Before Lucy can finish her sentence, her voice breaks. She sniffs and looks up at the ceiling, heavy tears falling down her cheeks.

'It's okay, take your time,' Emma says encouragingly.

Everyone sits in a tender silence waiting for Lucy to collect herself. I shift uncomfortably in my seat, wishing it didn't feel like she'd just stolen my thunder.

'We're both just excited about becoming parents. It's been a long, hard process to get here,' she admits, smiling demurely.

Cora passes her a tissue, which she uses to mop up her tears. Some of the others have welled up, too. Even after my initial jealousy, a deep ache nestles in my chest for Lucy as I imagine her story. Struggling to fall pregnant isn't something I'd know anything about.

The level of empathy within the group after less than ten minutes together is astounding. I guess that's what you get when you put a bunch of hormonal pregnant women in a room together. But still, there's a hopefulness at the prospect that this really could be the start of something life changing. These people I've been so quick to judge could actually have the potential to become lifelong friends, just like Alex's mum said.

I realize in a moment of clarity that these women, Cora, Rachel, Violet, Carmen and Lucy, are all more than their fancy cars, expensive handbags and diamond-laden ring fingers. Electrified, I can't stop my smile from growing. This is my chance. This could be the start of my happily ever after I've been romanticizing about since moving to Cornwall.

'Thank you for sharing that, Lucy,' Emma says, working a crocheted breast in her hands like a stress ball. 'As you can tell, you all have very different stories and reasons for joining these classes, but you all have one thing in common. In about two months' time, all of you will be first-time mothers. This group is going to help teach you some of the basics you need to know to keep that little human alive, but it's also going to do more than that. This group is going to be your support system. Over the next six weeks you will get to know each other, bond with one another as you all prepare for the arrival of your first baby.'

Emma looks at each of us individually, smiling. 'Now, let's chat breastfeeding.'

CHAPTER 3

Emma blows stock photos up on a projector screen, making them pixelate and blur. She stops on a picture of a syringe filled with yellow liquid.

'Anyone know what's inside that syringe?' she asks, looking around the group.

We all shake our heads.

'It's colostrum, the first breast milk your body produces during pregnancy. I like to call it the Golden Liquid because of its colour. It's usually yellower than breast milk,' she tells us. 'It's full of nutrients beneficial for your baby's immune system. For the first few days after birth, it's what your baby drinks before your actual breast milk comes in, but you can start harvesting it from week thirty-seven of pregnancy.' She passes around a big bag of syringes, telling us to take as many as we like. I grab a handful and stuff them into my bag.

'Don't be disheartened if you're only able to collect small amounts of colostrum, either. Any amount is fantastic. Babies need less than a teaspoon of it to fill themselves up and get the benefits,' Emma says with a smile.

'Sorry to interrupt, but if we're planning on not breastfeeding, is colostrum still important?' Rachel asks.

'Yes! We'll get onto formula feeding in just a moment. The choice is yours at the end of the day, but even if you are going to bottle-feed and use formula, all babies can benefit from colostrum. You can freeze it in these syringes and use it when they're unwell or put it in their bath if they have a rash. There's so much you can do with it!' Emma's eyes gleam enthusiastically.

'Now, hand expressing is done by making a C shape with your thumb and fingers, like this,' she says, using the crocheted breast to demonstrate. 'Then squeeze the area around your nipple slowly and steadily so you create a rhythm. It's not common, but if you want your partner involved, they can help by getting ready with those syringes and catch the liquid being expressed.'

The thought of Alex syringing something from my nipples is probably the least sexy and fun thing I can imagine us getting up to at night. *We're definitely entering a new phase in our relationship*, I think to myself as I squirm in my seat.

I glance around the room, wondering if everyone else is thinking the same thing, but they all seem completely engrossed in everything Emma's saying.

* * *

'How was it?' Alex asks when I get home.

'Interesting. I learnt a lot about boobs I didn't know before,' I say, watching him squeeze bubbles into the bath he's drawn for me.

'I'm sure you'll fill me in on that later.' He laughs. 'What about the group? Were the girls nice?'

'Again, interesting,' I say. 'We're all very different people. There's this one girl, Cora. She seems nice. Rachel's pretty glam, a typical Rock local, y'know?'

Alex nods, swirling the water around in the bath.

'Violet's quite shy, think she might have social anxiety like me, maybe. Carmen's a bit bland and Lucy . . .' I pause, considering her for a moment. 'She's . . . interesting.'

'Word of the day?' Alex laughs again, coming up to me and slipping my cardigan from my shoulders.

I let him undress me and kiss my neck.

'The house feels way too quiet when you aren't here,' he whispers. 'Now, enjoy your bath. Relax for a while. I'm sure tonight was a bit overwhelming for you.'

I nod, draping my arms over his shoulders, and kiss him tenderly.

'Thank you,' I say.

Alex closes the door to the bathroom for me as he leaves, and I step into the tub, enveloping myself under a blanket of bubbles. The baby rolls in my womb, and I place a hand on top of my tummy, enjoying the movements for a while.

I sigh happily, leaning back in the bath, wondering who this little human is and what they're going to look like. When the baby finally settles, I dry my hands and pick up my phone. Opening up Facebook, I scroll through the newsfeed for a while, not really paying attention until a section for suggested friends appears.

I squint at the picture of the first suggested friend. It's a selfie of Cora with a man standing in front of Niagara Falls. I click on her profile, wondering if it would be weird to press the big blue 'Add Friend' button.

With her profile set to public, everything she's shared on her page is visible. It's like gold dust, giving me insights into who she is and what she likes. I discover she likes to bake and read books, and hike on weekends with her husband, Jack.

I'll have to remember these things; they'll be great conversation starters if I need them. I could chat for hours about books, and the thought of having a friend who likes books as much as I do stirs something inside me that feels a lot like hope.

I carry on perusing her profile. Her latest post is a photo of her and Jack on Rock Beach at sunset, posted earlier today. The caption reads, *Quick stroll down to the beach before my antenatal class tonight*. A number of people have liked the post, far more than ever like anything I post, not that I have many people who follow me on Facebook.

I read through the comments people have left, unable to help myself. Most of the comments are pretty standard, complimenting Cora on how she's glowing or how happy she looks, but one stands out. It's a comment from Lucy Harold which says, *It was so lovely meeting you tonight! Looking forward to getting to know you more.*

I click onto Lucy's profile, but it's set to private. All I can see is her marital status and profile picture, a photo taken of her silhouette looking away from the camera. The woman in the photo could be anyone with long blonde hair blowing in the wind. She's married to someone called Arthur Harold. His profile is even less forthcoming than hers.

My insides burn with a white-hot rage at knowing some of the others in the group have already connected on social media. Why haven't they reached out to me? Why am I excluded? It's a familiar feeling that has reoccurred throughout my life and it triggers a jealousy which gnaws away inside me. I still don't send any friend requests, afraid they'll think I'm stalking them, even though that's exactly what I'm doing.

Lucy's profile is too bare to gather any information, but I have her surname now, which directs me straight to Google. I'm not entirely sure why I'm honing in on her, but she is the one that reached out to Cora on social media and not me. Maybe, like me, she simply got a friend recommendation thanks to social media's algorithm. Maybe there's nothing more to it, but it's still left a bitter taste in my mouth.

Oddly, she's a bit of an enigma on Google too, and every social media platform seems to be privatized. At a loss, I search her husband's name.

The website to an established legal practice is the first hit and beneath that is a shortcut straight to the biography of one of their most successful attorneys, Arthur Harold. The image accompanying the description of Arthur shows a classically handsome man being practically choked by an expensive-looking suit and tie. He looks full of self-importance. His biography includes a long, impressive list of credentials.

I backpedal to the search page and scroll down the page linking to various articles about him and the work he's done. One article catches my eye that seems different from the rest. It's an article from *Cornwall Live* dated a few years back. The title reads, *Attorney Arthur Harold's wife found dead in their coastal family home.*

I study the article forensically, learning that Arthur's first wife, Jessica, and her two children had been the victims of a terrifying home invasion five years ago. Arthur had been out of town on a work trip when it happened. The children had been left unharmed physically, but they'd watched their mother endure unspeakable horrors before her throat was slit in front of them. She'd bled out on the kitchen floor. There's a photo of her in the article, a meek-looking woman with the same blonde hair and grey eyes as Lucy. She's almost a carbon copy.

I have to stop reading the article at one point; it's too distressing to imagine. When I manage to stomach the rest of the story, it comes to light that the killer was never found. With endless possible motives and potential suspects arising from Arthur's line of work and substantial wealth, the case went cold. I quiver in the water; I've been in the bath for so long my skin has started to wrinkle. Realizing how close we live to the house Arthur's first wife was murdered in churns my stomach. Death follows me everywhere, it seems.

I scan through a couple more articles, but despite my best efforts, I can't seem to find anything on Arthur and Lucy in between the eruption of accounts on Jessica's slaughter. Giving up, I put my phone down and try to shake the eerie feeling that's settled in the pit of my stomach.

* * *

After trying unsuccessfully to collect colostrum for over half an hour, I pull the syringe out from between my teeth and chuck it to the floor. Climbing out of the bathtub, I towel dry my hair, thinking about Lucy and the article. I've never known someone with such a close connection to a grisly crime like this.

She's suddenly fascinating to me. I want to know more about her and more about the murder. Selfishly, it occurs to me that it's the most exciting thing that's cropped up since moving here. I have to fight the urge to sit on the side of the bathtub and carry on my research after I've moisturized and changed. Alex will wonder what's taking me so long.

Grudgingly, I swipe my phone from the corner of the sink and open the bathroom door.

'Any luck with the colostrum thing?' Alex looks up from his phone as I enter the bedroom.

'Nada.' I sigh.

'Just keep trying. I'm sure you'll get there,' he says, patting the bed.

I go to sit beside him. 'What's happening?' I ask, motioning towards his phone, which keeps lighting up with messages.

'Jack started a new group chat, just for the guys,' he says in mock excitement, opening up the chat for me to see.

'Cora's husband?' I ask, reading the exchange of messages, a smirk playing at my lips.

'Yeah, how'd you know that?'

'Oh, Cora mentioned his name at class tonight!' I try to hide the blush giving my lie away as I scroll through the messages on the guys' group chat.

Alex has agreed to drinks at a local village pub on Saturday afternoon.

'That'll be nice for you,' I say, masking my sinking heart with the best smile I can muster. Saturday is usually our day to spend together where Alex isn't distracted by work.

'Why don't you start a group for the girls and organize something?' he suggests.

I roll my eyes at him but grab my phone from the charger and tap in my passcode. As I open the instant messaging app, a new group request appears at the top of the screen called 'Rock Mummies'.

'Looks like someone's already beat me to it.' I accept the invitation and read the first message, sent from Lucy.

Hi, Rock Mummies. Hope you don't mind me adding you to this group. Arthur told me there's a guys' private chat going on already, so I thought I should make one for us, too! I hear there's drinks at the village pub on Saturday afternoon for the boys, so I wanted to invite you all over to my house around the same time if everyone's free. I'll make a lunch spread. Let me know if you can make it. Lucy x

Messages from the others are flooding in, accepting the invitation. I show Alex, and neither of us need to speak as our eyes connect. *It's happening. We're making friends.*

I don't tell Alex about the articles I found on Arthur and his late wife, frightened to ruin this seemingly perfect moment. Even though I can't shake off a creeping sense of foreboding, I don't want to damage things when it seems like we're finally beginning to slot nicely into our new lives.

CHAPTER 4

Arthur and Lucy's house isn't just a house. It's a phenomenal restored manor house that looks like the backdrop to a *Pride and Prejudice* film adaptation. I recognize it from the articles I'd read on Wednesday evening as I drive through the gothic gates, closing me in as my car creeps up the driveway. I give an involuntary shiver, knowing I'm approaching a property with such a dark and disturbing past. Yet, if I hadn't read about its history, the manor would seem absolutely marvellous to me with its alluring beauty.

The verdant, manicured lawn is like an infinity pool, the edges vanishing down the cliff to a private pathway that trails to the beach. The grounds are lined with beds of lush tulips that put even the Netherlands to shame. There's a table set up on the grass when I arrive with a vase brimming with an expensive flower arrangement. An array of French patisserie and cream cakes, fine champagne flute glasses rimmed with gold and six lotus-folded linen napkins are dotted around the table.

'This is quite the spread,' Violet mutters, leaning in close to me. She's wearing a poppy-red dress that matches her hair. We're all dressed in the colours of spring, I notice, looking down at my own warm orange ensemble.

'It's incredible,' I agree, my eyes roaming the property, enchanted.

'Everything looks too beautiful to touch!' Cora eyes the cream cakes longingly.

'Nonsense, dive in!' Lucy glides over, her blonde hair braided and draped over her shoulder.

I have so many questions for her, but I wouldn't know where to start. I wonder if it's weird for her, living under the same roof that Arthur's first wife was murdered in, having that constant shadow hanging over her home. I think about what it must be like for her, cooking in the same kitchen where Jessica's body was found. I know I can't possibly ask, but there's no hiding my curiosity as I study her closely.

She doesn't make eye contact with any of us, busying herself by rearranging roses in the vase at the centre of the table. She seems nervous, almost shy to be around us. I wonder if, like me, she finds it hard being around new people. I recognize myself in her, I realize, which piques my interest further still. I watch her float around the table in her powder-blue dress. Like Carmen, you can hardly tell she's pregnant.

'Have any of you started trying to collect colostrum yet?' I ask, a question I'd practised in my head before arriving. My attempt to engage and make an effort. 'I've tried so hard since the last class, but it seems impossible!'

'Why are you trying to collect colostrum already?' Rachel looks at me, shocked.

'Am I not supposed to?' I colour instantly, regretting having said anything at all.

'Only at thirty-seven weeks, I think?' Carmen says, looking at the other girls for confirmation.

'Yeah, Emma definitely said no sooner than thirty-seven weeks. Any sooner could cause premature labour.' Cora is already on her phone, googling it.

'I must have missed that bit,' I say, shrinking into myself.

'We can't be expected to remember everything. It's an absolute minefield!' Cora puts her phone back into her pocket and squeezes my arm reassuringly.

'It really is. You know, I only realized the other day that I shouldn't be cleaning out the cat's litter box while pregnant! I've been doing it the entire time. I felt horrified when my mother-in-law told me off,' Violet says.

'I'm sure we've all done something we shouldn't have done accidentally. Just before our first antenatal class I went for a spray tan because I had to fly to Ibiza the next day for a hen do and I honestly had no idea you're not supposed to spray tan when you're pregnant!' Rachel laughs. That explains the grotesque orange skin when we first met, I think to myself.

It's a comfort to hear stories from the other girls, to know that I'm not the only one that makes mistakes, but it doesn't stop me from feeling incredibly stupid in that moment.

'Don't worry about it, Darcy. I've been leaking colostrum for weeks already. Breast pads have become part of my daily attire,' Carmen says, and somehow the kindness from her is the most surprising but also the most appreciated.

Lucy sits down at the table, calling us all over to join her. Our names are printed on embossed place cards, showing us all where to take a seat. I can't help but think it all seems a bit excessive. It makes me wonder what an event like her baby shower or a birthday party would be like if this is just an impromptu Saturday gathering. I'm sat between Rachel and Cora, directly opposite Lucy, whose grey eyes seem even larger today.

'Would anyone like a drink?' she offers, holding up a bottle of Saicho Sparkling Tea that has been chilling on crushed ice. We all accept a glass, clinking them together in a toast. The tea tastes floral, of jasmine and apple. It's the nicest non-alcoholic drink I've ever had.

'Lucy, this is divine! So much better than some of the other non-alcoholic crap in the shops. I've never had Saicho before,' Carmen says, pronouncing Saicho as 'psycho', making Rachel laugh.

'You have to pronounce the "ch",' Lucy corrects her, smiling kindly.

'We stock this at our shop,' Rachel says, tapping the bottle before telling everyone about her and her husband's farm shop specializing in fine wines and cheese. I can't tell if she's bragging or not.

'We place an order with you every week, actually. The goats cheese you make is just beautiful. I miss it.' Violet gives a chef's kiss before patting her baby bump.

While we all sip our drinks, we learn that Rachel teaches horse riding and occasionally helps in the farm shop. Cora's a manager at a charity for children, and Violet is an artist currently exhibiting at Padstow Gallery. Carmen helps at her husband's architecture firm and Lucy is a housewife.

'Arthur's got children from his previous marriage. They live with us full time, so I take care of them when they're not in school,' she says, passing around a photograph of a bullish-looking man with two young children at his side. Arthur looks just like the image I'd found from my online sleuthing. He's suited and booted, his grey hair slicked back, with a receding hairline and strong jaw. The children look to be around ten years old, blonde with big grey eyes. Eyes that have seen far too much for their tender age. If Lucy hadn't told us she wasn't their biological mother, I'd have automatically assumed she was.

'What about you, Darcy?' she asks, shifting the attention onto me.

'I'm looking for work in the area,' I say, taking a big gulp of Saicho, wishing it contained alcohol. Compared to everyone else, I feel incredibly unsuccessful and boring.

'Oh! I'm not sure what sort of job you're after, but I might be able to help. My friend works in recruitment. I'll give you her details.' Cora whips out her phone and forwards me her friend's contact information.

'Thank you,' I say gratefully, glad she didn't ask me to elaborate on what my experience is. I can't tell these high-powered women I've been a barmaid and a receptionist, I just can't.

I wonder how Alex is getting on at the pub. He told me he'd send an SOS if he needed rescuing, but so far, I haven't heard a peep.

* * *

Hours later, once the weather has forced us to relocate inside, Lucy is giving us a tour of the manor. We haven't found our way into the kitchen yet and I'm not sure if I want to go there or not. On the one hand, I'm intrigued. I want to know more, but at the same time it chills me thinking about stepping into a room where such an awful thing happened.

Lucy's busy herding us around her indoor pool, talking about how nice it will be to teach the babies to swim here one day, when the guys all make an appearance.

'Forgot to tell you all the boys were on their way over.' She grins.

Their voices carry across the length of the water as they enter through the sliding glass doors, all of them laughing and slightly red in the face. Drunk. Alex weaves through everyone to find me, his arm snaking around my waist. He reeks of whiskey and cigarettes, reminding me of his mother.

'Have you been *smoking*?' I whisper to him, shocked. I've never known him to smoke, but then again, I've never seen him drunk either.

'If I say no, will you kiss me?' he drawls, puckering his lips. Out of the corner of my eye I notice Lucy rolling her eyes at us. I ignore her, batting him away and laughing at this different side to him I'm not familiar with.

I look around at the new faces, trying to figure out who belongs to who. There's a huge man wearing an olive-green lumberjack shirt, towering above everyone. He must be with Rachel. Another man in a lilac t-shirt makes his way over to Cora and gives her a kiss, his hands roaming over her bump. He must be Jack. There's a guy in a crisp white collared shirt with salt and pepper hair and a serious expression on his face. I genuinely can't decide if he's Violet's partner or Carmen's.

I don't know either of them well enough yet to know their taste in men.

I get my answer when an incredibly skinny woman with long hair down to her waist shimmies up to Violet and pecks her on the lips. She's so tiny I hadn't even noticed her walk in with the rest of the guys. I blanch slightly, wondering why Alex hadn't told me there was a woman in his group. Swallowing down my anxiety, I force a smile as Violet introduces her wife.

'This is Marie,' Violet says. She grins, showing a set of slightly discoloured teeth. Her whole persona seems to transform with Marie close to her. She seems brighter, more vibrant.

'Oh, introductions would be good, wouldn't they? This is Johnny,' Rachel says, nodding her head in the direction of the guy in the lumberjack shirt.

Johnny grins at us, holding two beer bottles in his hands. The smell of alcohol and cigars wafts over to me as he gets closer.

'Where's Arthur, Lucy?' Cora asks. I look around the room, noticing that he's missing from the group.

'Yeah, we'd love to meet him!' the guy in the collared shirt says, walking up to us and introducing himself as Grayson. His eyes linger on Carmen, who gives him a small insincere smile in return.

'Let me give him a call and check.' Lucy ducks out of the pool room with her phone in hand.

'Arthur wasn't with you guys?' I ask, though I already know the answer. Marie shakes her head no.

'I heard he's an attorney. Even more demanding job than mine to be working on a Saturday,' Alex says.

I wonder to myself if Lucy struggles with loneliness the same way I do. I know first-hand how tough having to constantly be without your partner is. If I was in her shoes, I'd probably be jealous of the other husbands being around today and showering their wives with affection too. I decide to let go of the roll of her eyes when she saw Alex and me together.

'Yeah, he's working apparently. Not even I work that hard! Messaged the group and said we should come up and enjoy the rest of the evening with you lot though.' Johnny shrugs, cracking open the beers. He hands one to Alex, who has a glazed look in his eyes as he scans the room.

'We should swim,' he suddenly says loudly and all of the guys cheer, ripping the shirts from their backs.

It amazes me how comfortable everyone seems here, in a house we've never been to before. The alcohol has obviously taken effect, worked its way into everyone's bloodstreams and loosened them all up. I take a moment to remember the sweet, warm sensation a glass of wine would have on me, how it calmed me and helped me to drop my walls. It makes me envious that I don't have that to fall back on as a crutch right now.

Surprisingly, I notice it's Grayson who seems to be the most intoxicated as he topples sideways into the pool with a splash. I can tell Carmen isn't happy about it, her legs shaking restlessly as she sulks at a table in the corner of the room. Rachel, on the other hand, has stripped down to her bra and knickers and is wading into the water from the steps. She's wearing huge Bridget-Jones-style underwear, stretching over her bump, but she seems totally comfortable in her own skin. One by one, the girls trickle into the pool.

Violet floats silently through the aqua water on her back, looking up at the raindrops pattering onto the skylight. Cora and Carmen have limited themselves to sitting by the top step and are chatting about what car seat they've each bought for their baby. I'm sitting alongside them with one foot dipped into the warm chlorinated water. They're comparing the features on the car seats from swivel functions to their compatibility with aeroplanes. It sounds like they're speaking a foreign language. I've had it on my To Do list for weeks to drag Alex to John Lewis for a consultation with one of their experts. We haven't even started decorating the nursery let alone purchased a car seat, pram or cot. I feel guilty, wondering if everyone else already has everything sorted for their baby.

Lucy reemerges in a strapless one-piece swimming costume, sleek and vibrant. Her willowy body reveals no signs of pregnancy. She is paper-thin but touches her hand to her stomach guardedly.

'I'm getting a little kick.' She grins, noticing me staring at her.

My own baby digs an elbow or a knee right under my ribcage at that exact moment, making me jerk from the sudden movement. I hold onto my bump, wondering how it's possible to be so much bigger than Lucy and Carmen when we've all got such similar due dates. *Every bump is different*, I repeat in my head while I side-eye Lucy again.

Her makeup looks like it's been touched up, the bronzer adding some much-needed colour to her face. Her lips look plump and glossy, and is that perfume she's wearing? As she passes me the unmistakable scent of Myrrh and Tonka drifts by. She's carrying the necks of more beer bottles, which she passes around to the guys, each of them giving her new appearance an approving glance.

She enters the water, her long legs slowly disappearing until I'm left staring at her backside. The costume has ridden up, revealing two perfectly round cheeks, free of dimples and pimples unlike my own. I can't help but think she's pulled the costume up like that on purpose. There's a newfound confidence to her since the guys arrived, and it has me chewing at my fingernails. She takes a sip from the remaining beer bottle in her hand, which staggers me.

'Want some?' she asks Rachel, who is also looking at her in bewilderment.

'I really shouldn't.' Rachel frowns as Lucy offers her the bottle, gesturing to her tummy.

'One every now and then doesn't hurt.' Lucy winks, taking another sip. I can't help but feel like she's trying to impress everyone, especially our husbands. She's barely recognizable from the sheepish woman who welcomed us into her home earlier today. Gone is the quiet, reserved woman I was starting to feel a certain kinship with. It's as though she's shifted the very essence of herself, of who she is beneath her skin.

'I've heard beer is good if you've got an iron deficiency actually, and the iron tablets the midwife's put me on make me *so* constipated.' Violet takes the bottle from Lucy. I catch Carmen shaking her head in disgust from the corner of my eye.

Two children poke their heads into the pool room at that moment, startling us. They're the children from the picture Lucy showed us earlier. They look even more like her in person, I think, watching them stare at Lucy with the same large smoky eyes she has. Lucy hasn't noticed them yet; she's too busy giggling at something Jack's said at the other end of the pool. She splashes him playfully, squealing as he dives beneath the water in her direction. I glance at Cora, watching them steadily.

'Lucy!' the young blonde girl calls, her voice fighting to be heard over the raucous men talking over each other.

Lucy turns to the children, her face visibly dropping at the sight of them.

'I've invited some guests over for the afternoon. You two head upstairs to your rooms and do your homework, please?' Her smile doesn't meet her eyes. The girl gives her a quizzical look, the boy shuffling his feet beside her.

'It's Saturday. We have sailing practice. You need to take us, remember?' the boy whispers.

'You'll have to give sailing a skip today. Now go inside and get your homework done.' She turns away from them, taking another sip of beer.

'Lucy,' the girl whines, making Lucy roll her eyes in irritation before she turns back to them.

'What?' she asks, her mouth a tight line.

'What about dinner?'

'I'll order us a pizza later, okay?'

The little boy's face lights up. 'Pepperoni?' The delight is adorable.

Lucy nods. The little boy grabs his sister's hand, and they scurry out of the room.

'Sorry. Sometimes having to be a mother to someone else's children is a bit grating,' Lucy tells us, a hand playing with her braided hair uncomfortably.

'I bet.' Rachel swims over to the side of the pool and takes a small sip of the beer Lucy offered her. I stare at Lucy, replaying her interaction with the children in my head. It's left me unsettled. Even if they aren't technically her children, they didn't deserve to be shooed away to their bedrooms like that, lured by the promise of pizza.

'Coming in?' Her eyes pierce me as she catches me studying her.

It happens so quickly I don't see it coming. My heart rate skyrockets, the blood rushing straight to my head. Alex snaps his head up in my direction.

'You okay?' he mouths.

I manage a curt nod. My vision blurs as my hands claw at my thighs. The ringing in my head gets louder and louder, blocking out everything else around me. I stumble away from the pool, towards the sliding doors. I try to slow my breathing, but I'm powerless to the fit of terror flooding through me.

'Whoa, everything alright?' Cora steadies me.

'Need air,' I gasp, getting my clammy handprints all over the glass as I pull the doors open.

I hear a laugh coming from inside; it's Alex's laugh. I look back and see Lucy leaning over him, passing more beers around. She's so close to him that her perky breasts are almost touching his nose. The way she looks at him is subtle, but I see it. There's a twinkle in her eyes, a risqué brush against him under the water.

I rub my eyes, transfixed. What is she doing? Alex glances over to me, noticing me staring. Our eyes lock, silently communicating. The silly boyishness to him evaporates as he sobers. Taking an unreasonably big gulp of his beer with his eyes still on mine, he swims to the other side of the pool away from Lucy.

* * *

I find my way to one of the guest bathrooms, pull up my dress and sit on the toilet seat. Staring down at the thick, shiny tissue that covers my thighs, I choke back a sob. I'll never be able to show my legs again, not without the gawking and questions that would follow, and what would I say? You'd think after all this time I'd have crafted the perfect lie, but then again, I've never had a good poker face. I couldn't have gone in that pool, even if I'd wanted to. My thighs show a story I'm not willing to share.

Cora taps lightly at the bathroom door. 'You okay in there?' she says.

I look up at the spectacular chandelier twinkling above me, wishing she would leave me alone.

'I'll be out in a minute,' I say, burying my face into my knees. This is *so* awkward. I can just imagine each couple going home tonight, talking about my weird meltdown in the pool room.

What bothers me more is that Alex still hasn't come to check on me. When I first heard the knock on the door, I'd assumed it was him, coming to wrap me up in his big sturdy arms. He's usually so attentive and considerate, especially when it comes to my anxiety. It makes me realize just how much of a bubble we've been in since we first met earlier this year. I've had his full, undivided attention. I've never seen who he is around other people because we've never been in a social setting like this. Now he's smoking and drunk. It's all new to me, and I'm not sure I like this version of him.

I try telling myself our bubble wasn't healthy, that this is what normal really looks like. A group of friends having a pool party on a Saturday afternoon, not two people isolated and constantly in each other's pocket. Collecting myself, I open the door to the bathroom where Cora and Carmen are standing.

'Everything alright?' Carmen eyes me cautiously.

'Yeah. Sometimes I get a bit overwhelmed around big groups of people.' A blush spreads over my cheeks, pronouncing my mortification, but at least I've spoken the truth.

'Bless you. I was worried about you,' Cora says.

'I'm fine,' I mumble, unable to look either of them in the eye. Their concern for me is overwhelming.

Ambling along behind Cora and Carmen, we explore more of the manor. I lose count of how many rooms we stumble across. It's eerily quiet and incredibly dark, thick curtains drawn shut at every window, depriving the house of natural light.

The floral-papered walls are crowded with framed photographs, mainly of Arthur's children. All of the shots are professionally taken; I can't seem to find one that isn't posed in a studio. They're all so forced and unnatural they could pass as Shutterstock photography. Not one candid shot from a family holiday or of the kids playing in a park hang on the wall. I can't even seem to find one from Lucy and Arthur's wedding day.

There's some of Arthur with the children, dotted around infrequently. Even more scarce are photos of Lucy. Carmen manages to find one, pointing it out to us. Arthur and Lucy are staring into the lens of a camera, unsmiling. They're posed rigidly with an elderly couple who I presume to be Arthur's parents. They look as straightlaced as him, pretentious, their expressionless faces giving nothing away.

'They look fun,' Carmen whispers sarcastically, scrutinizing the photograph.

'I wonder who this is.' Cora points at a sepia photograph of a smiling woman in a long-sleeved lacey wedding dress. It makes a refreshing change from all of the other photographs alongside it. I recognize the woman instantly as Jessica, Arthur's first wife. I wonder how Lucy feels having photographs of her still hanging up inside her home, or if there's so many photographs here that she hasn't even noticed.

I want to ask Cora and Carmen if they know about Arthur's past, about what happened in this house. Surely it must have been front-page news in a small village like this, but no one has mentioned anything. Perhaps, like me, they don't want to be the person to spread rumours. I decide to keep quiet, for now anyway.

We find our way to a ginormous staircase, peering up curiously. No sounds of children's voices float down, no televisions blare cartoons. It's as though the house itself is missing a heartbeat.

Cora carries on meandering through the hallway, stopping by a bookshelf to look at what appears to be hundreds of Folio Society classic hardbacks. Carmen sidles up next to her and picks up a Shirley Jackson novel with a hauntingly beautiful illustrated cover. The title *We Have Always Lived in the Castle* trails down the spine.

'These must be worth a fortune,' I hear her say, handling the book as if it could shatter as she places it back between more limited editions.

Sneaking away from them, I creep further up the gloomy hallway, the floorboards groaning beneath my feet. This side of the manor seems uninhabited, a stench of mildew lacing the stale air. There's a creak from one of the rooms up ahead, making me jump.

The door is slightly ajar, and a man's low voice coming from inside intrigues me enough to edge closer. I push the door open just slightly, trying to be discreet, but the door protests on its hinges, disturbing the man. He's draped dramatically over a deep red chaise lounge. He turns in my direction, a phone held to his ear with his shoulder.

It's Arthur, more cataclysmically handsome than his pictures led me to believe. I offer him a smile, one he doesn't return. Instead, he penetrates me with Arctic-grey eyes that seem lifeless. Frozen in the doorway, I watch as he pulls himself up, striding towards me. I open my mouth to say something, apologize for the interruption, but before a word is able to leave my lips, the door is slammed in my face.

CHAPTER 5

'Maybe he was on an important work call,' Alex suggests on the way back home. 'The bloke's an attorney. A good one by the sound of things.'

'He just seemed so *cold*.' I shudder, gripping the steering wheel tightly as I wind around a bend in the road.

'Like you always say I seem when I'm trying to work, and you disturb me?' he jokes, a slight slur to his words.

I narrow my eyes at him, deadpan. His hand is on my thigh, stroking through the fabric of my outfit. It's been there throughout the majority of the drive home. A peace offering. Not that we fought, but he knew I was a bit miserable with him as we'd buckled up our seatbelts.

I take one hand off the steering wheel now, finally relenting, and weave my fingers through his.

Night has fallen, the crescent moon shining a silvery light over the ocean. The roads are deserted, just how I like them. The residents of Rock have all turned in for the night. Smoke billows up from chimneys, into the star-scattered sky. It might be one of the last evenings chilly enough to enjoy a lit fire before spring gives way to summer.

'I just feel like he could've at least smiled at me. It's not the best first impression to give someone, especially considering we're in the same antenatal class.'

'Let it go, Darcy.' Alex turns the volume up on the radio to drown me out.

We drive the rest of the way home without speaking, but our hands remain interlaced as we endure an overplayed pop song.

* * *

That night, Alex lies comatose in bed, his snores reverberating throughout the house. Deep throaty growls that have somehow become comforting to me in the handful of months I've known him.

I can't sleep. I can't stop thinking about Arthur and the way he'd stared at me like I was nothing more than a nuisance. It makes me wonder what Lucy's relationship with him is really like. Perhaps that explains why she can be so timid sometimes, but then I think about how much she changed as soon as our husbands arrived at the pool. It was like she was a different person. Arthur and Lucy are enigmas I can't quite figure out.

I drift off eventually, lulled by the gentle rhythm of Alex's heavy breathing. I dream about an ominous ancestral manor that seems to be right out of a gothic horror novel. Dark secrets are imprisoned in the walls, closed off from the outside world so no one can hear the cries for attention. It takes me a while to understand that I'm not a person in the dream, but one of those secrets. My mouth opens wide as I try to shriek, but nothing comes out. My voice is stolen.

I wake, tearing at the skin around my neck. It takes me a moment to realize I'm not dreaming anymore, no longer trapped inside the manor. I turn towards Alex, but he's still fast asleep beside me, the smell of alcohol permeating the air around him. He must have had a lot more to drink than he had me believe. As I look at him, I realize just how much he looks like his mother right now. It's such a hideous thought that I have to look away.

I'll have to speak to him about the drinking in the morning. If I don't, it will only fester. I can't lose him to alcohol. We both know how dangerous it can be.

I can't get back to sleep. The sky is just beginning to lighten to a morning hue, midnight blue turning red. I tiptoe into the kitchen, pouring some pellets into Henry's food bowl. He comes skittering in, wrapping himself around my legs. Pulling a packet of ibuprofen out of the cupboard, I pop two pills out of the blister pack before pouring a glass of water, which I take to Alex's bedside table. With not a raincloud in sight, I seize the opportunity, grabbing a thick jumper, which I pull over my pyjamas, and head out the house towards the beach.

***

Something about the ocean has always calmed me. It's where I'd gone right after identifying my parents' bodies in the hospital that day. That awful day that has kept me away from hospitals ever since.

When Alex's job became completely remote, moving to the coast seemed to be the perfect solution to our problems. I had nothing holding me to the city and Alex was desperate to fix our relationship after I'd caught him messaging another woman, and so we moved. I'd been hoping the ocean would heal me and mend us. Yet despite being here for weeks already, we haven't once taken a walk down to the beach together at sunrise.

I sit on a sand dune, hidden in the thick morning fog, and watch the waves lap gently onto shore. The water looks intoxicating, and I realize that regardless of the cold, I want to swim. I want to submerge myself in the water and feel weightless in the waves as the sky turns from that moody red to cobalt blue. Looking up and down the shoreline, I see no one for miles, so I start to peel off my clothes.

It's so freeing that I bellow out a laugh as I stand completely naked, letting the numbingly cold water meet my toes. Every step I take makes me sink further into the ocean's embrace. The water wraps around my pregnant belly, so cold at first it makes me gasp in shock. I feel the baby wriggle, letting me know they're there too, enjoying this moment with me. A big wave swoops over me, and then another. Before I know it, I'm not only laughing, but I'm also kicking my legs about as I bob up and down in the Atlantic Ocean.

For just a moment, I forget everything. I forget the scars that riddle my thighs, I forget the nightmares, I forget the crash and everything that came after it. I even forget about Alex, about Arthur and Lucy and the rest of the new people that have come into our lives. I let the ocean wash it all away and for a moment I wish it wasn't temporary, but I can't run away from life. Not again. So as the first of the morning's beach strollers start to arrive in the distance, I force myself out of the water before anyone takes notice of me.

I've just slipped the jumper over my head when I hear someone calling my name. I startle, scrunching my pyjama bottoms in front of my dripping legs.

'Thought I recognized you. It's a gorgeous day for a swim,' Cora says brightly.

'Morning,' I mumble, my teeth chattering together as I dance on the spot in the sand.

'Bless you, your lips are blue!'

The wind picks up, flapping the pyjama bottoms around in my hands, revealing the scars on my thighs. I watch her look at them, see her eyes grow wide. I go as scarlet as the early morning sky.

'Sorry, I'll let you get dressed.' She turns on her heels, facing the ocean to let me finish getting dressed.

I jam my legs into the pyjamas quickly, remaining silent. The ocean rumbles, dogs speeding along the beach chasing balls. When I'm dressed, Cora turns to face me again and offers me an apologetic look.

'Want to grab a coffee?' she asks, nodding in the direction of the café overlooking the estuary. I nod, wrapping my arms around myself.

'How's Alex feeling this morning?' she asks, smiling knowingly.

'He's still asleep. Pretty sure he's going to be useless for the day,' I say, grateful she hasn't mentioned my scars.

She laughs, an easy, light-hearted laugh. 'Jack's the same. He doesn't usually drink, but I think he got excited about bonding with the boys.'

Up at the café we order decaf cappuccinos and a couple of almond croissants.

'I'm sorry if I surprised you this morning,' she says, biting into her pastry.

'It's fine. I just thought I was alone, and the water seemed so inviting.' I'm blushing again.

'Oh, don't be embarrassed! Jack and I often go for a little skinny dip when the beach is quiet.' She winks at me.

People slowly filter into the café, the smell of freshly ground coffee beans overpowering the air. I've suffered with nausea throughout this pregnancy, and the strong bouquet of caffeine turns my stomach.

'I noticed your legs this morning,' Cora ventures. Her words almost make me throw up. I look up at her, horrified.

'You don't have to tell me what happened, if you don't want to.'

Why did you bring it up then? I think, angrily. I pick up my croissant and stuff it into my mouth so that I don't have to speak.

'Is that why you panicked at the pool yesterday?' she asks.

I knead my fingertips into my forehead, feeling cornered. She carries on staring at me, waiting for an answer. I want to tell her she's a nosy bitch and walk away. It's what I would have done in the past, but that's why I've been left with no friends in my life. I pushed everyone who came close away and I promised myself that this time would be different, so very slowly I start to nod my head.

'No one would take notice, Darcy,' she tells me, as if she knows, as if she too has a body that makes people gasp out loud when they see it, pointing and ogling indiscreetly.

'Like you didn't?' I cock an eyebrow.

She has the decency to give me an apologetic look. 'I just thought maybe you could use a friend. You seemed so distraught yesterday and I want to help.'

'So, you're a fixer,' I say.

'Guilty,' she says, smiling.

Infuriatingly, she's impossible not to warm to. At first, I thought her over-friendliness and habit of getting involved in everything would annoy me, but I'm surprised to realize it doesn't. In a weird way, she really does already feel like a friend.

'It was a car crash. I was trapped inside, glass got into my leg when I managed to climb out,' I say, feeling the blood rushing to my temples. I don't know where to look. The pounding in my head is dizzying.

'Oh my God, Darcy. I'm so sorry,' she says, her eyes wide.

'Don't be. I got out. Other people weren't so lucky,' I murmur, struggling to comprehend that I've told Cora more about the crash than even Alex knows.

I've stunned myself, suddenly aware that I've said way too much. The truth about the accident needs to be kept a secret. I can't afford to start letting people in, not now, not when I've escaped my past and made a brand new life for myself that is finally working. If I open up about this, what else will I share? Alex will never forgive me if I tell her about why we really moved here, about him cheating.

The messages to another woman, someone he'd worked with, will likely always haunt me, even though he swore to me that's all it ever was. Messages. There's always been a lingering suspicion that more happened than he wants me to believe, but I guess now I'll never know.

I searched for her once, the girl I'd seen messaging him. Evie. Typed her full name as it had appeared on his phone into Google's search bar. She was elusive. No social media, not even a LinkedIn page. It had bothered me at first. I'd been desperate to find her, to get her side of the story — but I'm not sure I'd want to know now anyway. Whatever had happened didn't matter anymore, because he'd chosen me at the end of the day.

Alex doesn't want anyone to know about any of that, or to have a bad opinion of him. He isn't a cheater. He made that clear to me.

His words ring in my head, even now. *I just didn't know you were so serious about me; I didn't think you wanted something serious. I thought you'd hurt me, so I guess I hurt you to protect myself.* There had been so much regret in his eyes, and I knew all about needing a second chance, and so I took him back. What happened in the very beginning of our relationship is our secret, and he's tried every day since I found out to make up for it.

Cora must notice my torment because she swiftly changes the subject. 'So, have you and Alex started getting ready for the baby's arrival?' she asks.

'We were supposed to go to Wickes this weekend and choose some paint samples, make a start on the nursery. I'm not sure we'll have time to do it now,' I say, not wanting to tell her we haven't bought anything for the baby yet, but I can't help myself. 'I've looked at the gender-neutral clothes in Sainsbury's and Tesco's over the last few months, but I haven't bought anything yet.'

'Why not?' she asks.

'I thought as our due date got closer my anxiety would go away. I thought I'd start getting excited, but it's like I can't allow myself to believe it's finally happening, not until the baby is in my arms,' I say. 'I feel like only then it'll actually seem real to me, that I finally have a family. It's the only thing in life I've ever truly wanted.'

'What happened to your family?' Cora eyes me carefully.

I shiver involuntarily, a coldness sweeping through me.

'My dad fell asleep with a cigarette in his hand,' I whisper slowly.

Cora brings her hand to her mouth, tears springing to her eyes.

'Oh, Darcy,' she says, reaching out to touch my hand.

'The house went up in flames. By the time the firemen got there it was too late. I was away at university when I got the call. I had to come home and identify them in the hospital.' I swallow. 'I've hated hospitals ever since.'

The memory rips into me, the image of my family, what remained of them anyway. Their blackened, burnt bodies hardly recognizable, bubbled and swollen. I'd stood there beneath the harsh lights of the morgue as my entire world fell to pieces. When I'd done what I had to, I'd run out into the cool, sterile corridor of the hospital and vomited.

A silence follows, and we both know there's nothing that can fill it, so we let it settle.

'We could go together today if you like, to look at paint samples for your nursery. I *love* decorating. What sort of style are you wanting to go for?' Cora's face has lit up enthusiastically, and I appreciate her so much for quickly changing the subject.

'Thanks, but I think it's something Alex wanted to choose with me,' I say. The image of my parents' bodies in hospital has left me shaken, quivering.

'If it's just the samples, surely he'd be okay with it!' she says, seeming adamant.

'Okay,' I reply, smiling weakly.

I'm about to tell her I need to go home first to shower and change out of the pyjamas I'm wearing when a couple catches my eye at the back of the café. I recognize the man instantly. He doesn't have the kind of face you forget. It's unmistakably

Arthur, but I don't recognize the woman he's sitting with. A client of his, maybe.

'Hey, isn't that Lucy's husband?' I ask Cora, nodding my head in the direction of Arthur and the woman. They're hunkered down over their coffee cups in the middle of what appears to be a serious conversation. Cora subtly twists in her seat, taking a look in their direction.

'Yes! Who is *that*, though?' she asks, raising an eyebrow.

The woman he's with is stunning, with auburn hair far too perfectly waved for this time of morning and flawless makeup that looks airbrushed on. She's wearing beige designer loungewear, a Chanel handbag at her feet. She laughs at something Arthur says, throwing her head back to reveal a set of perfectly whitened teeth.

She has the power to make every other woman in here insecure, especially me in my salty, damp botanical-green pyjama set. I didn't really care about being out in public in my nightclothes until now. They seem close, too close to be merely acquaintances or even friends. We watch in horror as Arthur reaches out, a small smile playing at his lips as he places a hand over hers. Her stiletto-shaped nails tickle his forearms. Arthur looks over his shoulder hesitantly before taking her hand in his and kissing her bony knuckles.

'Poor Lucy!' Cora clasps a hand over her mouth, knocking over her coffee cup in the process. It smashes to the floor.

Arthur's head snaps up and his eyes lock with mine from across the room. The recognition is instant. He pulls his hand away from the woman, whispering something to her. She flicks her gaze to me with trepidation as they both get up from their table and leave hurriedly.

A waitress is blotting away at the spilled coffee — I hadn't even noticed it starting to drip all over my legs.

* * *

'We have to tell her, right?' Cora asks, driving me home.

'I guess so,' I say. 'I'd want someone to tell me if they'd caught Alex out with another woman.' The situation hits a little too close to home, a lump forming in my throat.

'How do you shatter someone's world like that? How do you tell them ten weeks before they're about to have a baby their husband is having an affair?' Cora seethes, shaking her head. 'What a vile man!'

She's driving over the speed limit, too caught up in her rage to notice. I want to beg her to slow down, but I'm frozen, gripping the sides of the car seat in dread as we careen through the sleepy roads. People don't realize the lasting impact a serious car crash has on someone. Even after all these years, getting into a car is hard for me. Closing my eyes, I will the drive to be over, thankful I live just around the corner.

After directing her, the Audi jerks to a stop outside the front of my house. I breathe out a sigh of relief, unbuckling my seatbelt. There's no sign of life coming from inside. The curtains are still drawn.

'We should call her,' Cora decides, pulling out her phone.

'Maybe we should think about the best way to approach this first,' I say, but she's already dialling Lucy's number.

Lucy answers after a few rings, making my heart stop. I don't want to be responsible for destroying someone's life, but Cora's roped me into this now and I can see no way out.

'Darcy and I were wondering if you were free for a little walk later today?'

'I could shuffle around a few things next week, maybe. Today's a bit short notice with the kids to take care of unfortunately.' Lucy sounds thrilled at getting the invite, if a little surprised.

I hate that we're about to break her heart. I hate even more that we have to wait days with this knowledge hanging over our heads.

CHAPTER 6

A screeching of tyres skidding across an icy road rings in my ears, car brakes failing miserably. The crunch of steel on steel, the smell of burnt rubber, leaking fuel. I feel the agony as shards of shattered glass bite deeply into my skin.

'Murderer!' someone screams.

I open my mouth and try to call out for help, but I'm hardly able to breathe let alone scream. I thrash and kick, whimpering as beads of sweat drip from my temple. It's the pitch black of night and there's someone restraining me. I fight against their firm hold, heart pounding, arms flailing.

'Darcy, it's okay!'

I hear Alex's voice close to my ear. The arms around me start to feel familiar, warm and safe. My eyes blink open, the thumping in my chest slowing.

'Another night terror,' he whispers, still clasping me tightly to his body.

My silk chemise has ridden up, revealing the scars that mar my thighs. Inching myself free, I mumble an apology, throwing back the bedsheets, and head to the bathroom. Alex sighs, readjusting the pillows and blankets.

I click the bathroom door shut softly behind me and press my sticky forehead against the cool glass of the mirror. It's humiliating, these night terrors. I splash cold water onto my face, trying to wash away the memories from that horrible day, the day I killed someone.

* * *

'Honey, we're going to be late!' Alex calls up the stairs.

I groan, giving myself one last glance in the full-length mirror. It's been an odd day, as days following a night terror often are. I haven't quite been able to pull myself out of my slump. A part of me wanted to cancel this week's class, but I had to remind myself that I'd begged Alex to pay for these sessions. I'd feel awful for wasting his money and so, after smoothing down my plaid sundress and touching up my lipstick, I take a breath and walk downstairs.

It's an uncharacteristically warm evening for late April, just the slightest breeze in the air. We drive to the hall in silence, Alex watching the road and me keeping my eyes trained on the ocean, as still as a lake. His hand, which usually always rests on my leg while we drive, is planted on the gear stick.

Our arguments are few and far between, but things got a little heated between us after my episode this morning. After a night terror, Alex always tries to prise information out of me. He interrogates me, asking me what it was about. I always lie and tell him I don't know, but it's got to the stage where he doesn't believe that anymore. I know he's upset that I refuse to open up to him about it, but he doesn't understand. I just can't. So here we are, on our way to our second antenatal class, the tension between us palpable.

Just what we need, these couples sensing something off between us, I think sardonically. The first class last week had been awkward enough, being slotted into small groups to work through activities Emma had given us. It had been clear right from the start who the alpha females amongst us were. Rachel had been the loudest and most opinionated by far, but Cora also seemed to like to take charge, which surprised me. For such complete opposites, they became the leaders of the groups throughout the night. It makes me wonder if they'll give anyone else a chance in tonight's class. The rest of us definitely seem more subdued, slowly coming out of our shells inch by inch, but perhaps tonight with our partners there it'll be different. I know if it weren't for the tension between Alex and me, I'd feel a lot more confident going into tonight's class having him there.

It'll be nice to see everyone again, too, particularly the guys now they aren't absolutely inebriated. I've been looking forward to seeing a different side to everyone. I just wish Alex and I could be in a better place, but we're already pulling into the car park.

I slump back in the car seat, our baby wriggling around inside me, clearly as uncomfortable as we are. I'm too stubborn to be the first to speak, but Alex is as infuriatingly stubborn as me. He always jokes with me that if our stubbornness is the worst part about our relationship, we should consider ourselves lucky, and I know we are, but right now I'm too annoyed to patch things up between us. I get out of the car and stalk towards the hall.

'Darcy, wait.' Alex runs to catch up to me. I turn to face him, my eyes blazing with more irritation than necessary.

'Is this really how you want to walk in there?' he says, taking my hands in his and gazing into my eyes. I sigh, shaking my head and taking a step towards him.

'I'm sorry,' I say as we fall into a hug in the middle of the car park.

'Me too. I'm just trying to understand you.' He kisses me tenderly.

'I know you are. I just can't talk about it,' I tell him. It's what I tell him every time I get a night terror and that much, at least, is the truth. I haven't spoken about what really happened in many years. It's something I've tried to bury deep down and forget about, and sometimes I almost think it's worked. Sometimes I can go weeks without a night terror, and I start to feel normal again, but then I wake up screaming and howling and get thrown off kilter again.

'If I say it out loud, I don't think I'll be able to handle it, Alex. It's something I'm really trying to wipe from my memory. I need you to stop asking me about it, please?'

He nods his head slowly, knowing not to push it further. The truth is that it would kill me if Alex knew the truth about my past. He would never be able to look at me in the same way again. I know that because I can't look at my own reflection anymore without thinking about what I did and who I am, who I will always be no matter how hard I try to run away from it.

The baby jabs out a limb, making me jump in surprise. I take Alex's hand and place it over my stomach so he can feel the movement. He melts with a smile, looking from me to my bump, and in that moment, I know we'll be okay. We always are. Neither of us can stay angry at each other for very long.

While Alex's hand is still pressed to my tummy, Cora and Jack appear beside us, Cora carrying that purple yoga ball she likes to sit on. She flashes us a warm, gap-toothed smile.

'How are we all?' Jack claps Alex on the back.

'Enjoying this lovely weather?' Cora asks.

'Yeah, Darcy was finally able to get down to the beach today, weren't you?' Alex looks at me encouragingly.

'We're new to the area. It's been pretty much raining nonstop since we arrived, besides the other day when I saw you, Cora. So, it was nice to do a bit more exploring today.'

Can they sense the simmering argument we'd had? Can they tell we're still licking our wounds? If they do, they hide it well. The way they're smiling and chatting to us is so friendly and warm it's an odd contrast to the day we've had.

'Where did you move from?' Jack asks. He seems genuinely interested, and I'm surprised this hasn't been brought up already.

'London,' I say, stealing a glance at Alex, afraid to say too much. 'Sorry, I thought we'd mentioned that.'

Had we really not shared we're new to Rock with anyone? I remember telling Cora I was looking for work, but maybe she'd just assumed I've been having a career break. It makes me think it may be easier to get away with not telling the truth about our past than I'd initially thought.

'Welcome to a better life! It's so much more relaxed here, away from the city.' Cora links her arm through mine, walking me in the direction of the hall.

The gesture surprises me. I've never known anyone quite as friendly as her. I look back over my shoulder to Alex, already chatting away to Jack as they follow behind us.

'We can't tell Lucy tonight, not during class,' Cora hisses in my ear when we're out of earshot.

It takes me a few seconds to realize what she's talking about. I'd completely forgotten about catching Arthur with another woman. The night terror and argument with Alex had eradicated everything else going on in my life. I feel awful for being so self-absorbed. I nod my agreement, not saying anything else in case the guys overhear us.

Inside, the others have already arrived. As I thought, everyone seems much more comfortable tonight now we aren't complete strangers. The guys are much tamer in their sober state; some even seem a little introverted. It's amazing what alcohol can do to a person.

Alex pecks me on the lips, squeezing my hand before he lets it go, leaving me to go and mingle with the guys who have formed a little cluster at one corner of the hall. I scan the room for Arthur, but I can't see him anywhere. I wonder momentarily if Lucy really didn't know her husband was home while we were having a party in their pool room. She clearly has no idea I'd bumped into him, or if she does, she's not giving anything away. Maybe Arthur hadn't told her I'd seen him, but why wouldn't he unless he didn't want her to know he'd been home? And where is he tonight? The questions are mounting up.

Nipping into the kitchenette, I pour a glass of tepid water and sip at it while I take in the group from the sidelines. The only person in the room not smiling is Carmen, who looks like she'd rather be anywhere but here. Her cheeks look even more sunken than they did before, the puffy skin under her eyes sagging low.

The other girls are sitting in their chairs, talking animatedly to each other, but Carmen hovers closer to her husband, Grayson. There's a tired scowl on her face, making me wonder if they've had some sort of argument before coming to class too. Once again she's wearing something oversized, a baggy button-up shirt that looks like it's been pulled from Grayson's closet.

Grayson leans in close to her, whispering something into her ear. She looks at him as though she's been burned, before flicking her hair back and strutting towards the girls. She attempts to smile when the girls look up at her, but I can tell it doesn't come naturally to her.

'You alright there?' Emma says, startling me from behind. I hadn't noticed her in the kitchenette; I'd been so absorbed in watching everyone else.

'Yes, I was just getting some water.' I take my glass and head back out into the hall.

When I reach the girls, I see Carmen and Lucy are huddled with their heads bent together. It feels cliquey, like they're forming their own special friendship away from the rest of the group. The only chair left is one next to Carmen, which I take reluctantly. It feels like I'm invading their privacy, but I have nowhere else to go.

'We're keeping the gender of our baby a surprise,' I hear Lucy say. 'We'll be happy with anything, as long as they're healthy.'

'That's all that matters,' Carmen agrees.

Lucy catches my eye, but I look quickly away, scared she'll sense the horrible information I know I have to tell her eventually. She beckons me over to join their conversation. I glance at Cora, but she's engrossed in a different discussion, so I have no choice but to slip in beside Lucy and Carmen.

'What about you, Darcy? It is Darcy, isn't it? So many names to remember!' Lucy says, giggling. Her big grey eyes watch me expectantly. I'm slightly insulted she can't remember my name, especially after having us all over to her house. It's not that hard to remember, surely.

'We're keeping it as a surprise, too,' I say. I don't admit both Alex and I are desperate for a girl. Something tells me this is the wrong crowd.

'Oh, are we talking genders?! I'm having a little boy,' Rachel says, slipping into the conversation. She's marginally less orange than she was last week.

'Same,' Carmen says, no amount of enthusiasm to her voice.

'Where is he?' Rachel jokes, staring at Carmen's body, still showing no sign of pregnancy.

'You don't mince your words, do you!' Violet sounds shocked at Rachel's bluntness. We must have all been thinking it, but none of us dared say anything out loud.

'I know, I'm still waiting to pop.' The monotone edge to Carmen's words doesn't falter. If she's offended by Rachel's comment, it doesn't show. She seems stoic, unmoved by any malice that may or may not have been directed at her. I wish I could be more like that, self-assured, oozing self-confidence.

'You'll get there. Every pregnancy is different,' Cora says before telling us she's having a boy, too.

'It was pretty obvious during the scan. There was no hiding that thing! Jack definitely had his first "proud dad" moment,' she says with a laugh.

'We're having a girl, we think. The sonographer seemed a bit uncertain, but she said she couldn't see anything between the legs, so I guess only time will tell,' Violet says, shrugging.

'Oh, tell me about it! At our first scan the baby wasn't playing ball at all. Had their little legs crossed the whole time. I was sent for walks up and down the hospital corridors and even jumped up and down, but they wouldn't budge! We found out the gender at a private scan we had to pay for,' Cora says.

'I'm so sad we don't get more than two scans unless we go private. Especially for a first pregnancy. I loved seeing them up on the screen, listening to their heartbeat. Watching her chew on her hand was incredible,' Marie says, coming to take a seat next to Violet.

'So, what's that between us, then? Three boys, a girl and two surprises?' Rachel asks, clapping her hands together excitedly.

I nod, stroking a thumb along my tummy. I can't wait to find out. Part of me is envious of the others who know the gender of their baby, but I'm also eager for the surprise. Not knowing until the baby's put into my arms is something I've been envisioning since I found out about this pregnancy. That one special moment where I'm told I have a son or a daughter as they do that cute little newborn scrunch, nuzzling into my neck for the very first time. Boy mum or girl mum, which will I be? The direction of my life will change forever, a road mapped out I've never navigated before.

'Can we guess the genders of your babies?' Cora asks, looking between Lucy and me.

'Sure!' Lucy smiles.

I nod, suddenly aware of everyone looking down at my bump.

'I'm guessing Darcy's got a girl. I mean, I've never seen you not pregnant obviously, so I don't know what you normally look like, but you're carrying pretty high. You're also carrying all around too,' Rachel says.

I flush, not wanting to tell her I'm just curvy in general, that it doesn't mean anything. Secretly though, her guess that we're having a girl makes me glow.

'Lucy's definitely got a boy. She's tiny,' Carmen says. My glow flickers and fades. I know I'm not as small as Lucy, I know I never will be, but it still isn't nice hearing how small someone is compared to me.

'I thought it was the other way round. I thought you were smaller with a girl?' Cora asks, her eyebrows furrowing.

'I think it's all just a myth. You can't actually tell the gender from the way you carry,' Violet says, catching my eye. I look back at her gratefully and mouth a thank you.

'Sorry to have to break up the party, but it's time to get tonight's class started,' Emma calls over our chatter.

* * *

'Welcome to week two, lovely to have you all here together and to meet the partners,' Emma says. 'Tonight's class is all about your labour and delivery. This will include some information on pain management and birth plans.'

Emma splits us up into groups, the guys in one group and the girls in the other. Once again, I can't help but feel all this time Alex has carved out to attend these classes with me is only making us have even more space from each other.

I try to not let it bother me and focus on growing my friendships with the girls, but I can't help but keep looking over my shoulder at Alex. I'm surprised how at ease he seems for someone who's always told me he doesn't do well in social settings. He's making it all look so easy, even if I know it is all a facade.

For our first activity, Emma dishes out a pile of old, tattered photographs capturing the different stages of labour and birth. 'I want you to place them in the order you think they go.'

Rachel instantly takes charge. She shuffles the photographs around on the table in front of us and steps back to admire her work. Cora switches the order around slightly, but the rest of us don't even have the chance to contribute.

I dwindle away in front of the other girls. They all have much bigger personalities than me. Marie, Violet and Carmen start an inane conversation amongst themselves, leaving me standing on my own. It feels like I'm on the outside, looking in at these other women already bonding with each other. I don't know how to insert myself into their conversations or activities, and I don't know how to relax and have fun. I end up hating the first half of the class, desperate to get back to sitting next to Alex so I don't feel so isolated.

Once Emma takes a look at the order of our photographs and tells us how many we got right and wrong, we all sit back in the main circle. Alex puts a hand on my knee and smiles. He looks so happy it makes me bristle. How can he be having such a good time when I'm struggling to stay afloat?

I try hiding my dismay as Emma comes around, handing out a set of laminated pictures and pamphlets. Alex and I are given an illustrated image of a baby inside the womb, its head attached to something that looks like a toilet plunger. We soon learn it's a ventouse suction cup, used in an assisted delivery situation. We have to read all about it and tell the group about it when we're done. When we've gone around the group, each couple discussing various birth methods from induced vaginal delivery to caesareans, Emma starts talking about the different types of pain relief available.

In the corner, Lucy's making notes in a little spiralbound book she's taken out of her handbag, the pen scratching across the page furiously as Emma speaks.

'So, what are you all thinking with regards to your own birth plans?' Emma asks us after she's dished out more information than I can possibly process.

'We're going to try and be as natural as we can. Vaginal delivery, maybe gas and air if it's needed,' Marie says, holding Violet's hand, nodding beside her.

'Yes, the great thing about Entonox is it's incredibly fast acting. It takes about twenty seconds to kick in and there's no harmful side effects,' Emma says.

'I've heard some funny stories from friends of mine whose husbands tried it in the hospital and ended up passing out,' Rachel says with a giggle.

'Well, it can make you feel very light-headed and sometimes quite ill. It's also a good idea to bring along some lip balm as it can really dry out your lips and mouth.'

'Johnny's sister swears by pethidine; she's had three children with it. It's lush, apparently. Helps you relax and it's just a little injection rather than having to be on a drip, so I'm probably going to opt for that.' Rachel shrugs.

'Can't pethidine be bad for the baby? I'm sure someone told me it can make them really sleepy or something?' Carmen asks.

'It does pass to the baby, and it has been known to make them sleepy. It can also affect their breathing, so they might require some assistance after birth.'

'Your sister didn't tell me that,' Rachel hisses to Johnny.

'Epidural for us, drip and all. I'm an absolute wimp and don't have much of a pain threshold, could hardly handle this tattoo on my wrist! So, I've already accepted the fact I'm going to be numbed up!' Cora says.

'It's important to note the side effects of both pethidine and an epidural if they're what you're considering. Pethidine can make you feel sick, sometimes even forgetful. An epidural, on the other hand, can cause headaches, you might need a catheter, and it can also extend the labour process,' Emma explains.

I squeeze Alex's hand, anxiety pouring into my bloodstream.

'Darcy, what about you?' Emma asks, fixing her eyes on me.

'I honestly don't know. I've been scared of giving birth since I found out about this pregnancy,' I admit.

'How come?'

'I'm not very good with hospitals.'

With my heart rate accelerating, I notice Alex's arm snake across my shoulders. He pulls me closer to him, protectively.

'It's okay,' he whispers, quietly enough for no one else to hear, but Cora gives me an understanding nod.

I look up at Alex gratefully, my forehead resting beneath his jaw.

'Have you considered a waterbirth? That's what I'm doing. My midwife told me because my pregnancy is low risk, she'd completely support the decision. You can do it at home and have gas and air to help,' Lucy says. 'You'd be able to completely avoid the hospital that way.'

'Lucy's right. As long as all the evidence indicates a low-risk pregnancy, you could definitely have a home birth. Water can help ease the pain of contractions, too.'

'I hadn't even considered that, actually.' I look at Alex to gauge how he'd feel about it. It's important to me that he feels involved and included in the birth, especially after nine months of him only getting to feel little kicks and wriggles here and there.

'I think it's a great idea!' he says enthusiastically, much to my surprise. I'd always assumed he'd want us to go to the hospital, to have the help of medical professionals straight away in case anything went wrong. Alex is usually a cautious guy, he isn't a risk taker, so seeing him seem almost excited about a home birth is the last thing I'd expected.

'There's also birth centres and midwifery units, if you're not a fan of hospitals, Darcy. I'm quite interested in that as an option myself actually. I've developed a really nice relationship with my midwife, and I like the idea of her delivering our son if she's available.' Carmen runs her hand through Grayson's hair as she speaks. I look away quickly when he shrugs her off, not wanting her to know I noticed.

'I just think that a home birth sounds *so* much more peaceful. You don't need to worry about your birthing partner leaving you afterwards and you're somewhere you feel comfortable,' Lucy says.

'Well, it sounds like you all have a bit of an idea about what it is you want and at some stage closer to your due date your midwife will discuss your birth plan with you. However, I'm sorry to be the bearer of bad news, but I want to be as transparent as possible in these classes. Don't get your hopes set on a specific birth. It almost never goes the way you want it to. I'm not trying to scare you in any way, but once you're in the throes of labour you might decide you want that epidural on top of just gas and air.' Emma looks around the room at us. We're all wide-eyed, like deer in the headlights.

***

Throughout the rest of the night, we're split up again into small groups to complete different tasks and get to know each other. By the time we leave, Alex is grinning and telling me what he's learnt about the guys during their activities. I feel so deflated but try my best to hide it for Alex's sake. I know how big this is for him. He lost all of his friends during his divorce because his friends had all been his ex-wife's friends and even though it was her who had cheated, they naturally took her side.

I want to be happy for Alex, but I can't stop the jealousy from festering inside.

CHAPTER 7

Alex and I are on our way from Porthilly Farm to Roscarrock in Port Isaac, passing picturesque woodlands and fishing coves that wrap around the countryside. It feels wrong to be going to look at wedding venues when Lucy's marriage could be crumbling apart at this very moment. I haven't been able to stop thinking about it. It takes the shine away from what should be the start of our exciting adventure of planning our wedding. It had been tough enough pulling Alex away from his laptop, but eventually he'd caved.

'We've been engaged for a few months now and we haven't planned a thing, Alex,' I'd told him when I asked him if we could finally go. 'I'd like to plan some of it before the baby gets here.'

'We've been a bit preoccupied with the pregnancy, Darcy. That kind of takes precedence, don't you think?'

I'd tried hard to hide how sad that remark had made me. I always knew once we started a family life would be permanently altered, but that didn't stop me from wanting that one special day to be about us. About me. I like to think that doesn't make me totally and completely selfish.

'I still don't understand why we can't just do a civil ceremony at a registry office,' he'd said, twisting the knife in an already open wound.

It felt like he'd lost sight of how much getting married to him meant to me and every time I tried to explain it, he just didn't seem to understand. I couldn't seem to link the guy who leaves me thoughtful love notes tacked up to the fridge and this guy, suggesting a bog-standard registry office wedding. It didn't add up. They aren't the same person.

I'd looked at him, my eyes welling up, and I saw his body sag, visibly softening. And so, we arranged a day of wedding venue viewings.

As we arrive at the rustic fourteenth century manor house surrounded by wild scenery, the setting sun has turned the endless rolling hills and valleys gold. My breath is stolen by the stunning views in the distance of The Rumps and Doyden Point. I've never seen anything look more like a scene from a fairy-tale.

'I love it,' I breathe as we trail along the stone hedges bordering the garden.

'It's lovely, but Darcy, don't you think it's a bit much? We don't even have anyone to invite to a big wedding,' Alex says, stopping at a viewpoint plummeting down a cliff to the churning sea.

'We have people,' I say defensively, but I can count on the fingers of one hand how many people we'd probably invite. Neither of us are close to anyone in particular, and Alex doesn't have a big family to come along. Just his mother, Debbie, who would either make an excuse not to come or get so hopelessly drunk at the event she'd ruin the entire thing anyway.

'It doesn't need to be a big, fancy wedding, Alex. I just thought it'd be nice to get married somewhere beautiful regardless. It would be nice if you were just slightly more enthusiastic about it.'

'A lot of wedding venues have a minimum number of people they'll host for. I just don't think a place like this is going to work for us. I don't want to start inviting random people just to fill up numbers.'

I look at him, remembering he's done all of this before. He's already looked at wedding venues and had the extravagant, special day. He spent thousands of pounds on a wedding that now means nothing.

He knows about planning a wedding in a way that I don't, and the way he's making me feel so naive about it irritates me. A family peers down at us from one of the arched windows back at the manor. They smile at us kindly, but we don't smile in return.

'We could invite everyone from the antenatal classes. I'm sure by the time we actually get married we'll be close with them anyway!' I try, looking at him with pleading eyes.

'We hardly know them, Darcy, don't be silly.' He starts to walk back to the car. I feel the vision of our ceremony here slip through my fingers like sand.

'It feels like you don't even want to get married sometimes, Alex!' I call after him.

'What does that mean?' he asks, turning back to me with a stern look on his face.

'It means we've done nothing to prepare for our wedding, literally nothing. You never even bring it up. It's like you've forgotten we're engaged!' I hold up my left hand, the dainty ring glinting in the remaining glow of the sun.

'Things are different now. It's not just about you anymore,' he says, his words landing like cement.

'It's never been about me,' I mutter behind his back, watching him continue back towards the car. I don't even know why I say it. I'm just overcome with a jealousy and disappointment I can't control. It feels like our whole relationship has been eclipsed by his previous marriage, even though I know that's far from true. He rarely brings up his ex-wife and sometimes I forget he was ever married before, so I know I'm being unreasonable and silly, but I can't seem to help it. It's like I want to punish him for something he hasn't even done.

Back in the car I look sulkily out of the window as we drive away from the venue, leaving behind the rich history inside those ivy-covered stone walls.

'Let's just get married at a registry office, then.'

'No.'

I frown, looking at him closely. Does he not want to marry me at all anymore? The fear of this is enough to send me into a frenzied panic inside my own head. I can't lose Alex; he's all I have. He's the closest thing I have to family.

The baby somersaults inside me, as though sensing my nerves. I rest a hand on my stomach, caressing my bump in an attempt to soothe the baby, but they end up only wriggling more beneath my touch. When I don't respond to him, Alex takes his eyes off the road for just a moment and looks me in the eye.

'We'll give you your big dream wedding, Darcy. If it's what you want.'

Even though he's placed his hand on my leg the way he usually does, he's somehow managed to make me feel like the most selfish person imaginable.

I choke out a sob, unable to control myself any longer. He jerks his head up, peering at me through heavy eyes.

'Darcy,' he whispers softly, squeezing my leg. 'I'm sorry. I know what this means to you, I do.'

'I'm sorry too,' I say, dabbing at the mascara running down my cheekbones. 'I don't know what's wrong lately, why we're arguing so much. I hate it.'

'There's just a lot going on, isn't there? Everything's about to change for us,' he says, casting his eyes back to the road.

The reminder of our impending parenthood makes my heart jump.

'It's like, even though we aren't getting to spend much time together at the moment, I feel like we've been living in each other's pockets at the same time. It's been making things so tense between us,' I mutter, fresh tears spilling down my face. 'I just want us to be okay.'

'We are, I promise. Things have just been a bit hectic lately, haven't they? I'll do better, and I'll try being more understanding about the wedding,' he says, stealing a glance at me. 'It means a lot to you, and it should. I never want to take that away from you. Sorry for being a bit of a knob sometimes.'

His apology is enough to settle the water between us. I catch myself smiling, the tears drying salty stripes down my face. My hand works its way into his.

'Come on, let's go do something nice. Ice cream?' he suggests.

'Pistachio?' I say, brightening.

'Always.' He smiles.

* * *

The invite for a girls' night at Lucy's couldn't come at a better time. My need for space from Alex is at an all-time high. While I'm not stewing from the disappointment from our wedding venue hunt anymore, I still need a distraction. So, when Lucy messages the girls' group chat to say she wants to organize something while Arthur's away with his kids, I jump at the chance.

I can't deny that the thought of getting a closer look into the manor thrills me. Is it wrong that I have a burning desire to set foot in the kitchen Arthur's wife was murdered in? To see it for myself and maybe get Lucy talking about what she knows about what happened intrigues me more than I'm sure it should. It hadn't at first. It had scared me, made me feel queasy inside. But now that I've met Arthur and his two children, I confess that I'm fascinated.

Cora starts a poll to find a date that would work best for everyone. I vote for every date she provides, not bothering to hide my eagerness. I watch the blue lines next to each date dance up and down as everyone else casts their vote, secretly hoping everyone chooses the earliest date there is.

Annoyingly, it's Carmen who can't seem to make most of the dates Cora suggested, which makes me wonder what on earth she does with her life that she's always so fully booked. Eventually, she decides she can commit to one night next week, a date that doesn't work for Violet. I read the messages as they come in with a quickening pulse, worried Lucy will postpone the night if we can't get the full group together. Co-ordinating us all seems like an almost impossible task. Luckily, Violet says she'll speak to Marie and let us know in the morning if she can make it.

I hardly sleep that night in anticipation.

By mid-morning I'm ripping the skin from my cuticles with my teeth. There's still no word from Violet. I swallow back the metallic taste of blood in my mouth as Alex hands me a decaf coffee.

'I'm sorry yesterday didn't go the way you wanted it to. We can carry on looking. I'm sure something will come up that's perfect for us,' he says, climbing back under the bedsheets.

The sun hits his eyes, turning them a light caramel colour. I stare into them, trying to smile, but all my mouth does is twitch. Even after our ice cream date by Padstow Harbour watching the fishing boats, my anxiety is at an all-time high.

'Sometimes it just feels like you don't want to get married, Alex. I know I've said that before and I know you hate it when I say it, but it's the truth. It worries me.'

'Of course I want to marry you, Darcy. I wouldn't have bought you this if I didn't.' He picks my left hand up and touches the ring with his thumb.

'Sometimes it feels like you don't remember this is my first marriage, so I still want some things to be special. I don't need some big fancy event, but I do want to get married somewhere special and look nice on the day. I don't even have a wedding dress yet.'

'Your first and hopefully your last marriage.' He smiles, scooting closer to me.

I rest my head on his shoulder and sigh.

'Darcy, I promise you, I want to marry you. I'm just a bloke. I'm never going to be overly excited about wedding planning, I'm sorry. But it isn't because of Harriet, okay?' Alex so rarely calls his ex-wife by name that I flinch when I hear it.

'Okay,' I say, wanting to change the subject.

'If it makes you feel better, why don't you take my card and go take a look at some dresses next week?'

I pull back from him slightly, unsure if I should be grateful or offended by the offer. The reason I haven't even started looking at dresses is because I know I can't afford one and I haven't been able to bring myself to ask Alex. For a moment I let excitement creep in, but it fades just as quickly.

'I can't try dresses on now, look at me,' I say, pointing to my bump.

'You could still look, get an idea of what you like. Go on, I know you'll enjoy it.'

'Who could I go with?' I ask, more to myself than to him. I don't have a mother to invite and there's not a chance I'd ask Debbie. 'Going alone would just be depressing.'

'Your new antenatal friends?' He suggests it jokingly, but it makes me wonder if that would be the perfect way to start bonding with them all properly. I could ask them at the girls' night.

'Alex, I love you!' I grin, leaning over to kiss him.

While I wait for there to be a consensus on a date for the girls' night, I call a bridal boutique in Wadebridge and ask if they have any availability for an appointment next weekend.

'How many people will be coming with you?' the woman on the phone asks me.

'Between four to six,' I say, invigorated even though I haven't asked anyone yet if they'll join me. For a moment while I chat to the shop assistant, I feel like a normal bride with friends and a life that isn't spent alone. It feels good.

I do wonder if the girls will think it's weird inviting them, especially as I've only known them two weeks. As I start thinking about how to broach the subject, Lucy messages the group.

> *Seems like the overall vote went to next Friday night! I'm arranging a private chef for the occasion, so if anyone has any allergies, please let me know in advance. Can't wait, but I'm sure I'll catch up with you all at the next antenatal class before then anyway!*
>
> *Lucy x*

Everyone gives the message a thumbs up. Excitement bubbles inside me. A date's been set and my friendships with these girls are going to start forming. Life is starting to work out for me at last. My phone vibrates and Cora's name appears on the screen. I wait a few rings before I answer.

'How're we going to tell Lucy about Arthur?' she asks me, sending my lifted spirits into a crash landing. I'd been so stirred up by everything I'd practically forgotten about what we'd seen Arthur doing at the café, about the crushing news we have to tell Lucy.

'We can't do it at the girls' night,' I say, selfishly not wanting to ruin what could be the most perfect evening.

'I agree. We need to do it when we have her alone, not in front of everyone else. I'll reach out to her and see if she can do something during the week, before Friday.'

'I can't do it before Friday. I've got a few job interviews lined up,' I lie. The truth is I haven't even heard back from any of the recruitment agencies I'd contacted, making me wonder if I shouldn't have been so straight up about my pregnancy in my email to them.

'I'm not sure I can do a girls' night with her without telling her something like this. She'll hate us for keeping it from her,' Cora says softly.

The nervousness in her voice has me thinking quickly.

'She wanted to organize a girls' night, so maybe she already knows. Maybe she's going to talk to us about it while

Arthur's away,' I say and hear Cora sigh down the phone in response.

'Maybe you're right. Let's leave it for now, then. If she doesn't say anything though, then we do need to tell her over the weekend. Okay?'

I promise her we will, and we end the call.

'Who was that?' Alex asks, coming into the kitchen and placing our coffee cups in the sink.

'Cora. Lucy's arranging a girls' night next Friday. We were just chatting about it.'

'Look at you.' Alex grins. I can't hide the smile on my face as I whack him playfully on the arm.

'Girls' nights, bridal shopping, group chats. I told you it would all happen for us eventually,' he says.

'It is starting to feel that way, isn't it?' I chuckle, caressing my stomach and leaning forward to kiss his cheek.

PART II
MAY

CHAPTER 8

By Wednesday evening, the excitement for the girls' night on Friday almost has me forgetting about the antenatal class.

'Aren't you ready? We'll be late, again!' Alex frowns, looking me up and down.

I'm wearing a soft fleece hoodie blanket and slippers, curled up with a new crime novel.

'Oh God, what's the time?' I jump up, tugging off my slippers.

The days have started blurring together the closer I get to my due date, especially without a job.

'We've got about twenty minutes before we need to be there.' He laughs, watching me dig through the wardrobe.

'I think pregnancy brain is officially a thing,' I tell him, hunting for something more appropriate to wear.

Throwing the blanket hoodie to the bed, I pull on a stretchy Primark dress in its place. Henry kneads into the hoodie at the foot of the bed, cosying up for a long nap on top of it while I rush from the bedroom to find my shoes.

* * *

We're in such a rush we leave our teddy bear and nappy at home and end up borrowing one of Emma's grimy dolls to practise nappy changing on instead.

'I can't believe we're already halfway through this,' Cora says when I sit next to her, nursing a strong cup of tea.

'It's gone so fast, but in a weird way it feels like I've known you all much longer than three weeks!' Violet says, taking a seat on my other side.

There's a table set up in the middle of the hall where Emma stands once we've all gathered.

'Can I get a show of hands, who plans on using disposable nappies?' she asks, looking around the group. Almost everyone raises their hands. 'What about cloth nappies?'

Violet and Marie raise their hands.

'We aren't sure yet,' Cora says. 'I'm interested to know more about cloth nappies, purely because I've heard how many nappies babies get through and if we can save a few pounds here or there, that's great.'

'I mean, it really depends how you look at it. The money you'd save on disposable nappies goes to the extra electricity for washing the cloth ones, surely?' Carmen says, looking at Emma.

'Like everything, there's good and bad sides to them. You have to change cloth nappies more often, they're less absorbent, so yes, you do end up with a lot of washing. They tend to be better for babies' skin, though,' Emma says.

She takes her doll and starts demonstrating how to put a disposable nappy on, though I'm only half paying attention. When she asks us all to give it a go on our own teddies and dolls, I'm confident I can do it.

While Alex wanders off into the kitchenette to get us both a drink, I start putting the nappy on the doll. It's ridiculous, practising on this weightless, motionless piece of plastic. I look over at everyone else, noticing Cora and Jack laughing with each other. They look so happy; my lips stretch at the sight at them. They're the picture postcard perfect couple, the ones everyone else wants to be.

When was the last time Alex and I laughed and joked around the way they do? The thought stills me. When had we lost the affection and playfulness we'd had in the beginning? When had the honeymoon phase ended? Before watching Cora and Jack interact, I guess I'd just thought it was the gradual progression of a relationship as you get more comfortable with each other.

My heart drops as I realize I miss Alex, a ridiculous thing to say when I see him every day, but I do. The baby jerks inside me, reminding me they're coming. It's an awful thought, but I keep thinking as soon as this baby gets here, my time with Alex will be even more scarce than it already is. I don't get his undivided attention as it is, but when we become parents will we ever have time for each other?

Sighing, I watch Cora and Jack, how connected they are. I end up having to look away. Most of the other couples seem to find the class hilarious, bent over their dolls and teddies, fiddling with a nappy. It's Carmen and Grayson who are breaking up the happy dynamic at the table next to ours. I keep my eyes glued to our doll, pretending to be working on my nappy-changing skills, but I can't help but overhear them.

'You're forgetting about the frilly bits,' Grayson mutters to Carmen when she's finished velcroing their nappy together with the side tabs.

'Frilly bits?' Her voice is clipped, and she wipes a sheen of sweat from her forehead.

'Here,' Grayson says, and I catch him rolling his eyes as I sneak a glance in their direction.

He scoops out the leg cuffs from the nappy and looks at Carmen, tight-lipped.

'She told us earlier; these need to be out. They work as leak guards. Pay attention.' He speaks so softly I'm not sure anyone else hears him, but his words jar me.

78

I look at him in surprise, and he notices me staring, raising his eyebrows at me. Carmen's eyes shimmer with tears; she looks like she wishes she could disappear. She waits a moment, refusing to look back up at me. Touching the leg cuffs with her fingertips, a heavy tear drops to her doll. Grayson grumbles something to her I can't hear, and she quickly scurries off to the bathroom before anyone else notices.

I can't understand why he's so irritated with her over something so trivial. The tension between them is palpable and I see the rest of the class has noticed it too. It makes my heart ache silently for them. It makes me see that Alex and I aren't the only ones that aren't perfect. Everyone else has their issues, too. Even Cora and Jack, surely. Fascinated, I want to discover the chinks in every relationship in the room and spend the rest of the class watching everyone closely.

* * *

On the way back to the car, we get stuck in the car park talking to Cora and Jack. It's already after nine in the evening and the salty coastal air nips at my arms. Jack's talking about a kebab van we have to try when I spot Lucy out of the corner of my eye walking out of the hall.

Cora elbows me and we watch as she unlocks her car. I try pushing down the growing apprehension inside me. It won't be long now until we have to tell her about Arthur.

'Bless her.' Cora sighs.

'I know, going back to that big creepy house all by herself,' I say without thinking.

'Creepy house?'

'Oh, you know. It's just such a big house to be in all alone,' I say, trying to backpedal. I'd forgotten the others don't seem to know about Jessica's murder.

'You know, don't you?'

I look her in the eyes and wonder how to answer. After a second's hesitation, I nod. Lucy pulls up next to us, her window sliding down. She glances over at Alex and Jack, but they're deep in conversation.

'Enjoy the nappy-changing class?' Cora says, her voice sugar sweet. She's smiling brightly, but I can still feel the conversation we just had lingering around us. She knows about Arthur's first wife being murdered. I have someone to talk to about it. Maybe she knows more, things that aren't available online. I'm desperate to talk to her, but right now I have to plaster on a smile and hold a conversation with Lucy.

'I thought the class was a bit daft to be honest. Raided Arthur's daughter's room for it, too,' Lucy says, gesturing to the bear sitting in the passenger seat of her car.

An uncomfortable silence follows at the mention of Arthur's name, neither of us knowing what to say.

'Oh, what was it you guys wanted to talk to me about by the way? When you called me the other day?'

My heart stops. I don't want to have this conversation now, not here. Not like this.

'Oh, nothing important for right now. We'll chat over the weekend about it.' Cora waves her hand about.

'If you're sure?' Lucy frowns, her grey eyes scanning us both so intensely it makes me shudder.

Cora nods her head, a little too enthusiastically.

'Okay then, have a good night,' Lucy says, putting her foot down and driving away.

'She's going to hate us for keeping this from her for so long,' I mutter.

'I think the best thing we can do is just show her we're her friends for now. So, when we do tell her, she'll know she isn't alone. She has us as support. If we tell her before we've had a chance to really connect, then she might not feel comfortable reaching out to us. I don't want her feeling completely alone.'

I take in Cora's words, and despite the niggling doubt in my gut about Lucy, my walls start to crumble. I should be able to sympathize with Lucy more than anyone. I don't want to become standoffish towards her. It's my blazing lack of self-confidence rotting inside me and my trust issues that could cause some sort of a rift and I know I need to let it go.

What Cora says makes sense, so I nod in agreement. She's right. Lucy needs to know she has friends to fall back on. I can't imagine how I'd feel if someone told me Alex was cheating on me right now, especially when I haven't had the chance to form the friendships I've been so excited about yet.

I look over at Alex now, still talking to Jack. I want to get back on the topic of Lucy's home, about the murder, while the guys aren't paying attention.

'I wasn't sure who else knew, about the murder, I mean. I didn't really want to say anything in case she didn't want people to know,' Cora says. 'I can only imagine how hard it must be trying to make friends with something like that hanging over your head.'

'I didn't want to say anything either. It'd be weird if the others didn't know about it though, right? It must have been pretty big news for a place as small as this.'

'Yeah, I'm not sure how new everyone is to the area, but for those of us who've been here a while, it's a pretty famous story. They call it the murder house. It's connected with a bunch of other murders from a decade or so ago, too.'

This surprises me. I hadn't read anything about other murders that had taken place there, and my curiosity intensifies.

'How did you know about it, anyway?' she asks.

'Oh. I'd read about it before we moved here, when I was researching the area,' I lie, hoping she can't see the blush working its way onto my cheeks.

'Right, you. We should be getting home,' Alex says, coming up behind me, his warm fingers squeezing the nape of my neck.

* * *

When we get home, he heads to the bar and pours himself a neat whiskey.

'I've got a few work things to catch up on, love. Why don't you head to bed and I'll be up soon,' he says, taking a sip from the tumbler.

I close the gap between us, my lips finding his in the dimly lit room. The smell of whiskey used to repulse me, but now my mouth lingers close to his hot breath for a few stolen moments. My hands roam, down his arms and across his chest, over to the ripening in his jeans.

'Baby,' he groans, leaning into me but grabbing my hands to stop me from going further. 'I'm sorry. I really need to get some work done.'

'Oh, sure. Sorry. Okay,' I whisper, backing away from him, keeping my eyes to the ground.

'Darcy, it's not you. I promise.'

'I know.' I force a smile, retreating upstairs. I don't even bother taking off my makeup before curling into a ball in bed and pulling the blankets over my head.

I'm so caught up in my own world I hardly think about Lucy and the Harold house with all of the murder attached to it until I'm asleep. That's when my dreams are full, full of blood and death and the macabre.

A decaying manor house with unknown shadows lurking in every corner traps me inside. My feet are thudding across groaning floorboards, I'm trying to hide. Someone is after me, a knife in hand.

I'm drenched in sweat, so much so that when I wake, the bed is soaked. It's gone four in the morning and Alex isn't in bed. Tiptoeing out onto the landing with Henry at my feet, I see Alex's office is in darkness. Nothing more greets me than an empty room holding his large mahogany desk and work folders.

Downstairs, the lounge is deserted too. On the bar top, I spot his whiskey glass. It's been drained, the bottle alongside it dry. How much has he had to drink?

I press my face up close to the door of the spare room, standing ajar. Alex is sprawled across the bed, his shoes still on. He's in a deep sleep, his breathing heavy. I close the door and leave him to sleep, then head into the kitchen and flick the kettle on, welcoming the rumble of the boiling water. Anything to fill the deafening silence around me. The isolation is the worst part of all.

***

I research the Harold house in its entirety, needing something to keep me busy until Friday. Things with Alex seem stagnant, so much so that I can't bring myself to remind him about my wedding dress appointment over the weekend. I haven't been in the right frame of mind to invite any of the girls to come with me anyway, so I postpone the appointment to the following weekend. I'll ask the girls if they'll come with me when we're at the girls' night. The closer Friday night gets, the more eager I am to get away from the house and the stifling atmosphere.

I need space, and so I retreat into myself, barely coming up for air from the articles I read. One article in particular is so harrowing my teeth chatter as I read it, but an obsession is building inside me.

DEVASTATION AT HAROLD FAMILY HOME AS HISTORY REPEATS ITSELF

Rock's historic manor home, belonging to the Harold family for generations, has claimed another victim. The site has stood as a haunting reminder of tragic, unsolved murders for many years. Now fascination over a property with such a dark past is at fever pitch as the area swarms with news crews and visitors trying to catch a glimpse of the grounds they claim to be cursed.

Jessica Harold, wife to Rock's local attorney, Arthur Harold, and mother to his two children was slaughtered on

17th August 2018. The massacre has been recorded as being chillingly similar to the murders that happened there decades ago, leaving the town questioning whether a copycat killer is afoot.

Many years ago, the previous owners of the house were found dead with their throats slit in the infamous kitchen where Jessica Harold was murdered. Jessica and Arthur's children watched the savage act unfold, which mirrors what happened all those years ago when Arthur and his younger sister were forced to observe the brutal attack on their own parents. While in both cases the children were left unharmed, one can only imagine the impact this has had on them.

At this stage of the investigation, there are no clues pointing in the direction of a suspect. This leaves the town wondering if, once again, the case will turn cold.

One after the other, the articles consume me. They take me in a vice-like grip and don't let go. I want to know everything there is to know about the place locals have been spreading stories about like wildfire. There are Facebook groups dedicated to it, people convinced the property's evil, doomed, the Harold family along with it, too.

CHAPTER 9

I wake on Friday morning with a nervous excitement, like it's Christmas morning. After researching the Harold house extensively, I've become more than a little obsessed. Seeing the girls has become more of an excuse to get closer to the house and explore its dark interior. I can't explain my interest in it, this compulsion that has completely taken me over. Part of me wonders if I'm trying to fill the void in my life where work and friendship should be.

Not one recruitment agent has returned any of my emails asking after any administration jobs in the area and with my due date quickly approaching, I don't even know if it's worth reaching out to them again, not until I'm ready to go back to work again anyway.

Will I ever be ready to return to a bland nine-to-five office job, though? I did extend feelers for other kinds of roles, but I don't like my chances. I'm not particularly good at anything, I don't have any special training or skillsets, so I already know I'm not the most desirable of employees. At my age, I do want to do more with my life than sit behind a front desk answering phones and responding to emails anyway. I sigh, knowing this a problem I need to deal with in the coming months, but not now.

Alex has been in the sourest mood since Wednesday evening, and I've noticed two more bottles of whiskey find their way into our recycling bin. He tucked them under other recyclables, trying to hide the evidence.

He's kept his head buried in work while I've kept out of his way. There's only so many times I can ask him what's wrong without it annoying both of us, so I leave him to it, assuming he'll come to me when he's ready to talk.

I've been dressed and ready to leave for Lucy's since lunch. By the time I slide into Alex's office to say goodbye, it shocks me that I haven't seen him all afternoon.

'You look nice,' Alex says.

I look down at what I'm wearing, smiling despite myself. Every part of me wants to remain angry at him for the way he's been over the last few days, but I feel the ice starting to melt between us.

I've gone for a black-and-white-striped twist tank dress. Every time I wear it, Alex says I look Parisian. It's one of his favourites. Wondering if I'd subconsciously put it on to grab his attention, I twist a lock of hair around my finger. I'd tried to tame my wild head of curls, spritzing in some leave-in conditioner and twirling it up out of my face, but some strands have already escaped.

'I'm sorry I've been such a knob,' he says.

I sigh. 'I don't really have time for this right now,' I say, despite knowing it will make me feel better if we sort everything out before I leave. 'What's going on, Alex?' I look down at the tumbler of whiskey resting by his keyboard.

'I'm just stressed, Darcy, but I don't want to talk to you about it when you're so close to giving birth,' he says, taking my hands in his. 'You don't need that kind of worry right now.'

My mind races. Are we in debt? Did we severely underestimate our budget when we moved here and bought this house? The only thing I can think of that would make him so anxious is money, and we both know it's the one thing I can't help with.

I look at him, guilt-ridden. He's trying to protect me from something that's clearly distressing him so much he's turned to drinking to cope and I've just let him be.

'I'll reach out to the recruitment agents again,' I say.

He shakes his head at me.

'Just focus on having our baby, please. It isn't about money, anyway. It's nothing for you to worry about, alright? It's just silly niggling doubts I have.'

'Doubts?' I ask, my chest tightening.

'Not about you. Doubts about whether I'll be a good dad or not. That kind of thing,' he says.

I flood with love for him, closing the gap between us and wrapping my arms around his shoulders.

'Alex, you're going to be an exceptional dad. I just know it,' I breathe.

He blushes, his hand stroking the small of my back.

'I have to go, but please don't worry about something like that, my love. You're already an amazing dad. Look at everything you've done for us. Just don't get too caught up in this,' I say, gesturing towards the whiskey.

'I know, I need to be careful. I'll stop, I promise,' he says, his finger circling the rim of the glass.

He's promising me he won't end up like his mother, and I want to believe him, but do I? I don't know. I've been seeing her in him more and more lately, and alcohol addiction is ingrained in his DNA.

I want to talk to him about it some more, but if I do, I'll be late, so I settle for a kiss. It's tender, and I feel his lips on mine long after we've pulled apart.

'Don't wait up.' I wink, feeling a thrill as I say those words. I have a life. I'm doing something without being attached to Alex's side. Debbie would be proud, right?

As I'm leaving the room I catch Alex pick the tumbler of whiskey up and knock back the contents.

***

The Harold house is lit up with ground lights flooding the exterior. They glow invitingly as I pull up outside. The gate screams out for oil as it parts. With the large front doors standing wide open, I step inside without knocking. I'm early by twenty minutes, purposefully done to try and get some one-on-one time with Lucy, to see if she'll tell me about the house.

'Hello?' I call out through the foyer, my voice reverberating around the bronze sculptures balancing precariously on plinths all around me. The silence is ominous. My low platform heels click against the marble floor as I venture deeper inside, letting the house inhale me with its musty atmosphere and buried secrets.

I follow a rich, buttery smell down the corridor, passing by the dusty framed photographs that hang perfectly straight on the walls. I stop at the photograph of Arthur and Lucy with an older couple who I'd previously assumed were Arthur's parents, but now I know they must be his grandparents. Now I look more closely I can start to understand their withdrawn, uptight appearance. They were in a constant state of grieving the loss of their family, Arthur's mother and father, who had been taken from them in such a brutal way. Their glacier-like eyes and the deep creases scored into their faces tell stories I wish I knew. I hold my hand over my bump, thinking about the unnaturalness of losing your own child. How wrong it must feel to have to say goodbye to them and carry on living. Looking at Arthur's grandparents encapsulated in this frame, I wonder if they're still alive today, if they ever healed from their loss or if that's the sort of sorrow that forever weighs you down.

Their eyes follow me as I continue down the corridor. There's a nutty, creamy fragrance getting closer as I edge further into the bowels of the house. I let my nose guide me, my pulse quickening the closer I get to what must be the kitchen, the scene of all of those blood-soaked horror stories. When I finally get to the entrance, I curl my fingers around the doorframe quietly. Inside, a man in a white chef's uniform slices effortlessly through the body of a fish. I watch his thick fingers move the fish around a chopping board as he fillets it, discarding the bones into a neat pile to the side. He's so engrossed in his work he hasn't noticed me. I give myself the chance to take in the room. Besides the overall structure, there's nothing similar about it to the photographs I'd found online. It's been completely remodelled with reclaimed oak floors, stunning stainless-steel appliances and a mosaic tile finish. I guess I'd been expecting this big, sinister atmosphere when I finally got here, traces of the murders embedded into the structure perhaps. I'm left a little underwhelmed.

I stare at the kitchen island where the chef is working, trying to figure out if that's where the murders would have taken place. I don't even realize I've stepped into the room when the chef startles, looking up at me knife in hand.

'Forgive me,' he says, slipping the blade down beside the salmon carcass.

'Hi, I'm looking for Lucy?'

'Lucy?' He knits his hairy eyebrows together, wiping his hands on his apron.

'I'm here for the girls' nights. I'm a little early,' I admit.

'Ah, of course.' He rinses his hands in the sink, grabbing the stem of a wine glass, and pours a deep crimson drink from a cocktail shaker.

'Alcohol-free, don't worry,' he says, handing it to me as he takes in my bump.

I politely take a sip, trying to avoid the pierced cherry placed as a garnish over the rim of the glass with a cocktail pick. My tastebuds burst to life with a zingy cranberry flavour.

'This is amazing,' I say, thanking him.

'Ms Harold should be down shortly. In the meantime, please make yourself at home.' He smiles at me, but the way he looks at me suggests it's time I get out of the kitchen.

The open window lets in a chilly breeze that strokes its way up my arms, leaving me covered in goosebumps. I look down at the severed fish head, my stomach flipping. Stealing one last glance around the kitchen, I retreat back out into the hallway with my mocktail. Checking my watch, I know the others will be starting to arrive at any moment, but I don't go back the way I came. Instead, I carry on further down the hallway until I reach the bottom of a staircase spiralling up to the second floor. Hesitantly, I grip the banister and slowly start the climb.

It's a different world upstairs, dark and confined. Paintings and sculptures have been covered up, not that there's any sunlight exposure up here to protect them from. Every window is closed, leaving the space stuffy and in a state of early decay. The closed curtains look thick with dust mites, as though they haven't been touched in years. Upstairs, the house looks forgotten about, neglected, as though someone just gave up on it one day.

As I slink across the landing, I notice one of the doors is slightly ajar. The door groans as I push it open, displaying a soulless room clearly meant for a little girl. In the centre of the room is a bed covered in a ripped hanging netting. There's a framed photograph on the pink bedside table of a little girl and her mother. I recognize the woman in the photograph as Arthur's first wife instantly. The little girl, full of cheeriness and smiling with her eyes, can't possibly be the same diffident girl I'd seen here a couple of weeks ago. I step closer and pick up the photograph. She has the same blonde hair and grey eyes as the little girl I'd seen, but that's the only thing they have in common. The girl who sleeps in this room now isn't the same girl in the photograph. The girl I saw here last time I came, with her pinched expression and downcast eyes, was a girl in mourning, tortured by grief and vivid memories. I know the feeling, and my heart aches for her. Next to the frame there's a notepad. I put my mocktail down and flip through the crinkled pages. They're filled with scribbles in blue ink. One page stops me in my tracks. I open the notebook up properly, the spine crackling, and stare at the page in alarm. Lucy's name is scrawled again and again on every single line of the page. The next page is exactly the same, and the next. It looks like some sort of twisted punishment she'd had to do. A tremor works its way down my back as I return the notepad and step cautiously out of the room. I'm about to hurry back down the staircase when a door right across from me swings open.

'Oh my God!' Lucy gasps, covering herself quickly. She's in a towel, steam billowing out from behind her.

'I'm so sorry, the front door was open, so I let myself in,' I say, cringing.

'It's fine. I'll be out in a moment,' she says, reversing back into the bathroom and slamming the door shut.

This is not how I'd envisioned tonight starting off. I scurry back down the stairs where the other girls have already started to gather in the foyer.

* * *

'Sorry about that. I was running a bit behind and had to jump in the shower!' Lucy says about twenty minutes later when we've all been served a new mocktail from the chef. She's wearing a tight white dress with a rose gold sash strung across her shoulder that says, *Mama to Be*. Her bump is a perfectly round mound on her otherwise tiny frame.

'I hope you don't mind, I decided tonight's going to be a bit of a joint celebration for all of us as mamas to be.' She points to her sash as the chef comes out with a handful of other sashes. He drapes them over our shoulders like some sort of Hawaiian garland before calling us all into the dining room. Blue, pink and green balloons bob up and down at every corner of the room, fabric bunting decorating the walls.

'Oh Lucy, this is so nice!' Cora squeals, touching the pearl chiffon table runner.

I take in the room, finding it a complete contrast to what the house looks like upstairs, out of sight from guests. There isn't much time to dwell on it though as the chef wheels in a trolley bearing our first course. A thick creamy soup swimming with dill is placed in front of me and I swear an eyeball is floating in the centre of it. Bile rises in my throat as I spoon the contents of the soup around in the bowl.

'What is this?' I lean over to ask the chef.

'It's fish soup,' Lucy replies for him, smiling sweetly. The image of the severed salmon's head in the kitchen fills my mind. 'Packed with goodness, especially when you're pregnant. So many people don't realize how beneficial the eyeballs and cartilage are for you when you take them from the skeleton.'

Rachel freezes, the spoon halfway to her lips.

'I'm sorry, eyeballs?' Violet pales.

'I think it's great,' Carmen says, shovelling another spoonful into her mouth.

'Don't worry, you don't have to eat it if you don't want to. The next course is going to be fun. He's coming in to do a bit of a teppanyaki-inspired thing,' Lucy says after swallowing a mouthful of soup.

I push my bowl to the side and look down at the mocktail, no longer sure I can trust what's in that either.

'I had my latest midwife appointment earlier today,' Lucy says.

'Oh my God, so did I. How difficult is it to pee into those tiny containers they give us to check our urine for protein and signs of infection?' Cora says with a chuckle. 'My bump's so big now I can't see what I'm doing down there, and they give me the tiniest little container, so I end up peeing all over myself!'

'Yes! I always make the mistake of wearing a dress to appointments so when I have to get up onto the bed so she can measure my bump and have a feel, I end up giving her a full-frontal view of my horribly neglected bikini line!' Violet says.

'I'm sure they've seen far worse things,' I say, meaning to sound reassuring, but it comes out more condescending. Luckily, we're distracted by Lucy, who starts handing out a nappy to everyone.

'You always play games at baby showers, right? So, I thought we'd play one now. My lovely chef, Philemon, is going to come out with a few different concoctions for the nappies. They're supposed to resemble the different types of baby poo you get. If you can guess what ingredients were used for the dirty nappy, you win a prize!'

The chef comes in to take away our first course, bowls and cutlery clattering back onto his trolley. 'You didn't like it?' he asks me as he clears my bowl away.

'I'm pretty sure I got one of the eyeballs,' I say meekly.

'Ah, but that's good for you! It will see you through the rest of the week!' He chortles at his own joke, taking the bowl from me with a flourish and replacing it with a dollop of something that looks remarkably similar to mint sauce, which he plops into the nappy. I look around at the other girls. Cora is reluctantly bringing her nappy up to her nose and giving it a tentative sniff.

'Oh! I know what this is,' Violet shouts, pointing down to her nappy. 'Peanut butter!'

'You didn't think I'd make it that easy, did you? There're at least two ingredients in every nappy. Get sniffing!' Lucy giggles.

'Can we taste it?' Carmen asks, peering down into her own nappy filled with some sort of thick and sticky dark brown sauce. Lucy nods, her shoulders heaving up and down with laughter.

'I never ever thought I'd be picking stuff out of a nappy and putting it in my mouth. How revolting!' Rachel grimaces, but there's a smile on her face.

We all dive into our nappies. Mine definitely has mint sauce in it, making it green and bitty, but there's something else in there too. Mushy peas, perhaps. We keep guessing for ages, slowly figuring out the ingredient in each nappy between us while the chef sets up an electric grill at the other end of the table. I'm having such a fun time genuinely laughing and connecting with everyone that I almost forget where we are until the chef brings out a set of razor-sharp knives. He performs for us, tossing the cleaver around with unfaltering grace. There's a sizzle of hot oil as each piece of meat hits the grill. Everyone cheers while he prepares small slithers of food he throws into our mouths.

When the evening is in full swing, I seize the chance to ask the girls about joining me at the dress appointment.

'I have something to ask you all. It might be a bit weird as I know we're all relatively new to each other, but I have a wedding dress appointment next weekend and no one to go with. I wondered if any of you would want to come?'

'Yes! I'd love to join you, Darcy,' Cora says, bouncing up and down in her seat. I swell with happiness.

One by one the girls all say they'll be there, and they all seem genuinely excited to help me choose a dress. Everyone but Carmen. She's busy next weekend, she says, but she doesn't go into any detail about her plans.

'That's okay, I know it's short notice,' I tell her, trying to offer her a smile, but she doesn't return it. She doesn't even look at me.

* * *

Towards the end of the evening the chef invites us all into the kitchen for an alcohol-free nightcap. Re-entering the room, which has been meticulously scrubbed clean, gives me an exhilarating thrill. I hadn't had enough time in here earlier and felt rushed to get out of the chef's way. We all sit around the island while he prepares us a decadent-looking hot drink.

'I thought it would be fun to play a little game of truth or dare to end the night,' Lucy says, looking around at each one of us.

'What are we, twelve?' Rachel scoffs.

'We'll start with you then, Rachel. Truth or dare?' Lucy counters, staring directly into Rachel's acidic green eyes.

'Dare.' Rachel stares back.

'I dare you to eat one of those fish eyeballs.' There's a wicked glint in Lucy's eyes. The chef sifts through the soup, finding an eyeball and placing it down in front of Rachel. She swallows hard.

'This dare would've been much better suited for Darcy. Didn't you see how pale she went when the chef put the soup in front of her?' She laughs. 'But . . . those who know me know I never turn down a dare.' She parts her lips and spoons the eyeball into her mouth. Chewing slowly, an involuntary gag makes her convulse.

'Vile!' She retches, sticking out her tongue to show us it's all gone.

Everyone but Carmen seems impressed. She seems miserable tonight, hardly making an effort with anyone. I wonder if I'm the only one who's noticed.

Rachel asks Lucy next, who chooses truth.

'Who do you think the most attractive guy is in the group, besides your husband obviously?'

Lucy leans back in her chair, thinking about it for a moment, then her eyes land on me.

'Sorry, Darcy. It's got to be Alex.'

I blanch, trying to cover my reaction quickly as a murmur of agreement spreads through the room. I should find this flattering, but it leaves me nauseated thinking of the other women looking at my fiancé that way, especially Lucy. I don't even need to guess who Alex would choose out of the girls if the same question was posed to him. Lucy with her blonde hair and light eyes is exactly the kind of woman he would usually go for, so very different to me with my dark curls, curves and olive skin tone. I remember being so surprised in the past when he'd tell me which contestant on *Love Island* or *Married at First Sight* he found the prettiest. It was never the most striking beauty, always someone more understated, finespun. Someone just like Lucy. It vexes me that they'd choose each other as the most attractive people in the group. I'm still agonizing over it when Rachel's voice snaps me back into the present.

'I have a better truth question. Tell us about this house, Lucy. What really happened here?' Her eyes are challenging, defiant almost.

I'd been reaching out for my drink but still instantly, watching Lucy. So, Rachel knows about this house too. Lucy takes a quick sip of her drink, delaying her response.

'Do you all know about the history of this house?' she asks quietly, the gentle flicker of a flame from a candle casting a menacing shadow across her face. Surprisingly, everyone starts to cautiously nod their heads.

'It's the murder house.' She shrugs. Even the chef looks up from his station as she speaks. 'It's true, what they say about this place. A lot of people have died here, more than a lot of people are aware of, actually.'

I start to wonder who else died here besides Arthur's parents and his first wife, and why people aren't aware of it. I tremble in the silence that follows Lucy's words.

'Doesn't it creep you out, living here?' Violet shudders, the air in the room growing frosty.

'Sometimes. That's one of the reasons I wanted to invite you all here tonight. It's not the nicest place to be alone.' She looks at us apologetically. I'm not sure if I should be mad at her for admitting she's using us so she's not alone here. Was that all this evening was about to her, or is she actually interested in our friendship?

'It all happened here in this room, didn't it?' I can't help but ask.

'Every single death,' she says.

'That's my cue to leave, ladies. I hope you enjoyed your dinner.' The chef's smile doesn't meet his eyes as he gathers up his things. We all thank him, giving him a round of applause. As soon as he's gone though, there's a shift in the room.

'I think we should carry on playing the game. Lighten the mood a bit. Violet, truth or dare?' Carmen sits up straight in her chair, her hand placed over her tiny bump. The irony of her wanting to lighten the mood isn't lost on me.

'Oh, go on then, dare!' Violet smiles.

'I dare you to imagine you were in labour right now. Look around the kitchen and find something you'd be willing to let us use to help get the baby out of you in the case of an emergency.'

I think about the chef's cleaver, my stomach churning sickeningly at the thought of it.

Violet meanders uncertainly around the kitchen, peering into drawers. She's about to grasp the handle of one of the cupboards when Lucy shouts at her to stop. Violet flinches away as though she's been burnt.

'Not that one.' Lucy readjusts her face, trying to smile, but she looks nervous.

Violet pulls open a drawer and retrieves a filleting knife.

'That'll do it!' Cora quivers, staring at the knife in disgust.

'Lucy, truth or dare?' I raise an eyebrow at her.

'Truth.'

'What's in that cupboard?' I ask, pointing in the direction of the cupboard she hadn't wanted Violet to look inside. She sits there glaring at me for a few seconds before she stalks around the island with predatory elegance. When she opens the cupboard door, my eyes travel down the shiny black barrel of a gun.

'Art's hunting rifle. Don't worry, it isn't loaded,' Lucy says, noticing our horrified faces. She retrieves the gun and places the butt up to her shoulder. She hovers the muzzle over each one of us before eventually landing on me. 'Darcy, truth or dare?'

'Dare,' I say, my voice coming out as a croak.

'I dare you to trust me,' she says, stepping towards me with the gun still pointed at my head.

'Alright, Lucy, enough. This isn't funny,' Cora squeaks.

Lucy doesn't listen. She keeps the gun trained on me as she walks towards me.

'Open wide,' she whispers, pointing the barrel of the gun at my mouth. I ram my lips shut, starting to shake as the cold steel greets my jaw. I look at her, trying to figure out if she's making some sort of sick joke, but she's not smiling anymore.

'Go on, she said it's not loaded.' Carmen hoots with laughter.

'That would be illegal,' Violet says, as if that has any relevance, as if no one's broken the law before.

'We're supposed to be forming friendships, right? And friendships are built on trust. Do you trust me yet, Darcy?' Lucy's snigger is malicious, making my skin crawl. I nod my head at her, still refusing to open my mouth.

'Clearly not,' Carmen says, swirling the remnants of her drink around in the bottom of her glass. Fury rattles through me along with disbelief. How can anyone think this is a game? With every sense heightened, I wonder if I'm sitting right where Arthur's first wife was killed. Is this where she'd taken her last breath? All of a sudden, it's not hard to imagine me being the next victim.

'You do it then!' I snap at Carmen, twisting my face away from the gun and refusing to play.

'Fine.' She beckons Lucy over to her. Lucy's eyes linger on mine fleetingly before she turns her attention to Carmen.

Carmen rolls her eyes playfully and opens her mouth, letting Lucy put the barrel of the gun between her teeth. With her finger on the trigger, Lucy looks around the room, at our terrified faces.

'You all need to relax.' She returns her attention to Carmen and steadies herself. As her finger tightens around the trigger, I squeeze my eyes shut, bracing myself for a deafening bang. It doesn't come.

'Click.' Lucy smiles sweetly, releasing her finger from the trigger and dropping the gun from Carmen's mouth. 'Told you it wasn't loaded. At least Carmen trusts me!'

A nervous laughter ripples through the kitchen, everyone's shoulders beginning to sag in relief. I'm amazed at how amusing everyone seems to find it that Carmen just had a gun shoved down her throat in the very kitchen people have been murdered in.

At the other end of the island, Lucy looks at me in disappointment. I want to tell her this proves nothing; it doesn't mean I don't trust her at all, even though I don't. I want to tell everyone I just didn't want a gun in my mouth, that it isn't a game to me. It's stupid and dangerous. I want to scream out and ask why I feel like I ruined the fun, but the girls have all moved on already. The game of truth or dare has come to an end.

Lucy shepherds us all back into the foyer and hands us each our jackets and bags. I realize it's too late to salvage the night; it's already over. Saying goodbye, I get the sense I've disappointed not just Lucy, but everyone.

* * *

Leaving despondently, I hate the feeling that I've soured the night. As I buckle up, I keep wondering if letting Lucy put the stupid gun into my mouth would have made the night turn out any better. If I'd done that, maybe I wouldn't be feeling this way right now. Wishing I could turn back time, I put my car into gear and drive away.

The roads are slippery from another downpour of rain. I can hardly see through the thick fog that blankets the evening. By the time I see the deer standing in the middle of the road, it's too late. I swerve, slam on the brakes, my car skidding. That sound, the sound of tyres screaming as they struggle to grip the tarmac, makes me shriek, propelling me back into my car accident from years ago. The car jolts to a stop and I can't breathe, too afraid to open my eyes. Scared I'll be back there, my car wrapped around the snow gum tree in Australia. Every muscle in my body is tense, unmoving. I'm overcome by a nauseating dizziness making my head spin. Very slowly, I peel my eyes open and squint out into the darkness. Somehow, I've missed the deer. Large black eyes blink at me in stunned silence. We both carefully start to move our limbs at the same time, the shock beginning to settle.

The deer skitters off into the woodlands, leaving me alone in the middle of the road with no other cars in sight. Tears stream down my blotchy cheeks. I hit the steering wheel repeatedly, no longer sure if I'm crying about the near crash or about the girls' night I ruined. Or about something else entirely.

***

It's only the next day I realize I left my first mocktail glass in the little girl's bedroom, next to the notepad. If Lucy notices it, she'll know it was mine. No one else had been upstairs besides us. She'll know I was snooping around her house, and that I found Arthur's daughter's notepad filled with pages upon pages of Lucy's name.

CHAPTER 10

On Sunday morning, I meet Cora in the car park by the beach.

'How are you feeling after Friday?' she asks.

'Fine,' I lie. How can I tell her I haven't been able to stop thinking about that night ever since? That I've replayed the moment Lucy prodded my mouth with a gun over and over again until my head ached. No matter how many times I try to justify her actions, I can't. It wasn't funny, it wasn't a joke. It was cruel and stupid and anyone in their right mind would have reacted exactly as I had. Besides Carmen.

'I had the most awful stomach the next day, but I didn't want to say anything and offend her,' Cora says. When I don't reply, she looks at me a little more closely. 'You're upset about what happened, aren't you? I would be too, you know.'

I glance up at her, my eyes welling with tears.

'It feels like I upset everyone or ruined the game, but it didn't feel like a game anymore when that happened,' I say.

She touches me on the arm, her hand warm and comforting.

'I know. It wasn't right. The other girls think so too; I've spoken to them. No one wanted to say anything at the time. We were all a bit creeped out.'

'Even Carmen?' I ask sceptically.

The silence that follows answers my question. Of course, Carmen doesn't care about what happened with the gun. She found the entire thing hilarious. It was one of the only things that had made her smile the entire night. She'd been laughing at my expense. My temper flares.

Even so, it should be consoling that the others felt the same as me, but for some reason all I can think about is how much I must have upset Lucy. What she said when the gun was pointed at me rings through my head, *'Do you trust me yet, Darcy?'*

No. I don't trust her, and I never will. It isn't even her fault; it's Alex's. She doesn't know that. She doesn't understand that if he hadn't done what he'd done to me, I wouldn't have this deep-rooted insecurity ruining everything. I've tried again and again to heal from his cheating, but no matter what I do there's always a trigger. Unfortunately, right now, Lucy seems to be the trigger. Someone who seems to bring out the worst in me, the jealousy and confidence issues. I hate that I wish she wasn't a part of our antenatal group, that I know I'd be feeling so much better without her presence there. It isn't fair on her. Besides the weird game of truth or dare, Lucy has been lovely, and she seems so excited to come wedding dress shopping with me too.

'Carmen's a tough nut to crack. I think she's going through some personal things at the moment,' Cora says. 'I've had a few chats with her privately.'

I let out a breath and attempt a smile.

'Whatever she's going through, I just wish she wouldn't take it out on me.'

'I promise you it isn't intentional. It's not my place to say what's going on in her life; she's trusted me. So, I can't share what I know, just like I wouldn't share anything you tell me in confidence.'

'Thanks, Cora,' I say. I look into her kind eyes, a warmth spreading through me. I know in that moment I'm lucky to have Cora in my life. She's the sort of friend I'd always wanted.

* * *

Lucy meets us on the dunes, kitted out in khaki Lululemon hiking gear. She's carrying a cardboard carry tray with three takeaway hot chocolates, topped with whipped cream and mini marshmallows. Packets filled with toasted coconut flapjacks, carrot cake and Oreo brownies get passed around.

'I couldn't choose,' she says with a grin, offering the drinks to us as we start the walk to Daymer Bay.

I let the cup warm my hands, listening to Cora and Lucy chat about their pregnancy cravings. So far, Lucy seems completely normal. She even hugs me hello, wrapping her bony arms around me so I can breathe in that signature perfume she always seems to wear. It sticks to my skin long after she's let me go.

She hasn't brought up Friday night or the game of truth or dare. It makes me start to think that I imagined her bitterness when she'd accused me of not trusting her.

'This is great. Thanks for the invite. I really should be doing more exercise while I'm pregnant.' Lucy's hand rubs her stomach, which appears to be noticeably bigger today in such tight activewear. She looks almost as big as me and Cora, making me wonder if she's just incredibly bloated from the beer she clearly still drinks in her pregnancy or if she's genuinely just popped.

For a while we walk in what Lucy must feel is a comfortable silence, but to me it's excruciating. A gannet swoops over us, looking for food. Its powerful black-tipped wings almost graze our heads. We all duck, shrieking with laughter as our hot chocolates spill. For a short time, I forget the purpose of this walk, that we need to have a very serious conversation with Lucy. To anyone looking at us from afar, we must seem just like three friends out for a Sunday stroll. I wish that could be the case.

I cast my eyes out into the distance at Trebetherick Point, where the rusted remains of shipwrecks scatter the rocks.

'When we first moved here, I did some research. Did you guys know this place has a reputation for being a graveyard for ships? Apparently, there's something like six thousand shipwrecks off the shores,' I say, taking a bite of the flapjack in my hand. In truth, I'm only talking to avoid the conversation we all came here for.

Cora and Lucy both nod in unison, looking out at the rusty remnants of ships with me.

'Have you heard some of the creepy folklore stories about these waters?' Lucy looks at us, giving a devilish smile.

'I've heard something about a mermaid's curse before?' says Cora.

'Yeah, it's said that some Padstow local shot this gorgeous woman when she refused to marry him. He hadn't realized she was a mermaid when he did it. Before she died, she doomed the harbour from here to Hawker's Cove and that night there was this awful storm. It left heaps of shipwrecks in its wake,' she tells us. The icy undertone to her voice chills me.

'So that's why it's called Doom Bar,' I marvel.

'Exactly. Some people also like to call this area Death Bay.' Lucy smiles at me, her hair whipping around in the strong wind picking up.

We carry on walking up the Greenway path, Cora shooting me a look when Lucy isn't watching. I know we need to talk to her about Arthur, but I'm struggling.

'How've things been at the house by yourself, Lucy?' I force myself to say.

'Lovely! Art and the kids came home last night actually, so I didn't have to spend too much time completely alone there. We ordered a pizza and watched a film. It's nice to have them back. When they're gone I miss their noise.'

'And things with you and Arthur are good?' Cora asks.

'Of course. Why wouldn't they be?' Lucy gives Cora a perplexed look.

'I'm really not sure how to say this.' Cora starts to fumble with the knitted headband she's wearing, the nerves finally getting to her.

Lucy looks from Cora to me, her eyes full of concern.

'Lucy, we saw Arthur the other day,' I say, biting my lip.

'Okay?' She frowns, an anxious edge to her laugh. We've ground to a stop by Broadagogue Cove, the coarse sand biting at my exposed ankles as it gets picked up in the wind.

'He was with a woman, Lucy. They were being quite . . . intimate.' Cora winces at her choice of words.

Lucy looks away from us, out towards the few surfers bobbing up and down in the waves. Her eyes are curtained by thick blonde lashes that flutter furiously. When she turns back to us, tears threaten to spill down her rosy cheeks.

'I know,' she whispers, brokenly.

* * *

'Art believes in open relationships,' she tells us with a sigh.

'And you don't, I presume?' Cora asks.

'I mean, I don't *like* it. I've always found the whole polyamory thing a bit weird, to be honest. But I love him, and we have an understanding. The women he sees don't come to our home and it can never be anything serious, just sex.'

I want to tell her that the woman we saw him with definitely seemed like more to him than 'just sex'. They seemed cosy, but I keep quiet.

'So do you ever, you know, get involved with other men?' Cora asks sheepishly.

Lucy seems to think about this for a while before responding. 'Sometimes. I just feel like if he's allowed to do it, why can't I?'

I think back to the pool party and the way she was interacting with our other halves, how much her demeanour had seemed to shift. She'd turned seductive, self-possessed. She had definitely been flirting, and that skimpy one-piece had almost certainly been planned with seduction in mind. I'm sure of it. It's all starting to make some sort of sick, twisted sense. I look at her, so fragile and timid standing by the water's edge, and I think how harmless she looks on the surface. At the same time, I'm alarmingly aware that on paper she is exactly Alex's usual type. With her long blonde hair and big grey eyes, she could almost be the mermaid from the folklore tales. I feel a strong sense of possessiveness over Alex take hold of me, knowing I can never be comfortable with her around him anymore, not that I was to begin with. My gut had been telling me something from the start.

Alex is my happily ever after, my home. He's the man that gave me a family. I have to protect that at all costs.

CHAPTER 11

At our fourth antenatal class the following week, Emma is clearly surprised to see how close we all seem after a handful of classes. We all greet each other with hugs and it's a struggle for her to break up our conversation to begin the session. Lucy is by herself; this time she uses a flaky babysitter as her excuse. I'm almost certain it's a lie, and I wonder what her story will be next week. She's dressed in a low-cut dress tonight, revealing her cleavage. I notice more than a couple of the guys staring as she arrives, and I'm grateful that Alex has kept his eyes away.

'Has she always worn such revealing clothing?' I mutter under my breath to Cora. 'Or am I only just starting to notice now I know about her and Arthur's polyamory?'

Cora crosses her legs in response, pretending not to have heard me. The hall is humid, every window cranked open, so the sweet aroma of peonies floats in with the evening breeze. I fan myself with a pamphlet Emma's handed out, trying to ignore Lucy's breasts, but they're like two big hilltops shimmering on display. May has brought about warmer, sunnier weather already and it's starting to make me worry just how hot summer is going to get this year.

'Tonight's class is going to be focused on First Aid. It's all about raising your confidence so you feel you know what you should do in the case of an emergency with your little one,' Emma says. She's holding up the same grimy doll she'd used at the breastfeeding class.

Using the doll, she shows us how to open the baby's airway and make a seal around the mouth and nose so we can start giving rescue breaths. I try to focus, to take in everything she's saying, but I can't stop glancing over at Carmen and Grayson. I know she'll ask us to perform the rescue breaths on our own doll or teddy once she's finished the demonstration and I'm worried Grayson's going to get upset with Carmen again. She's distracted, looking out of the window. My pulse pounds.

* * *

The First Aid class is enough to instil a new anxiety in me, suddenly having me worried about all sorts of things from febrile seizures to meningitis. It's impossible to take in everything Emma tells us, and I feel like it's my duty to be able to retain it all, so I end up feeling totally overwhelmed by the time I drag my feet out of the hall.

Out in the car park everyone mingles for a while. I join the girls circle, dipping into the middle of a conversation about birth.

'Lucy's really starting to sway me into considering a waterbirth,' Cora's saying. Lucy is standing alongside her, and I wonder just how much the two of them chat privately.

My friendship with Cora has been slowly building, and I feel a rush of jealousy at the thought of Lucy being closer to her than me.

'I'd just be worried I'd get to the hospital and there'd be no birthing pools available or something,' Violet says nervously.

'That's why I'm renting my own birthing pool and doing it at home.' Lucy touches Violet on the arm. 'I can send you the details for the company I'm using if you like?'

While Violet nods, Cora asks for the details too. I want to ask for the information as well, but I won't allow myself to do it. I just can't let Lucy close. My walls are rising around her, brick by brick.

The couples all trickle away until it's just Grayson, Carmen and Alex and I left in the car park.

Grayson and Alex are still caught up in a conversation, leaving Carmen and I lingering at their sides. Neither of us seem to be interested in making small talk, but eventually she's the first to speak.

'Oh, while I remember. I've been given some wiggle room, so I can come to your dress appointment on the weekend after all,' she says.

I almost groan out loud. Her expression is jaded, like she couldn't care less about joining the others for the appointment. It makes me want to ask her why she's even bothering to come. She clearly has no desire to do so.

'That's great,' I force myself to say.

She gives me a tight-lipped smile, her beady eyes looking from me to Alex.

Alex catches her eye and gives her a friendly smile, but she looks away from him too, her eyes darting down to her feet. Maybe it's not just me, maybe she's like this around everyone. But then I think of what Cora said, how Carmen had opened up to her and told her some things I'm not privy to. Perhaps she just doesn't like me and Alex. She's never particularly warmed to us, but she's had some sort of meaningful conversations with some of the other girls. I wish I could work her out.

Eventually, Grayson unlocks his Tesla and Carmen pulls herself inside. We wave them off before getting into our own car and heading home.

* * *

That evening, while Alex watches the latest season of *The Bear*, I google home births. For years when I started thinking about having a baby of my own, I'd always assumed I'd have to go to a hospital to give birth. I'd never imagined it another way, and the idea of having to be back inside the walls of a hospital was enough to put me off wanting kids for a long time.

Everything I read makes me even more excited about the idea of having our baby here, at home. Looking around, the lounge is big enough to hold a birthing pool. It's a calming room, the walls painted shades of green and blue with cream curtains and a dark stone floor. If we shifted the large L-shaped sofa, we'd have plenty of space. I try to imagine it, giving birth right here, welcoming our child into the world without all of those doctors, machines and sick or dying patients everywhere. Or dead patients for that matter. The hospital mortuary isn't a place I ever want to be close to again. Just the thought of it makes bile rise in my throat.

I touch my bump, a silent ache ripping through me. It's a pain that doesn't come often, but when it does, it very nearly destroys me. My mum and dad will never get to meet their grandchild. The silver locket containing my parents' photographs dangles from my neck, and I stroke the delicate engraving along the back. Inhaling deeply, I gulp back a sob. I try to fight the thoughts of my family from my head, replacing them with plans for a waterbirth. I won't allow myself to think of my family. I can't. It hurts too much.

I make a few enquiries with some companies that hire out birthing pools, wondering if any of them happen to be the one Lucy's using. While I type my email to them, I gently stroke Henry purring on my lap. His warm body stretches lazily across me.

I look over at Alex, engrossed in a montage of Jeremy Allen White cooking. He's trussing a chicken, basting it, preparing fresh sprigs of rosemary with bright purple flowers for it.

'I've been looking into home births a bit more,' I tell him, keeping my eyes fixated on the screen.

He pauses the television and puts a hand on my leg, waiting for me to say more.

'It just seems perfect for us. I love that I wouldn't need to be around that kind of sterile medical environment. You know how much I hate it,' I say.

'I know, I can't even begin to imagine what you've been through,' he says, taking my hand and stroking my fingers slowly. 'I don't like hospitals either, never have. Maybe you should speak to Lucy about it a bit more. She might be able to offer you some advice?'

A flicker of annoyance washes over me at the mention of Lucy's name. I wanted to like everyone in our antenatal group, and I've really tried to, but Lucy has made it incredibly hard to trust her. Especially around Alex. I'm too insecure around her. As soon as I fell pregnant, as soon as my body was hijacked by our baby and my boobs began to swell and the stretchmarks had started to snake their way up my stomach, I sensed that Alex had stopped looking at me like I was something to be desired. I guess I'd been so busy growing our child that I hadn't even realized I missed it until I felt threatened by another woman.

'Yeah, I'll reach out to her tomorrow,' I lie, not wanting him to sense my insecurity.

'It'll be good for you to have her to talk to about it. I know you're scared of giving birth. I would be too, Darcy. Honestly, thank God you're doing this and not me. Can you imagine?'

We both laugh softly.

'Alex, you can barely handle a headache let alone childbirth,' I say with a smile. 'I don't even know how you're going to cope during the birth with your fear of blood.'

'Hey! I fainted one time.' He grins at me.

It's always been a running joke in our relationship, but as the time has drawn closer to give birth, I have to admit that it has worried me.

'It's really important to me that you're there, in the room, when I give birth,' I say. 'You're all I have. I don't think I'll be able to do it without you.'

'Darcy, you know I'll do my best. I promise,' he says, kissing me on the cheek. Somehow his promise only makes me feel even more uneasy.

'Anyway, if you and Lucy are both planning on having your babies the same way, it could be a great way to connect with her, don't you think?' he says. 'I think she needs some friends from what I've seen. She seems pretty lonely, with Arthur always working.' He's rubbing my stomach as he talks, soothing my itching, stretched skin.

I try to hide my irritation, snuggling into his chest and pressing play on the remote. We'd got through the antenatal class without bickering, and I don't want to start now. I don't want to respond to him or talk about Lucy anymore. I want to enjoy this moment with my fiancé. We spend the next twenty minutes finishing an episode of *The Bear* with Henry squeezed between us.

Before we go to bed that evening, a message comes through from Carmen and Grayson.

> *Sorry for the short notice, but we'd like to invite you to our baby shower this weekend! It was supposed to be a surprise, but my mother accidentally sent me a message about the party that was meant for someone else, so the cat's out the bag! I'd love for you all to come if you can make it. It's going to be at the same hall we use for our antenatal classes, this Saturday at 12 p.m. Hope to see you all there. C.*

I read the message again. I can't believe it. This Saturday. The Saturday I'd invited everyone to my dress appointment, the dress appointment she said she could come to just hours ago. Her baby shower is at exactly the same time as the dress appointment, too. She hasn't even acknowledged it.

I tell Alex, battling not to let my emotions run wild.

'That's a bit rubbish,' he says, frowning. 'But it's fine, Darcy. You can just reschedule, no? It's not like she planned it on purpose. She's said it was supposed to be a surprise for her, look.'

I can just reschedule. Again. My shoulders droop. It feels like everything to do with our wedding is never a priority. Alex doesn't seem to notice my disappointment.

'I better start looking for a baby shower gift.' I sigh.

'Imagine if we get invited to everyone's baby shower. That'll get expensive.' He raises his eyebrows at me as I scour the internet for the perfect gift.

***

Although Carmen's party is at the village hall, it's nothing short of exceptional. They've hired a pizza van and inside there's a fully stocked bar manned by a handful of young girls pretending to know how to mix cocktails. The entire hall is done up to the nines, blue bunting banners draped from every beam, and there's a huge balloon arch over a lit-up neon sign with the words *Oh Baby* glowing from it.

Each table has a framed photograph of Carmen at every month throughout her pregnancy. Somehow even with all of the tacky décor, the place looks refined. She doesn't strike me as someone who would want this level of attention, but nevertheless, she seems thrilled when she sees us arrive. I try to hand her our gift bag, but she points me in the direction of a corner table already overflowing with presents. Next to all of the other beautifully wrapped gifts, ours looks ridiculous. I tuck it at the back, a wave of resentment taking hold of me. If Alex and I were to have a baby shower, we wouldn't have even half of the number of gifts laid out on this table. We wouldn't have nearly as many guests either. In fact, besides Alex's mother, I doubt there would be anyone to invite except for our new antenatal friends.

Carmen and Grayson's friends are boundless, with more people rolling in by the hour. Alex heads off to grab a cocktail with Jack and Johnny, leaving me sitting alone at a table, staring at a photograph of Carmen at six months pregnant.

'This party puts mine to shame!' Cora pulls up a chair and sits down next to me, rubbing at the swell of her ankles.

'I'm glad I'm not the only one thinking that.'

Violet, Marie and Rachel zigzag through the crowd, making their way over to us with virgin mojitos in hand.

'You're swelling up too, I see.' Violet lifts up her skirt, revealing bulging legs. Her entire face looks puffier today and her dainty fingers have expanded, too.

'It must be the heat. Summer has definitely arrived early this year!' Cora grimaces. Outside, the sun is beating down onto the village hall playground. The climbing frames and slide radiate heat, a blurry haze obscuring my vision of the ocean in the distance.

'I used to be such a warm weather person. You couldn't get me out of the sun! Now, I'm already desperate for winter to come back,' I say.

Cora looks at me, her skin dewy. She's wearing a grey dress with unforgiving sweat marks pooling under her armpits. 'I'm sorry about your wedding dress appointment today, Darcy. Was it rescheduled? I'd still love to come.'

'Yes, me too!' Rachel says.

'They haven't got back to me yet. It's the second time I've had to postpone, so I think I've annoyed them a bit.' As soon as I speak, I wish I could take it back. I don't want it to seem like I'm complaining about Carmen ruining my dress appointment.

'Well, just let us know when it is, and we'll be there.' Cora grins as the others nod in agreement. I smile at them gratefully.

We all twist in our seats as the doors to the hall open again.

'It's Lucy.' Marie smiles, beckoning Lucy over to us. She's holding a ginormous present wrapped in shiny gold paper, which she pops proudly on display right at the front of the table with all of the other gifts. There's no need for her to feel embarrassed about the size of her gift. Today she's dressed in a stretchy sundress that hugs her baby bump and shows off her long legs. She makes her way over to us, giving us all a kiss on the cheek as she says hello. Her perfume claws its way up my nose, so overpowering I can't even smell the pizza dough baking outside anymore.

We all catch up for a while, and then she notices the bar. I see her eyes lock onto the guys and within seconds, she's up and out of her chair.

'I need to get one of those mocktails, I think,' she says, smoothing down her dress before walking towards the bar.

'Off to the boys, I see,' Rachel mutters. I'm glad to know it isn't just me that's noticed the way she gravitates towards our partners. I look over at Cora, but she gives me a subtle shake of her head. She doesn't want me to tell the girls about the polyamorous lifestyle Lucy leads, even though I don't think Lucy would even care if we did. She seems pretty open about it.

I peer at Lucy as she edges closer to Alex after getting her drink. I see him say hello to her, and I flinch as she kisses him on the cheek in return. Does she always do that when they see each other? Is that why I always seem to smell her perfume on his skin? Why hasn't he told me she kisses him hello? But then, why would he? It's normal. It's my insecurity that isn't normal. I exhale, calming myself.

They fall into easy conversation, and I'm crushed by how effortlessly it seems to flow. I watch as Alex laughs his deep throaty laugh at something she says. I can't remember the last time I made him laugh like that. She leans in close and says something into his ear and at the same moment they both look up and stare at me from across the room. Alex has the decency to look shamefaced, but Lucy narrows her eyes at me, a tiny cruel smile playing on her lips. She's toying with me, dangling my fiancé in front of me. She has to be, but I don't understand why.

I turn away from them quickly, not wanting them to see how paranoid they're making me. Bitterness sweeps through me. I've never seen Alex around another woman like this before; it's making me territorial and suspicious. Surely Lucy wouldn't be intentionally flirting with Alex. I try and tell myself I'm imagining it all, but it doesn't stop me from wanting to march over there to tell her to leave Alex alone. I'm stopped by a strange sound coming from Violet, who has her head in her hands at the table.

'You okay, hon?' Rachel asks her.

'Sorry, I've had this headache for days. It just won't go away.'

'I think maybe we should go.' Marie looks concerned. They gather up their things and make an early exit. When I sneak a glance back over to the bar, Lucy and Alex have separated.

***

'What were you talking to Lucy about?' I ask Alex along the drive back home. I can't help it. I have to ask him or it will only start a new fear rotting inside me.

'I knew you were going to ask me that.' He sighs. There's rum on his breath, filtering into the air. How many cocktails did he have today?

I grip the steering wheel tightly, clenching my jaw in frustration. I can feel the evening starting to curdle already.

'Why won't you just answer the question?' I say.

'When are you going to start trusting me, Darcy?' he says, snapping his head in my direction. 'You promised me you'd try. I've done everything to fix us.'

'I try. You know I try,' I whisper, on the verge of tears. How has he turned this around onto me? I feel attacked, like my anxiety is unjustified when we both know it isn't.

'You know the things that can trigger me, Alex,' I say. 'If roles were reversed, wouldn't you be bothered by me talking with another man?' After what had happened with his ex-wife, I'd always assumed so. He'd thought Harriet had been filling her days finding purpose, helping out at a charity in Brixton. Little did he know she'd started seeing the guy running the organization. She'd been sneaking around behind his back for months before it all finally came out following a New Year's Eve party when she'd never come home. She'd said she'd booked a hotel room for one because she'd been too drunk, as though taxis didn't exist. A look at her credit card statement revealed a little more than he'd anticipated.

Her cheating had crushed him; that's why him cheating on me has never made any sense. I've never been able to understand how he could do that when he knows exactly what it feels like.

Now I wonder if he's somehow managed to heal in ways I know I never can because as hard as I try to ignore it, I can feel Lucy impinging on our relationship every time we see her.

'No, because I trust you implicitly,' he says, turning away from me with a sigh.

I take a sharp breath in and hold it until I'm desperate for air. 'You trust me implicitly because I've never done anything to damage your trust,' I say. 'What were you talking to her about?' I hate that I can't let it go.

'We were just talking. I didn't take notes; I'm not a scribe,' he snaps, looking out towards the setting sun over the ocean. He's never spoken to me so harshly before.

'Please don't snap at me. You know how hard it is for me seeing you around another woman after what happened,' I say, a tremble in my voice. 'It's like you've forgotten everything that happened.'

'Oh, I remember. It's the biggest regret of my life and I have to live with what I did every day,' he croaks. 'Seeing how I broke you as a person absolutely kills me, Darcy. I'll never ever do anything to hurt you again. I wish you believed that.'

When we get home, he skulks off to his office and closes the door behind him, leaving me standing in the hallway alone. I don't see him for the rest of the day.

* * *

That evening, I make a beef stroganoff, his favourite dinner. The smell of the creamy mushroom sauce eventually lures him into the kitchen. He heads to the fridge and cracks open a cider before sliding into his seat at the table. I blink in surprise. How can he still be drinking after all the cocktails he's had today? In any case, he'd promised me he was going to stop drinking.

'Is everything alright?' I ask sheepishly.

'Just work stress. Nothing for you to worry about,' he says, tipping the can of cider to his lips and taking a long sip. I can't shake the feeling that he's keeping something from me.

Neither of us bring up the issue we both know is there between us, my growing insecurities. Moving here was supposed to make everything better, fix what he'd broken, but I guess we're both starting to realize it was naïve to think it would be that easy. I try and think of things from his perspective, imagining how upset he must be. He's tried everything to make it up to me, including relocating. He must feel disheartened.

I glance at him now as he takes another long gulp of his drink. He looks twice his age, massaging the deep wrinkles in his forehead. His hair is starting to grey, his beard too. When had that happened? Despite everything, I have to fight the urge to go over to him and wrap my arms around him. Even in his darkest moments I seem to want to please him.

Draining the pappardelle, I offer him a small smile, hoping the tension between us can start to fall away. There's been so much of it lately. I plate up the dinner and sit down at the table across from him, neither one of us seeming to know what to say.

'What's that?' I ask, looking down at his phone constantly lighting up with messages again. I can't help myself; the question slips out before I have a chance to stop myself. I instantly wish I hadn't said anything. He slams the cider can onto the tabletop in irritation. It's already empty.

'Nothing. Just Jack sending a bunch of random crap to the group chat.' He doesn't show me his phone screen the way he usually does when I ask him about the messages he receives. Instead, he gets up from the table, leaving his dinner untouched, and heads back to his office.

CHAPTER 12

That night, Alex sleeps downstairs, again. From barely ever sleeping apart, he's been starting to do it a lot lately. The bed feels desolate and cold, even with Henry snuggled at my feet.

It isn't a night terror I experience during the night, but one of the most vivid and sickening nightmares I have ever had. I dream of Arthur's two children, their young grief-stricken faces permanently etched into my memory. In the dream, they're in a kitchen, watching their mother die. A blade makes a clean slice at Jessica's neck, turning the room into a gory bloodbath. The children cry, shoulders heaving. When the person holding the knife turns to them, I see eyes the colour of gunmetal smouldering through a balaclava mask. Lucy's eyes. Her name is carved into the walls, over and over again like it was in the little girl's notebook.

It's as Lucy strides towards the children, knife in hand, that I wake in utter panic. The bed is so soaked in my sweat I have to strip off the covers and change the sheets.

* * *

In the morning, the gurgle of the coffee machine sputtering to life wakes me, followed by footsteps coming across the landing. Alex nudges the bedroom door open with his knee, two steaming mugs of coffee in hand. He looks dishevelled, grey tracksuit bottoms hanging loosely from his hips, scruffy hair and puffy eyes.

'Hey,' he says, standing in the doorway, his voice coming out croaky. He glances down at the pile of dirty sheets on the floor. 'Night terror?'

'Something like that,' I reply.

'Let's move on, please?' he says. 'I hate it when we fight.'

I nod my head slowly. We've both calmed down now. The moment, whatever it had been, has passed. He climbs into bed beside me, kissing me on top of my head.

'I'm sorry I got so worked up yesterday,' he says, sighing as he settles down next to me. 'I wish you could just trust me again, and I wish you could understand how much I regret what happened. If you could just see yourself through my eyes, you'd know I'd never do anything to jeopardize us again. Ever.'

I lean into his shoulder, exuding heat. 'I'm sorry I still struggle with it all,' I say.

'Do you think you'll ever get there? To a point of trusting me again?' he asks.

'I hope so,' I say, and I mean it. I bite my lip. 'I want that more than anything. I'm just so scared of getting hurt again.'

'I'm your family, remember? Your only family. I'm never going to let you down again,' he says, cupping my chin and looking me in the eyes. 'I'm here to stay, Darcy. You and this little person are my entire world, okay?'

He moves his hand from my jaw to my stomach, stopping as the baby rolls beneath his touch. We both smile.

'I do trust you,' I say. 'It's other people I don't trust.'

'You honestly don't need to worry about Lucy.' He laughs, running a hand through his hair.

'I know. You were just being friendly,' I say. I'm not sure if I'm telling that to myself or to him.

I unhook my phone from the charger and unlock the screen. The Rock Mummies chat is flooded with messages. I rub my crusty eyes and start trying to scroll to the top of the message thread while Alex hands me my coffee.

'Oh my God!' I gasp, almost dropping the mug onto the bed.

'What?' Alex asks, looking panicked.

'Violet had her baby last night. She's the tiniest thing I've ever seen,' I say, tears springing to my eyes. Stickers cover the little chest, with wires and monitors all around her.

'What do you mean? That's early, isn't it?' he says, craning his neck to see the photo.

'*Welcome to the world, Holly McAllister. This little girl couldn't wait to join the world. Born six weeks early and weighing just three pounds, she's already showing us her fighting spirit.*' I read the text aloud to Alex, my voice breaking.

Three pounds. Violet and Marie are both petite themselves, but three pounds for a newborn sounds terrifying. The tears freefall, and I burrow into Alex. Seeing their tiny little baby out in the world is like a reality check. I marvel at the picture, realizing that must be what our baby looks like right now, too. Violet was only about a week ahead of me in pregnancy. My hand goes instinctively to my bump.

'There's more,' I say, continuing to read through the message. '*Violet's in recovery. She developed high blood pressure, and the midwife noticed protein in her urine sample, diagnosing her with pre-eclampsia. She went into preterm labour yesterday. It's all been a bit of a shock, and we have a long road ahead, but overall, we couldn't be happier.*'

'Wow. That'll be us soon.' Alex looks up from my phone, a film of tears in his eyes. I don't think either of us know what else to say, so instead, we hug. Alex pulls me into his arms, and I breathe in his familiar patchouli scent. All of the animosity brewing between us falls away.

'I don't think I'll ever be able to stop thanking you for making me a dad,' he whispers into my neck.

'I'm sorry, for everything. I guess the thought of losing you is just unbearable,' I say. I want to say more, but he places a finger on my lips, silencing me. I nuzzle into his chest and let him hold me close.

* * *

The Rock Mummies group chat is a constant stream of messages of congratulations and updates from Marie. Midmorning, she sends a photo of a huge gift hamper filled with lily of the valley flowers, a bundle of Tiny Baby babygrows, the most delicate champagne-pink cashmere baby blanket, a bunch of different snacks and a selection of magazines. The caption reads, *OK, who did this?!*

A few of the girls respond to say it wasn't them, with promises of bringing a gift with them when they're allowed to visit. I'm about to respond that it wasn't me either when I see Lucy typing. I wait a while, then put my phone down to pour a glass of water. When I come back her message appears on my home screen.

Guilty.

Of course it was Lucy. Irritation rumbles in the pit of my stomach, the jealousy rearing its ugly head once again. Marie can't stop thanking her for how kind and considerate she's been. I feel bitter that I hadn't thought to send a gift to the hospital, but it would only have been overshadowed by the extravagance of Lucy's gift anyway. It must have cost an absolute fortune, too. Resentment oozes through every pore as I chuck my phone down, startling Henry, who hisses and stalks away grumpily.

* * *

Once the news sinks in that the first baby has arrived, I slink into Alex's study with a cup of coffee and slide it onto his desk. He's squinting at his computer screen so intensely he hardly registers I'm there. Even though it's Sunday, he's still hard at work.

'Sorry, I know you're busy. I just . . . I think after today with Marie and Violet's news, maybe it's time to start preparing for this baby.' I perch on the armrest of his chair.

'You're right. We can't put it off anymore. We literally have nothing. Let me wrap up a few work emails and we can go shopping this afternoon?'

I'm pleased he's finally carving out some time for me. I want to thank him as I run my fingers through his unwashed hair, but he says something that ruins the moment completely.

'Have you spoken about waterbirths with Lucy yet?'

'No,' I say, my voice clipped. 'Why would you bring her up again?'

'Sorry, I know you're sensitive about it,' he says.

I scoff. 'Sensitive? I'm not sensitive.'

'You sure about that?' he says, cocking an eyebrow at me.

'She just upsets me, Alex.' I still can't decide if it's the pregnancy hormones making me feel this way or if it's just repercussions from before we left London.

'Darling, I promise you there's nothing to worry about,' he says, reaching out for my hand.

'Maybe it's all in my head.' I sigh, shaking my head. 'I just can't seem to gauge what her true intentions are. It's making me anxious because I'm usually such a good judge of character.'

'Her true intentions? Darcy, she's just another pregnant woman trying to make friends,' he says. 'I guess she can be a bit overfriendly with the guys, but maybe she's just got a flirtatious personality. Either way, that isn't my fault, so please don't take it out on me.'

'I'm trying not to, I promise. I'm just struggling,' I say, looking down at his hand resting over mine. 'Please just stop bringing her up.'

'I've only brought her up when we're talking about a waterbirth,' he reminds me, squeezing my hand. 'Do it, Darcy. Reach out to her. It'll be so good for you to have her to talk to about it.'

Unable to hide how livid I am, I harrumph, storming out of the room. I head to the dressing room to get ready to look at an abundance of baby paraphernalia and hopefully forget all about Lucy Harold.

* * *

'I'm astounded by the sheer number of functions and features prams can have. What happened to simplicity?' Alex mutters under his breath in John Lewis. 'I started feeling like we're buying a car when that assistant was explaining the four-way suspension.'

I let out a half-hearted laugh, giving him a tight-lipped smile. I want to enjoy this shopping trip with him, but I'm still angry.

There's a lot of pressure to have the newest and most stylish model to fit in with everyone else when it comes to prams. The Silver Cross brand seems to be the Rolls Royce of the pram world. If I had it my way, we'd be finding a reliable second-hand one, but Alex is adamant that he wants everything shiny and new.

I have to mute my phone to be able to concentrate on what the shop assistant is saying. Throughout the day the Rock Mummies chat has been exploding with messages, gushing over Lucy's fabulous hamper. Everyone suddenly seems to want to be her best friend. It repulses me. This blonde woman loaded with money who sleeps around with men and is a seemingly awful stepmother has become a hot commodity amongst the group. Even Cora's being overly friendly to her, and I know she saw the way Lucy was with Jack in the swimming pool that day at her house, so I just can't understand it. I snarl at the mere thought of her, frightening the woman trying to talk to us about the durability of the polished chrome chassis for a particular pram that has caught Alex's eye. It all sounds like gibberish to me.

'What's got into you?' Alex asks me when she nips into the office to ask her manager something about non-puncturing wheels.

'I'm just not having a good day,' I say, knowing I could easily try harder to make this experience nicer. Shopping for our baby is supposed to be exciting and fun, and I don't want to cause another fight with Alex, but I just can't seem to help myself.

I refuse to admit that Lucy has riled me up again. I'd rather blame the pregnancy hormones than admit another woman has got under my skin, and maybe it *is* the pregnancy hormones. Lucy hasn't actually done anything with any of our partners, most importantly Alex. She's been nothing but nice to all of us, and that's what seems to annoy me most of all. But who am I to judge a woman for the way she chooses to live her life with her husband? I've done far worse things than swinging, and it isn't like Lucy tried to hide her lifestyle from us either. In fact, she was pretty open about it. Surely, she wouldn't actually make a move on one of our partners when we're all forming friendships built on being first-time parents together. That would just be wrong.

Once Alex has chosen a pram, he heads in the direction of the baby monitors to cater to his technology obsession. He's evidently fed up with me for being in a mood once again. I don't follow him. Instead I mooch around the aisles, lost in an abundance of breast pumps. Like prams, the breast pumps seem to come with an array of functions I can't understand. One even boasts about multiple rhythm options like it's some sort of fancy, sensual vibrator for breasts. I almost choke when I see the price of them, chucking a manual handheld pump in the shopping basket instead. How different could they be?

***

We're busy loading up the car with what seems to be half of the John Lewis baby and nursery section when I hear her voice behind me. It makes the hair on the back of my neck prickle.

'Darcy, Alex! Small world.'

'Small village!' Alex jams a boxed activity mat into the backseat, turning to grin at Lucy. She's wearing a low-cut cream knitted jumper. Her cleavage is on full display again. She laughs, making her breasts jiggle.

'Getting ready, I see,' she says, pointing towards our shopping.

'About time. Until today I'm ashamed to admit we didn't even have a pack of muslins. Left things to the last minute, didn't we, Darcy?' Alex squints in the sunlight, his hands on his hips.

'I guess Marie and Violet's news gave you a nudge?' she says, her perky breasts distracting me as they bounce around. It's making me acutely aware of my own cheerless breasts, currently bolstered up in the most unflattering nursing bra.

'Yeah. I can't believe the first baby is already here! That was a bit of a surprise this morning.'

Alex and Lucy are so engrossed in their conversation that I feel practically translucent. I watch Lucy bite her lower lip as Alex shows her our selection of baby goods.

'These are all such good choices, Alex. I'm impressed,' she says, eyeing the Silver Cross pram that has taken up the entire boot of the car.

I clear my throat and watch both of them look up in surprise.

'You're lucky, Darcy. I hope you know that. Art's been way too busy to come baby shopping with me.'

We stare at each other, and I swear there's as much hostility in her eyes as there is in mine.

'I'm glad we bumped into you actually,' Alex intervenes, shifting Lucy's attention back to him.

'Oh really? Why's that?' She's clearly flattered.

'Darcy's started to think quite seriously about having an at-home waterbirth after what she's heard from you. We thought it might be a good idea if the two of you got together to chat about it a bit more?' As he speaks, he snakes a hand around my waist and pulls me in close to him.

'Wow, yes! Of course, I'd love to help. Let's get something in the diary, Darcy?'

I nod, not sure what else I can do. It's bothered me that Alex felt the need to speak for me, but I can't get out of it now.

CHAPTER 13

I try to postpone meeting with Lucy for as long as I can. I make excuse after excuse, which is surprisingly difficult to do when you don't work. I fill the days before our fifth antenatal class by preparing the nursery, installing the car seat, packing a hospital bag in case of emergencies and generally nesting around the house.

I find myself spending hours just sitting in the nursery once the paint has dried and the fumes have faded. We went for a beautiful terracotta orange colour, and I hand painted green botanical art over the walls, trailing down to where the cot and changing table will go once we've built them. Though when I'll be able to pull Alex away from his work again to help me put furniture together is beyond me. He seems in no rush. Even without it all built, the nursery is now my favourite room in the house. The cream nursing chair has a light green knitted blanket from Alex's mum draped over it and a soft toy tucked in the corner. There's even a mounted wall bookshelf stacked with books I've already been reading aloud to the baby. Sometimes, I feel the baby wriggle to the sound of my voice reading Julia Donaldson's books. There seems to be a bit of a preference for *The Gruffalo*.

It makes me sad to think the baby won't actually be spending much time in the nursery for the first six months. I almost want to sleep in here myself it's so lovely, but we already have a palm leaf moses basket set up on its stand next to my side of the bed. Henry has assumed it's his new bed, making a cat net push its way into my next bulk Amazon order. It's become an unhealthy obsession, trawling through Amazon at all hours of the night, adding things to my basket and proceeding to the checkout armed with Alex's credit card. He never once complains about the money spent or the constant stream of delivery drivers churning up our garden after dropping off more parcels. Now, with just weeks left to go until the due date, I sit in the nursing chair and wonder what else I could possibly do to prepare for this baby.

* * *

I do eventually have to face Lucy at the next class, but I do my best to keep my distance from her. Instead I immerse myself in the lesson on bonding with our babies, though as all the classes seem to do, it leaves me with a sense of dread that I'll fail at this whole parenting thing. This class has me worried that bonding won't come easily with my baby once they arrive, even though Emma assures us that it can sometimes take some time.

'It isn't always instantaneous, and I want you all to be aware of that so it shouldn't be something for you to be ashamed of,' she tells us.

I've been trying so hard to bond with the baby while they're still in the womb. I've been reading books to them, singing to them, talking while driving alone. At first, it felt bizarre and a little silly, but gradually it started feeling more natural to me. Now, I can't wait for my alone time with my bump so I can talk to them.

Emma spends the first half of the class talking about the different ways you can bond with your baby before they're born, and it makes me feel good knowing I'm already doing almost everything she suggests. It's when she starts talking about the parents that struggle to bond with their baby once they're born that I start getting doubtful. What if that happens to me? What if the baby gets here and I'm terrible at everything? What if nothing comes naturally to me at all? There's no real way to tell how it's going to go until my time comes.

I want to voice my concerns to the group, but it's Carmen that beats me to it. It's as though she's invaded my head.

'I'm so worried I won't feel connected to him right away,' she says, her fingers laced in her lap. Grayson looks uncomfortable sitting next to her, his long legs stretched out. They aren't touching or interacting with each other at all, and they don't throughout the entire class. They must have had a fight before they arrived. They're frigid, detached from one another even when we're split up into our couples to practise the bonding exercises which Emma talks us through.

It's a strange class without Marie and Violet there, quiet and small. I didn't realize what a gap they'd leave in our group, but without them the whole dynamic is off somehow. I wonder if it would be the same if Alex and I were to miss a class.

For the last half of the class, Emma makes us all a cup of tea and lets us mingle between ourselves for a change.

'Were you able to get another dress appointment sorted, Darcy?' Cora asks, blowing at her cup of tea.

'This Saturday. Did you still want to come?' I ask. It was tough work securing another appointment and the way the manager spoke to me over the phone made it seem like they didn't hold much hope that I'd actually show up.

'Hell yes we want to come!' Rachel jumps in, grinning. 'Have you started thinking about the kind of dress you want? Let me show you mine.'

She flicks through photos on her phone until she finds some from her wedding day. 'I'm biased obviously, but I think you'd look great in something like this.' She zooms in on a black and white photograph of her standing by a horse in the middle of a field. The sun is casting rays around her, her veil dancing in the wind. The dress is the furthest thing from anything I'd ever wear. Rachel is curvy, like me, but unlike me she likes to show her curves off. Her dress is figure-hugging, a V-neck trumpet gown with a lot of tulle. It's stunning on her, but I could never imagine myself in it. My pear-shaped hips have always made me a bit self-conscious, even though Alex says he loves them.

'I've just always thought of something with sleeves, a bit of lace maybe,' I say, trying not to offend her.

'Absolutely, you do you. I'm just saying you might try something on that's totally different from what you'd envisioned and end up loving it! That's what happened to me.'

While we finish our drinks, Rachel, Cora and I go through the bridal boutique's website, looking at the different designers and dresses in stock. I take screenshots of some of the dresses I'd love to try on, starting to feel that little glimmer of excitement spark to life inside me again.

'I won't be able to make it this Saturday, but I hope you have a good time,' Carmen says before we leave. She and Lucy have been having their own chat in another corner of the room.

'I'll be there, Darcy. I'm looking forward to it.' Lucy smiles.

I'd feel better if it were just Cora and Rachel at the appointment, maybe even Violet too. It doesn't bother me that Carmen can't make it, though it does amuse me that she wanted me to come to her baby shower, but she won't make the effort to come to something for me in return.

'That's great. Thanks, Lucy,' I say with no amount of enthusiasm in my voice.

'We still need to have our chat about waterbirths. Maybe we can grab a drink somewhere together after the dress appointment?'

'Yeah, sounds good,' I lie, calculating that I've got a few days to come up with some sort of reason to avoid spending more time than I can take with her.

* * *

Things with Alex have been good, better than good really. It's the longest we've gone without some petty argument getting in the way for a while.

On Saturday morning it's sunny and warm enough to be able to sit outside and enjoy our breakfast together before I go to the dress appointment. He's made blueberry and bacon pancakes, drizzled with maple syrup.

'Are you sure you don't mind?' I ask when he slides his solid steel credit card to me.

'If you find your dream dress, go for it. I'm glad some of the girls can come with you,' he says, rubbing his beard, almost ginger in the sunlight.

'Yeah, I'm sad Violet can't be there. It was weird without them at class the other night too.'

'When do they get to leave the hospital?'

'I don't know. I think they've still got a while to go. It's only been a week.' I gather our plates and empty coffee cups as we head back inside.

'God, a week in hospital. I can't imagine anything worse.' Alex shudders grimly.

'Last I heard she might be there a couple more weeks,' I say, pulling a face.

'Don't you dare come out early, then!' Alex bends, planting his lips over my bump. I giggle as the baby kicks at the sound of his voice.

'I'm going to go get ready for the appointment,' I say, smiling at Alex as he washes the dishes. 'It's silly because I can't even try the dresses on, but I want to look nice.'

'You always look nice,' he says, fishing cutlery out of the sudsy water.

'I do not.' I laugh and retreat upstairs.

I dab on my best makeup and straighten my hair. There's a flutter in my stomach. I blink at my reflection, smile with painted lips, but it's a sad smile. My breathing is slow. I chew skin away from my fingernails, unable to shake the heavy feeling in my chest.

'I'm going wedding dress shopping, Mum,' I whisper. 'I wish you could be there.'

When I pull a dress from the wardrobe, I notice the peachy material trembling in my hand. The ache of not having my parents with me today is excruciating, and memories of seeing them lifeless in the hospital are at the forefront of my mind — but I have to pull myself together. I have to make the most of this.

Alex wolf whistles as I walk down the stairs.

'Thank you again,' I say, holding up his bank card. It feels cold and weighty in my hand.

'Go find your dream dress.' He smiles down at me, and it makes my heart soar.

'God, I wish my mum and dad could've met you,' I say.

He kisses me, holding my chin gently in his hands. 'Me too,' he says.

Walking me to the car, he pulls something out of his pocket. A small white box. I stare down at it, then look up at him questioningly.

'Open it,' he says.

I snap the lid of the box up and peer inside. Nestled in the velvet cushioning is a pair of pearl earrings.

'Alex,' I say softly. 'They're—'

'They were my mum's. I know you don't have the best relationship with her, but she's still my mum and she always told me to give these to the girl I was going to marry,' he says. 'I want you to wear them when that day comes.'

'I will,' I promise him, and touch the pearls gently before closing the box again. 'That's so special.'

Although the thought of wearing Debbie's earrings doesn't exactly fill me with joy, I know it means a lot to Alex.

* * *

Cora, Rachel and Lucy are already waiting for me inside the bridal boutique when I arrive. The shop assistant pours everyone a glass of alcohol-free bubbles while we sift through an endless maze of bridal gowns.

When I see the dress dangling on the sale rail right at the back of the shop, it's what I imagine love at first sight feels like. My eyes come to life, my breath is lost, my mouth left hanging open.

'This one,' I whisper, touching the delicate lace sleeves with handsewn 3D embroidery applique worked into it. The satin crepe skirt feels light and soft in my arms as I take it over to the round bridal podium.

The shop assistant draws the silky curtains around us and helps me into the dress while the others wait on the cream sofas by the rail of gowns we've selected.

'We won't be able to fasten all the buttons up because of your bump,' she says. 'But I can do my best to pull it tight and you can get a feel of what it'll look like.'

I know it's my dress the moment I look up and see myself in the floor-length mirror. I twist my body to look down at the gorgeous puddle train and satin buttons that would fasten at my waist.

'I've never seen a bride look as good as you do in this dress,' she says.

I'm sure it's what she says to every bride that comes in, but I don't care. I'm too busy wiping tears from my eyes.

When she pulls back the curtain, the other girls make a commotion I'm not expecting. I'm sure I even notice Lucy welling up. For the first time in my life, I like the feeling of all eyes being on me. I feel radiant, sparkling almost. It feels good.

'I don't even think we need to try on the other dresses, do we?' Rachel says, looking me up and down. 'I mean, I still think you'd look great in the kind of gown I had, but this one does look incredible on you!'

'Stunning.' Lucy nods approvingly.

The assistant beams proudly. 'The best part is it's in her size and on the sale rail!'

'That's amazing. Alterations can be so expensive!' Cora says. 'Can we see it with a veil?'

When the veil is clipped into my hair, it seals the deal. I've watched enough episodes of *Say Yes to the Dress* to know this is the moment all brides dream of, but I'm still overwhelmed when it finally happens to me.

We clink our flute glasses together in celebration when I punch the numbers of Alex's pin into the card machine and the sale goes through.

'I can't believe how quick and easy that was,' I say, flushing with happiness.

'The dress needs a bit of a clean, which we include in the price, so it should be ready for you to collect early next week if that's alright with you?' the assistant tells me before we leave.

I arrange to pick the dress up the following Tuesday, then leave the boutique with the others in a bubble that can't be popped.

Rachel treats us all to afternoon tea while we're in Wadebridge to celebrate. To my surprise, Carmen's there when we arrive. She's set up the table and there's a Bride to Be garland strung up along the wall. I stare in wonderment. Has this been planned all along? Is that why Carmen couldn't come to the appointment?

She hugs me and smiles, and it's one of the few times I've seen her truly smile. It alters her entire face.

'I hear congratulations are in order! Can I see the dress?' she says.

Cora waits for me to say yes before showing Carmen the photographs she'd taken of me in the dress. I glow as I look through them, already wanting to be back in it.

'Gosh, it looks amazing on you. It really does.' Carmen sighs, swiping through the photos again. They're beautiful photos, capturing moments of me looking at the dress from all angles. As she stares down at one of the pictures, one where I have the veil on, I see a subtle shift in her demeanour. It's the clenched jaw and narrowed eyes, the way she folds her arms across her chest when she's handed the phone back to Cora, that sends a sudden shiver down my spine.

* * *

On Tuesday morning I arrive at the bridal boutique bright and early, desperate to pick up my dress. The shop assistant blinks at me in surprise when she sees me. She finishes helping another bride purchasing a pair of bridal shoes before turning her attention to me.

'Is something the matter with your dress?' she asks.

'No. I'm here to collect it?' I say, confused. A sense of dread is already building in the pit of my stomach. Something feels off. She looks bewildered, thumbing through the diary on the desk.

'The dress was collected yesterday,' she says.

CHAPTER 14

'I'm not sure I understand you. You gave my dress to someone else?' I speak slowly, trying to remain calm.

'Yes. She came in, gave us your details. Said you'd asked her to pick it up for you,' the shop assistant stammers.

'I didn't ask anyone to pick the dress up for me. Did you recognize her? Was it one of the girls I was with on the weekend?' My heart is beating erratically.

'We get a lot of customers, Ms Holloway.'

'Do you have CCTV or something?' I ask, exasperated.

'I'll see what I can do,' she says, slinking off into the back to speak to her colleagues.

While she's gone, I message Rachel, Cora and Lucy to ask if any of them picked it up for me. One by one, they all say no.

'We've managed to pull some security footage from yesterday evening, but I don't know if it'll be much use to you.' The assistant ushers me into the back and plays back the footage. We watch as a woman enters the shop just before their closing time, her face hidden beneath a peaked beret. She's small, pint-sized, wearing tight activewear showing off an impressive physique. Her hair, unnaturally black and shiny, is pulled up into a high ponytail.

I watch as she's handed my dress. The exchange is brief. She isn't even in the shop for two minutes, if that. Then, she's gone.

* * *

The police arrive and look through the footage, take some statements and seem positively bored by the situation.

'We'll do what we can, but I'll admit there's not much to go on here.' The policewoman flips her file filled with our statements closed. 'I'll open a theft case. Look through other CCTV in the area, see if we can locate her and follow her movements to get some car details or something more to go on.'

'Can the boutique not be held liable? They literally just gave the dress to some random person. They didn't even make her sign anything!' I hiss, though the shop assistant hears and looks mortified.

'She gave us all the correct details we needed to give her the dress.' Her voice is nothing more than a whisper. 'This has never happened to us before.'

'Let me go away with the information I've got and see what we can do first, alright?' The policewoman yawns, not bothering to put her hand in front of her mouth as she beckons for her partner to wrap things up.

As they leave, I feel something very similar to heartbreak setting in. My dream dress is gone, and I have no idea who has taken it.

* * *

I can't bring myself to tell Alex the dress is missing. That over a grand is gone with nothing to show for it. So, when he asks me where the dress is when I come home empty-handed, I lie.

'It's at a seamstress they recommended,' I say. 'I have to make an appointment with her after the birth.' I watch him easily digest my words, and lying to him splinters my heart even further.

'Can you believe it's the last antenatal class tomorrow?' he asks, twirling his finger around one of my loose curls as we snuggle on the sofa together that evening.

'Mm,' I grunt in response. My entire day has been spent chewing on the fact that my dress is missing. Alex seems completely oblivious to my mood.

'Thanks for suggesting we do the classes. I know I wasn't interested in them in the beginning, but I think they've been good for us,' he says.

Any other day I'd have revelled in the joy of being right, but not tonight. Tonight, I nuzzle into his neck and pretend to fall asleep so I don't need to talk anymore.

* * *

I'm not expecting any news from the police anytime soon, but it still upsets me by Wednesday evening when I've heard nothing. We head to the last class early, carrying with us a batch of freshly baked scones. We all decided to bring a little something to turn the last class into a bit of a party after spending six weeks together learning the ins and outs of parenthood.

I lay the scones out on the table along with tubs of clotted cream and local jam. There's already a bunch of nibbly bits spread out, but I can't bring myself to eat anything.

'Tonight's class is all about mental health,' Emma tells us when we've taken our seats in the hall. There's an image shining up on the wall from a projector. It's an illustration of a tree with a bunch of stick figures doing different things around it.

'I want you to look at this image and tell me which stick figure you feel best describes how you feel right now about becoming a parent.'

I look at the picture closely, feeling particularly drawn to a stick figure getting pulled up onto a low-lying branch by another stick figure.

Emma goes around the circle, and one by one we all give a brief reason why we relate to a certain stick figure. It doesn't surprise me when Rachel and Johnny choose the figures way up at the top of the tree.

'I guess it's because we feel like we're winning at life in general. Everything is just great right now,' Rachel says, smiling.

'I feel like the stick figure on the left there, just sitting with their feet dangling over the branch. They look relaxed and happy with where they are and that pretty much describes me,' Lucy says when it's her turn.

Once again Arthur isn't here, not even at the very last class. This time Lucy explains that it's because he's taken the children away to Disneyland. 'I could have gone, but I told him the doctor wouldn't give me a fit to fly letter, so I could have a bit of time to myself,' she'd told us earlier before the class had started.

Cora meets my eyes now as we listen to Lucy talk. She sounds so placid, so carefree. Yet looking at the figure on the branch, it's hard not to notice the loneliness it depicts. They're sitting isolated, whereas almost every other stick figure has a partner interacting with them in the image. I wonder if Lucy even realizes that, or if I'm just reading way too much into it.

When it gets to me, I point to the stick figure being pulled up onto a branch.

'I chose this one because I feel like I'm still learning so much about becoming a parent. I feel like Alex is my rock, which is why he's lifting me up onto the branch.'

Alex reaches out and squeezes my knee. I don't say how I really feel, which is that Alex is up in the branch already because he seems so much more ready than I do. He's connected so well with the guys and doesn't seem to be worried at all that our entire lives are about to change when our baby comes.

I guess I do feel connected to the girls, especially after the dress appointment and the surprise bridal shower high tea they threw me, but it still doesn't feel as natural as it seems to be for Alex and the guys.

Once everyone else has answered, Emma starts talking about how different baby blues is from post-natal depression and tells us how we can spot the signs. Jack seems to be taking the class incredibly seriously, scribbling into a notebook on his lap as she lists a bunch of symptoms that sound like how I already feel on a day-to-day basis. Sleep troubles. No energy. Tiredness. It's like she has the wrong set of notes in front of her; she must just be talking about pregnancy symptoms, but then she starts talking about low moods and finding no enjoyment in life anymore. I still feel a bit like she's put me under a microscope and is detailing exactly how I feel on an average day. It makes me squirm in my seat slightly and I wonder if Alex is thinking this all sounds like me, too.

***

I'm glad when the class ends, wanting nothing more than to scurry away back home.

'That was a pretty heavy class to end on, wasn't it?' Alex says as we're driving home.

'Definitely not as fun as the others. At least there was cake,' I say, staring numbly out of the window, still thinking about my dress.

***

I get a call from the police a few days later apologizing for the wait.

'Council CCTV couldn't track her from the boutique,' the policewoman says, sounding like she's got her mouth full. 'CCTV black spot, I'm afraid.'

'What happens now?' I ask. I've gone to hide in the garden while I take the call. My stomach feels stretched to capacity. It's itchy and tender to touch as I gently stroke my fingers along it.

'The theft case is still open, and we'll do what we can,' she says, but there's not much hope in her voice.

PART III
JUNE

CHAPTER 15

After three weeks, Violet is finally allowed to take Holly home from the hospital. Marie invites the girls over to meet her and catch up with Violet, who starts weeping the moment we all arrive.

'I'm sorry, these hormones are absolutely insane,' Violet says, rubbing at her nose with her sleeve. Holly is attached to her breast, suckling away quietly.

Marie and Violet's living room is scattered with muslins, wads of wipes, balls of used nappies and abandoned nursing bras. There are half-full coffee cups forgotten about on every available surface.

'I had a membrane sweep today. Hated it. I swear the midwife had her entire hand jammed up in there!' Cora says with a shudder.

'I've heard they're awful. Friends of mine have had them and said it did nothing. I've got mine booked. Not hopeful but maybe it'll kickstart things before they have to induce me.'

'After almost nine months of tolerating constipation, haemorrhoids, backache, varicose veins and a blistering hot, dry summer that arrived early, I bet you're all ready to have your babies,' Marie says. 'You lot are superwomen, honestly. I couldn't have done it.' She squeezes Violet's shoulder.

'Oh, I am so ready. I've started snipping leaves from my raspberry tree and trying to make my own tea!' Rachel laughs.

'I've heard that can help. I'm still just incessantly bouncing on my yoga ball,' Cora says, rolling her eyes. The dark rings under her eyes give away how tired she must be.

'I've been ordering vindaloo from the Indian, asking for extra chilli,' Carmen mutters. 'It was so spicy the other night I was literally pacing around our lounge sweating.'

'I've literally tried every trick in the book,' I say. 'Nothing seems to want to encourage this baby out of me, though I haven't reached my due date yet. The midwife keeps telling me she thinks my baby is coming early, but I don't want to get my hopes up.'

'The midwife said that to me too, and look where I am,' Violet says, gesturing to Holly.

'Guys, I know this is a bit soppy, but I'm genuinely so grateful for you all,' Lucy says. 'We're all so different I don't know if we'd ever have met if we hadn't been put in these classes together, but I feel like we've really bonded.'

'Agreed! The last few weeks have been special, haven't they?' Rachel grins.

'They have. You guys have actually kept me sane,' Carmen says. 'Things with Grayson have been rocky for a while. You might have noticed.'

'I did think things were a bit icy between you two.' Violet winces. 'What's up?'

'To be honest, they've been icy since before we found out about this pregnancy. But the pregnancy has only made things worse. It wasn't planned.' She swipes furiously at her eyes.

'Oh, Carmen.' Cora sighs, reaching out and touching her knee.

'He won't even touch me anymore. I'm a complete turnoff to him now,' she says, sniffing.

Hearing her open up about her relationship with Grayson makes me understand her frosty personality in a way I hadn't been expecting.

'You're beautiful,' I find myself blurting out, and she looks up at me in surprise.

'Thank you,' she whispers, a tiny smile appearing on her lips.

I nod my head at her, and it's like all the tension between us fades away.

The only person I'm still not thrilled to have in the group is Lucy. Even after the stretch of time away from her, the feeling of weariness she gives me is not one I enjoy. At the classes I found myself watching her too closely, her every move, analyzing her every word. I just can't trust her, not at all, and yet everyone else seems to adore her. It makes no sense to me.

Today, she's plastered on her sweetest smile, going nicely with the pastel pink maternity dress she's wearing. She's talking to Rachel about Arthur, about how he's been away for work a lot recently. I find myself wondering if that's when she usually finds other men to keep her company and then my imagination spirals, envisioning some sort of group for men with a fetish for pregnant women. I'm being ridiculous and I know it, but I can't help myself.

While the rest of us coo over how incredibly tiny Holly is, Cora busies herself by starting to clean up the living room. Marie tries to object, but Cora tells her to take a break and relax while she can. I can see how grateful Marie and Violet seem, watching how Cora soundlessly blows from room to room, tidying every nook and cranny like she's been here before.

'How's it all going then, being a mum?' Rachel asks Violet, who is wiping thick milk from Holly's little chin.

'Amazing, honestly. It's more than I could've ever asked for. I'm becoming quite adept at sniffing out a dirty nappy too, like a bloodhound!'

I watch as Violet lays Holly down on a soft mat, holding her dainty legs up by the ankles as she swiftly changes her nappy, which looks ginormous on her tiny frame.

'Gosh, she's so delicate and small. I'd be scared to break her.' Carmen sighs, watching Violet button up the rainbow-print babygrow.

'You'll see when your baby arrives; you just sort of get on with it. I don't even think about it anymore. They're not as fragile as you think,' Violet says, nuzzling into Holly's neck.

'At this rate I feel like this baby is never coming out. He seems so snug in there.'

I look dubiously down to Carmen's bump, still confused as to where it is. Considering we're due in the same week, she's still so suspiciously small.

'I know it's the worst possible thing to say to a pregnant woman, but he'll come out when he's ready!' Cora pokes her head into the lounge, grinning at Carmen, who rolls her eyes back to her.

'Don't,' she says, but she's smiling.

'Cora, come sit down. You shouldn't be up on your feet so much; you need to rest too!' Violet says.

'I'm fine! Jack's banned me from doing any more nesting and reorganizing at home because he can't find any of his things anymore, so let me help you guys out at least. I have this burning desire to tidy at the moment!'

'They say that's a sign of your body preparing for labour, you know?' Lucy winks. She's brought over a week's worth of frozen homecooked meals in posh Tupperware boxes.

'Just a selection I whipped up for the kids this week. Spaghetti Bolognese, a chilli, some slow-cooked stew,' she says proudly.

When Marie takes them off her hands and loads them into their freezer, Lucy slips into the seat next to Violet. Her eyes don't leave Holly's delicate little body, curled up snugly on Violet's chest.

'Can I hold her?' she asks after a beat, and I notice Violet blink up at her in surprise.

'Um, sure.' It sounds like the last thing Violet wants to do is part with her baby. I wonder if anyone besides Marie and

Violet have held her before now. It's an awkward exchange that Violet seems far from comfortable with from what I can see, but how do you say no to someone who has just asked if they can hold your baby? Especially someone who has showered you with such lovely gifts. I feel sorry for Violet, looking down at her baby gurgling softly as she's lifted away from Violet's chest.

Holly drowsily opens and closes her eyes as she's placed into Lucy's arms, her tiny fingers stretching wide as she searches for Violet again.

'Oh, wow.' Lucy draws in a breath, tucking the baby in close to her as she strokes a delicate chubby cheek covered in milk spots and baby acne. Holly has short tufts of dark, fluffy hair and the sweetest cupid's bow lips with a dribble of breastmilk sliding down her little chin. She's extremely small, with not a roll in sight on her fragile arms, which are moving around involuntarily. Lucy starts making a repetitive shushing noise, craning down to plant kisses on the baby's head. We all watch as the baby starts to make an unsettled grunting noise that quickly turns into a cry. The skin beneath her eyebrows reddens as she grows more angry.

'Oh no, don't cry, little one,' Lucy says softly.

She pulls her in closer, making continual shushing noises while rocking back and forth. Violet seems out of sorts, unable to take her eyes off Lucy and her baby. I want to rip the baby away from Lucy and hand her back to her mother, but instead I sit with bated breath, waiting for Lucy to realize she needs to give the baby back. As the crying intensifies, Marie hurries back into the room. She takes in the situation, her eyes roaming from Violet to Lucy. The baby squirms, her tiny head so smothered in Lucy's bosom that for an alarming moment I start to think she can't breathe.

Lucy is so absorbed in holding Holly that she hasn't even noticed Marie.

'Lucy, I think it's time to give Holly back to Violet now.' Marie speaks slowly, calmly.

'Just one more minute,' Lucy whispers, still trying to soothe Holly, who has now started to shriek. The sound is hair-raising, so loud for such a tiny human to make.

Rachel and Carmen exchange an anxious look. Holly's skin is turning an angry shade of red.

'Lucy,' Marie says, more forcefully this time. Lucy snaps her head up, her hair falling around the baby like a blanket. 'Give Holly back to Violet now, please.'

It's as though Lucy comes out of some sort of trance. Very slowly, she peels the baby away from her chest, which is now glistening with tears. Blue veins bulge from Holly's head. She seems distraught, flailing her little legs about.

'I'm so sorry. I don't know what came over me.' She looks mortified, holding Holly out to Marie, who takes her back to Violet.

No one knows what to say. We just watch as the baby nestles herself back onto Violet's breast and gradually lulls into a fitful sleep.

'Well, I think we've all overstayed our welcome!' Rachel slaps her hands to her knees, breaking the silence. Scooping up her handbag, she pulls herself up from the sofa and ambles out of the living room with the rest of us following closely behind her. We just get to the front door when Lucy turns to us, regret written all over her pale face. She looks sickly, a sheen of sweat giving her forehead a lustrous glow. Her hands are shaking as she takes her car keys out of her bag.

'I'm sorry,' she whispers.

For a moment it seems like she wants to say more. She shifts from foot to foot, glancing at each one of us and then down to our pregnant bellies. She places a hand onto her own bump before gulping back a sob. We all remain mute.

When none of us respond, she hurries to her car. Before any of us can say anything to stop her, she climbs in and drives away.

'That was weird,' Carmen mutters, running a protective hand up and down her stomach. We all leave Marie and

Violet in peace and for the rest of the day the mummies chat is lifeless.

It's only after midnight that a long, harrowing message arrives to the group from Lucy.

> *Ladies, I am so sorry for the way I behaved today. I overstepped and I feel awful for it. The truth is, holding Holly just blew my mind a little. Everything hit me all at once. Art and I tried so hard to have a baby, but it just wasn't working. We started fertility treatment to help us, but the quality of my eggs was terrible. We ended up with only two healthy embryos for transfer. We were amazed when the first transfer was successful. I couldn't believe I was finally going to have a baby! Some people dream of becoming bestselling novelists or actors, but my dream has always been to be a mother. The pregnancy was going well. I suffered a lot with morning sickness, but I didn't care. I was just grateful that I was pregnant. I lost the baby in the first trimester. We'd used the top-quality egg we had, and I went into a really dark place. There was a stage where I really thought it would never happen for us. This whole pregnancy, since discovering the transfer was successful again, has been one of complete unease. I can't relax, I'm so afraid of something going wrong and losing my baby. I don't think I'd be able to handle it. So, holding Holly today, it just churned up my insides. I'm so close to the finish line, to holding my own baby in my arms at last, and I guess for a moment today I just pretended that Holly was mine, that I'd made it. I'm so sorry for making all of you feel so uncomfortable, but most of all I'm sorry to you, Marie and Violet. I hope you can find it in your hearts to understand. It would mean a lot to me to be friends with you all and I hope I haven't ruined that chance.*
>
> *Lucy x*

CHAPTER 16

The more Lucy shares about her life, the less I trust her.

Unfortunately, the same can't be said for the others. They flock over her after reading her message. But as for me, the constant stories seeking sympathy from the group are becoming tedious. If it isn't her strange polyamorous relationship with her husband, it's her fertility struggles. She always seems to have a story, a means to wangle her way into being the centre of attention, and if it isn't a sympathy vote she's after, she seems to try and win everyone over with expensive gifts.

To make things worse, she forwarded the message to the main antenatal group chat as well, so Alex read the message too. Ever since, he's been badgering me to reach out to her even more.

'She's fine,' I say over dinner.

Alex has opened a bottle of wine and poured himself a generous glass. The spicy pepper aroma is rich and inviting. *Not long to go now*, I tell myself as I watch him take a sip.

'Darcy, she's clearly not. She needs friends . . . some company,' he says. 'You're in a very similar boat. I don't understand why you can't just make an effort with the poor girl.' He harps on at me for hours, spoiling our dinner and the entire evening until eventually, just to shut him up, I agree to send her a message.

He watches while I type it.

Hey Lucy, hope you're okay? I wondered if you'd be up for that lunch date soon. I'd love to chat more to you about waterbirths. D x

Before I send it, I look up at him to make sure he's satisfied. He nods his head, urging me to press send. Once I do, I can't take it back. It's out there, in the universe, and soon I'll have to endure a day of being with Lucy one on one. I'm not looking forward to it.

* * *

Trying to cram my purse and lipstick into my satchel, I'm getting progressively more fed up. We've arranged to meet at the café, the one I'd spotted Arthur at with another woman. The thought of having to endure an hour or more with Lucy has me pacing around the house like a caged animal. I think about feigning illness, but that would only set back the inevitable for so long. I feel on the verge of tears when Alex comes to find me.

'Almost ready to go?'

'No,' I snap, giving up on fitting everything I need into my satchel. I fling the bag over my shoulder grumpily, discarding the makeup.

'I don't understand why you're being so unreasonable.'

'I just don't like her, okay? And I don't need someone who isn't a trained professional talking to me about an at-home waterbirth. That's what my midwife is there for.'

'You're being ridiculous, Darcy. Lucy has been nothing but nice to you and everyone else. She's been through a lot. I thought you of all people could sympathize with that,' he says, staring me down. 'I just thought it would be nice for you to have a *friend* to talk to about it, someone who is about to go through the same thing. This childish behaviour needs to end.'

I glower at him, feeling like a scolded child. I march from the bedroom and out towards the car. He doesn't follow me.

On the drive over to the café, I let my rage simmer. What he'd said had hurt my feelings. The way he'd said that I could use a 'friend' implied the one thing he knew would sting, that I don't have any. The last few weeks had been nice, getting to know the girls in our antenatal class, but none of them, not even Cora, could be classified as a friend. Not yet anyway.

I still crave that closeness with someone other than Alex, a girlfriend I could sit and drink wine with, talk about the latest episode of *Love Island* with, and moan to each other about our partners. That's the kind of friendship I'd hoped to gain from moving to Rock and joining these classes, but I feel like my relationship with each of these women will always be bound by our one and only thing in common, our babies.

Perhaps that's where I'm being silly, I think. Maybe if I just open myself up a little bit more, connections will actually form even if they are built on pregnancy. School children make a best friend based on nothing more than being in the same playground. They always make it seem so easy, too. They just walk up to another kid and start talking, sharing toys, bashing each other about, and it just works. It gets harder as you get older to make solid friendships. People are more guarded, cliquey. You can't just go up to a random table of women in a pub and join their conversation, not really. The world, at some point, just stops working that way as you get older.

I sigh, retrieving my phone from my satchel on the backseat, but there's no text from Alex. We always text each other right after an argument. I want to call him, but if I do, I know I'll burst into tears, and I don't want Lucy to see I've been crying. I have one of those faces that stay blotchy for hours after shedding even the slightest of tears.

Things have seemed so tense with Alex over the last few days. I don't like it. I want to fix it. He doesn't know what I know about Lucy. He doesn't know how threatened I feel by her, about how much it kills me when he has a conversation with her or gives her attention, even if it is just friendly. His attention is hard to come by as it is, but when he's talking and laughing with Lucy, I can't help but think how good they look together. How effortlessly their conversation flows. How easily he laughs with her. I could tell him how I feel, that would solve everything, he'd finally understand . . . but I also know it would open a can of worms I don't want to dig up.

My emotional state has me remembering things that I don't want to, things I keep buried inside. The second phone Alex had for work creeps into my memory, making me shiver as I recall the evening we'd been in my tiny flat in London, drunk on wine with bellies full of cheese and olives. His work phone hadn't stopped vibrating. When he'd gone to the bathroom I'd leaned over and pressed the screen out of curiosity. There were several messages from someone called Evie on there. I couldn't see what they said, but already my gut instinct was telling me they were bad. All I could see was a tiny blurred image of a woman with blonde hair on the screen. When he'd returned from the bathroom I'd thrust his phone in his face, demanding to know who Evie was. The look on his face was all I'd needed to see to hurl my glass of red wine all over him and kick him off the boat. We had only just said we loved each other the day before and then suddenly, abruptly, it was over.

Alex had been persistent over the next few weeks, constantly knocking at my front door, which I refused to answer. He'd leave flowers, notes, occasionally food too, which I'd shamefully squirrel inside and eat once I was sure he'd left the dock. Eventually, I met up with him to talk. He'd told me how sorry he was and promised me something like that would never happen again. He'd said he'd never done anything like that before and he didn't understand why he had. It was the first time I'd ever seen him cry. Knowing that I was the first girl he'd ever cheated on was almost a bigger slap than actually being cheated on. It made me spiral into a depression so colossally deep that I never fully recovered from it.

I try every day to tell myself I'm enough for him, but I don't know if I'll ever fully believe it, especially not after what he did to me before we left London.

The last few months have been predominantly incredible between us. By the time I'd calmed down enough to hear Alex out weeks after I'd caught him cheating, he'd already deleted the messages from Evie. He'd promised me he'd ended things, that it was nothing more than a few flirty messages anyway. He'd told me he just wanted to be rid of anything to do with her and to make me his priority from there on in, which I'd thought he'd done. Until I caught him again, that is. A message from Evie reappeared after I found out we were pregnant. If I hadn't checked his phone when he was in the bathroom one evening while we were watching a movie, I'd never have seen them. Checking his phone isn't something I'm proud of, but I couldn't shake the gut feeling I had.

I'd demanded he open the message in front of me when he got back into the room. He looked horrified as he typed in his password and handed me his phone. I'd snatched it from him and was surprised to find there wasn't a chain of messages, only a handful.

The exchange baffled me. I didn't understand it. He'd told her we were pregnant. One simple text message, just two words. *She's pregnant*, it read. When I asked him to explain, he'd told me he still saw Evie sometimes, that they worked in the same building. This was news to me and made me instantly furious. He'd been working with her for the last couple of months of our relationship after promising me he had nothing to do with her. I felt betrayed, lied to.

'Why did you tell her of all people? We haven't even told your mum!' I'd spat at him.

'I know you won't understand, Darcy. Evie's always felt terrible for almost splitting us up and always asks how we are whenever we bump into each other,' he says. 'So, I guess when I found out you were pregnant, I didn't think and just wanted to share the news. I wanted her to know she hadn't completely broken us.'

I'd kept looking at the messages on his screen for what felt like hours. I hated him for having messaged her, for lying to me about working with her. Not one part of me believed that in the months we'd been together, nothing more had happened between them, and so we moved. We left London to get away from Evie and start fresh with our baby.

So, if I tell Alex why I feel so threatened by Lucy, it will remind him of what he did, and I know how enormous his regret is. When I'd finally taken him back, I'd made a promise to myself that I wouldn't use what he'd done against him as ammunition in arguments. I'd trained myself to completely forget it had ever even happened.

***

Reluctantly I step out of the car and trudge up to the café. Lucy's already there, sitting by the window looking out to the estuary. From a distance, she looks so sad. There's a morose longing on her face, complementing her milky complexion. This is the real Lucy, the one I feel I could potentially, perhaps in another world, connect with. Seeing her sitting there, absorbed in her own thoughts, feels so real compared to the banal illusion she puts on as the happy housewife to some attorney who never seems to be there. When she notices me in the doorway, her entire face morphs into a smile that stretches from ear to ear. Whatever gloomy thoughts were roaming around in her head are seemingly forgotten about in an instant. She waves me over, crushing me into a startling embrace before kneeling in front of me so she's eyelevel with my stomach.

'How's bump?' she asks at the exact moment the baby gives a mighty kick, putting an intense pressure on my bladder.

'Good, wriggling around like crazy.'

'Oh really! Can I feel?' she asks, but she's already pressed her hands firmly against my stomach. The baby kicks again, making her squeal in delight. I glance around in embarrassment as she whispers softly to my belly.

'How long until you're due again?' she asks, those grey eyes looking up at me.

'Four weeks,' I say, stepping away from her touch. People around us are starting to stare.

'Gosh, so soon! How exciting. Sorry, anterior placenta. I don't get to feel much movement with this one.' Her eyes are glistening as she motions to her own belly. I can't help but notice it's another excuse, a reason for her complete disregard to personal space.

When the situation with Marie and Violet's baby happened, she'd excused it by sharing how difficult it had been for her to fall pregnant. When she was being flirty with our partners, although not a direct excuse, she told us about Arthur being polyamorous shortly afterwards and now, kneeling here with her hands plastered over my bump without my consent, she's excused it with an anterior placenta. I make a mental note to remember what the next inevitable excuse will be for her bizarre behaviour.

We take a seat at the table, and I watch as she pours my tea into a tiny ceramic cup. She hands it over to me shakily.

'You okay?' I ask, gesturing to her trembling fingers.

'Oh, yes, just low blood sugar. Really knocks me in pregnancy. The doctor told me my body struggles to process glucose or something. Anyway, what about you? You're really considering doing a home birth?' She drops cubes of brown sugar into both of our teacups.

I nod, stirring my tea. 'Yeah, I'd much rather be comfortable at home. I'm speaking to my midwife about it at our next appointment. I guess I really should have arranged all of this a long time ago, but the move here kind of threw everything off. I haven't had any complications with this pregnancy though, so I'm hoping she'll support my decision.'

'I'm sure she will.' Lucy nods vigorously. 'It's the best decision you'll ever make. Think about it, no long journey to a hospital or having to worry about Alex getting kicked out the ward after visiting hours are over if you have to stay in. I've heard so many great things about waterbirths, how gentle they are and how relaxing it is for the baby. Someone told me it makes labour go faster, too.'

'You're pretty set on doing it too, then?'

'Without a doubt. Who knows, with it being a home birth, maybe Art will actually be there too,' she jokes, but it falls flat.

'I went to a hypnobirthing class the other day. It's made me feel way more confident about the whole thing,' she says when I don't respond. 'I'll teach you how to do some of the techniques, so you don't have to pay for the classes. It's really easy.'

I raise my eyebrows at her, choking back a laugh. How can she assume I can't afford classes myself? I can't remember telling her that I was in a bad situation financially. I fold my arms across my chest, then I remember I'd mentioned being unemployed and looking for work.

'Thanks,' I mutter.

She sighs, leaning back in her chair as she stares at me. 'I'm trying here, Darcy. I want to help you. Let me and you'll see, everything will be so much easier. I'd love to be friends with you.'

I want to tell her that I don't need her help, and that I'm definitely not interested in being her friend. I don't want someone in my life that I can never trust fully around my fiancé.

'I'm not really sure why you seem to have your guard up around me. If I've done something wrong, I'm really sorry.' Her intense grey eyes search mine.

I twizzle my engagement ring around my finger, thinking about being honest with her about why I'm so uncomfortable, but pride wins, and I refuse to let her see my vulnerable side.

The sun hits the tiny diamonds dotted around my ring, shining right in Lucy's eyes. She looks down at my ring finger, her face opening up with a smile.

'It's the polyamory thing, isn't it?' she asks. 'Darcy, I'd never dream of doing anything with Alex. You know that, right?'

I can't tell if I'm imagining it, but I'm almost certain there's a condescending tone to her voice.

'It's not—' I start, but she cuts me off.

'I just want to help you. I know you're new here. That must be pretty lonely, not knowing anyone, not having any friends.'

My skin starts to prickle at the cold truth behind her words. Her nails rap against the wooden tabletop as she waits for me to respond. When I don't, she seems vexed.

'You might not believe me right now, but I'm just like you,' she says. 'All I want to do is make friends. It hasn't been easy for me here as Art's new wife. This place is cliquey. A lot of the women were friends with his ex.'

A lot of women probably have husbands you've screwed, I think. The way she's looking at me though makes her seem truly genuine. Her huge eyes look so devastatingly desperate that I find myself starting to feel sorry for her again.

Despite everything, what she says resonates with me. I'm still wary of her, still have my guard up, but a part of me is starting to think that maybe Alex has been right all along. Maybe my behaviour has been childish. Those nightmares of Lucy murdering Arthur's first wife, the paranoia of her stealing Alex; it's all been in my head. I'm starting to see her in a new light, and in this light, she's harmless.

'You promise me you won't do anything with Alex, or anyone else in the group for that matter?'

'You have my word.' The smile on her face is euphoric.

* * *

'You've had a bit of a change of heart,' Alex remarks after I wave Lucy off from the front door.

I smile at him sheepishly.

'If you want to hear it, then fine, I'll say it. You were right, Lucy's lovely,' I say, perching on the armrest of his chair and letting him scoop a hand over my bump.

'I'm sorry, can you repeat that, please?' he asks playfully.

'You were right.' I prod him, laughing contentedly in his arms. Our recent arguments forgotten about.

I enjoy the simple, quiet moment between us in our lounge, realizing it's the first day we haven't been breathing down each other's necks in a while. I can't help but think maybe it's better because I finally have someone else in my life, a friend. I'm no longer solely relying on Alex and the cat to keep me company. As hard as it is to admit, listening to Alex and letting Lucy in has done me the world of good. I feel healthier and better for it.

Lucy has visited every single day this week and to her credit, whenever Alex is in the room, she keeps her distance as promised. Surprisingly, she hardly makes eye contact with him and besides quick friendly greetings, Alex tends to keep away from us too. It's like an unspoken pact has been made between the three of us and it's working beautifully.

Lucy and I burrow away, leaving Alex to work while we focus on hypnobirthing techniques. Each day she teaches me different things from breathing techniques, affirmations and visualization methods. At first it all feels a little silly. I find myself struggling to concentrate, wanting to burst out laughing as she tells me to repeat chants about how strong I am, how my body knows exactly what it needs to do. The breathing techniques don't seem to be doing anything more than making me feel dizzy, either. But through this shift in my relationship with Lucy, an unexpected calmness runs through me about labour. I don't realize it straight away, but Lucy's help has been invaluable to me. I'm ready.

As Lucy suspected, my midwife seems happy with my decision to have a waterbirth at home when I speak to her at my check-up.

My friendship with Lucy flourishing quickly, we decide to go together to meet Rachel and Johnny's baby when they're home from hospital. Unlike Marie and Violet, who delivered early, Rachel gave birth four days after her due date. I find myself braced with so many questions to ask her by the time we arrive.

'I didn't really want to share the whole birth story on the group chat, not yet anyway. If you want to know, then I'm happy to tell you about it, but equally if you'd rather wait until after you've given birth yourselves, I completely understand that!' Rachel tells us when we arrive.

She's feeding a bottle to her son, who guzzles it down at an impressive speed. It's messy business, milk dribbling from both corners of his tiny mouth. When he's demolished the bottle, Rachel lies him across her lap face down and rubs his back until he lets out a tremendous burp.

'I'd love to know everything,' I say, wanting to prepare myself for every kind of possibility.

'Well, two days ago I thought I had my bloody show when I went to the bathroom. I didn't feel great though, something just felt off. So, I took a picture of it and sent it to my midwife,' she says. 'She called me back pretty quickly and told me it was a clot, not a bloody show. Johnny had to take me to the hospital and after waiting for ages they told me they wanted to induce me. I really didn't want to be induced, so when the doctor went away my midwife said if that's how I really feel, I should go under twenty-four-hour observation. She literally told me to stick to my guns, so I did.' She smiles, hoisting her baby up on her shoulder. 'Anyway, I went into labour only a few hours later and then Joey arrived really quickly to be honest! No one could believe it; he kind of just shot out! The doctors were really surprised I didn't have a bad tear because of how quickly it all happened and the size of him.'

I look down at Joseph, at the enormity of him. He's the spit of Johnny, already looking like he belongs out on a rugby field. I can't fathom how he came out of her naturally. Just the thought of it makes me feel queasy. It's an eye-opening moment, knowing that in just a few weeks I'll be pushing out my own baby.

'Oh God, I'm starting to get nervous,' I say, biting my lip. 'What if I can't do it? What if something goes wrong and we have to get to a hospital?'

'You'll be fine, Darcy. We both will. We can do this!' Lucy says, touching my leg softly. It makes me jump in surprise. I pull at my dress to make sure it doesn't ride up to show off my scars.

'Of course you will be. You'll smash it.' Rachel winks.

We all smile as Johnny lumbers in carrying a tray of coffees and biscuits for us. Joseph burps again as Rachel rubs his back. I can tell she's watchful of Lucy while we're there, but Lucy doesn't step a foot out of line. Much to my surprise, she's actually pretty quiet the entire time we're there. She seems timid, like she's terrified of disgruntling Rachel in any way.

'Would you like to hold him, Darcy?' Rachel asks me, handing Joey over to me.

'Wow,' I breathe. 'I can't believe he was eleven pounds. Well done you!' I smile at Rachel, then let my eyes drift down to Joey. 'I've never held a baby this new before.'

I breathe in his delicate powdery scent, trying not to get overwhelmed. I don't know what I'm doing. I feel awkward, afraid to move, but at the same time I can't stop grinning. His buttery soft skin is riddled in rolls of the most adorable baby fat, his chunky fingers gripping hold of mine tightly. I can tell Lucy is envious, but she doesn't ask to hold him, and Rachel doesn't offer.

It's when we're in the car on the way back to her house that her mood becomes acidic.

'She could've let me hold him. It's not like I'm going to make the same mistake I did with Holly again, am I? The bitch should give me the benefit of the doubt,' she spits.

I'm taken aback by her animosity and the swift change in attitude. When we'd left Rachel and Johnny's, she was all smiles, hugging everyone goodbye. Now that we've rounded the corner and are alone in the car, her nastiness has come from nowhere.

'You think she was being a bitch too, don't you, Darcy?'

I don't respond, feeling uncomfortable at how pushy she's being. I don't want to talk about Rachel behind her back. She continues to stare at me, wild-eyed.

'You agree, right?'

I keep my eyes locked on the road, but her relentless stare is making me lose my concentration. Her eyes are burning into me, making me feel trapped.

'Say Rachel was being a bitch. I know you're thinking it too.'

I'm not thinking it, but I want her hounding to stop. I also don't want her to be upset with me when we've had one of the loveliest weeks together and I feel like I'm finally making a friend. It might not be the exact friendship I'd wanted from the antenatal classes, but the last week has felt so nice, having a girlfriend to see every day, someone to talk to when Alex is stuck behind his laptop. It's made me feel normal, like just an average person going for walks and meeting a friend for coffee, something I've never experienced before. Selfishly I don't want to lose that, so when she probes at me again I give in.

'Rachel was being a bitch today,' I say.

The words feel nasty and wrong, but Lucy seems satisfied. Her approval is somehow addictive, like a drug to me. I find myself not wanting to disappoint her, filled with fear of losing the first proper friendship I've had in years.

Somehow my desperation to feel like I finally fit in exceeds all else, and so whatever Lucy wants me to say, I say. It doesn't make me feel good, but I shove that thought to the back of my mind.

CHAPTER 17

When I get home, Alex is in the bedroom packing his Fred Perry barrel bag. My first thought is he's leaving me. He's had enough of the bickering and negativity. Despite a few better days lately, I'm not convinced they're enough to pull us from the wreckage our relationship has become recently. For a moment I find myself thinking I don't blame him for leaving me.

'I've got to head back to London for a few days for work,' he tells me, using his ridiculous t-shirt-folding board he's had since I've known him to crisply fold another shirt that he adds to his bag.

I watch him methodically pack in the same shirt in varying colours, his shiny work shoes and his leather washbag. A part of me wants to beg him to stay. I'm not ready to be alone in this new house yet, and he'd always promised he'd never leave me this close to our due date just in case I went into early labour. But another part of me knows that maybe some time apart will do us the world of good. Perhaps this is the perfect time for me to bond with this place anyway, without feeling like I'm tiptoeing around and walking on eggshells while Alex works.

I nod, doing a sweep of the bathroom to make sure he's remembered his toothbrush and deodorant. While he loads up the car, I settle on the bed and count the kicks coming from my womb, still thinking about Lucy's strange behaviour. I've started to enjoy spending time with her now, but the switch in her attitude after leaving Rachel's has left me rattled. I think about telling Alex about it, about trying to talk to him about how strange she can be sometimes, but I know it will just end in yet another argument.

I sigh, noticing Alex's wallet on the bedside table. I roll my eyes and grab it for him, wondering what else he's forgotten to pack. He's notoriously forgetful when it comes to packing. I smile, remembering one time we'd booked a week away in New York, but when we'd got to the airport, he'd suddenly realized he'd left his passport behind.

I'm about to push myself up from the mattress when I notice just how thick his wallet seems. It feels squishy and weighty in my hands. Out of curiosity, I flip it open, expecting to see wads of cash folded up inside it. What I do find is something far harder to try and understand. I pull out a strip of thin-feel condoms. They tumble out, hitting the bed, leaving me with my mouth hanging open. Alex and I stopped using condoms early on. There'd been no need after that condom had broken and I got pregnant.

His footsteps thud up the staircase. I can't move. I'm frozen solid, the shock debilitating me. When he gets to the bedroom, he looks down at the condoms scattered across the bed and then up to me. He's turned deathly pale.

'What the fuck is this, Alex?' I grasp a handful of the foil packets, waving them in his face.

'Darcy, it's not what it looks like,' he says. The cliché line a man always uses when he's been found out. What has my life become?

'Oh really, then what is it, Alex?'

'They're old.'

'Old? Then why would they just wind up in your wallet when you're about to go away?'

'I found them in my toiletries. I wanted to get rid of them without you seeing them. I knew it'd upset you, make you think the worst, which it clearly has,' he says, still standing stock-still in the doorway.

I tear off one of the packets from the strip and turn it around in my shaking hands, looking for an expiration date.

'Ha! See, these don't expire for *years*, Alex! You're lying to me,' I shout, pointing down at the stamped date on the packaging.

'Okay, fine. They're from the day at the pub with the guys. We'd all had a few pints and got a bit silly in the bathroom when we saw one of those vending machines selling condoms. We were just a bunch of drunk idiots being stupid, Darcy.'

'Were you planning on using them somewhere?!' I spit.

'No! Never. Grayson was just throwing them around to everyone. It was just a bit of fun.'

'Do you think I'm stupid, Alex?' I narrow my eyes at him.

'God, you still don't trust me, do you? What do I have to do, Darcy?'

'Not show up with a massive roll of condoms hidden in your wallet, maybe! Especially when I'm carrying your child and look like this,' I yell, loud enough to frighten Henry, who skitters away. I'm on my feet now, gesturing wildly down to my booming baby bump. How has he somehow managed to twist this all around to be my fault?

'If you don't believe me, then ask the guys!' he snaps, knowing full well I wouldn't reach out to the guys about finding a bunch of condoms wedged into my fiancé's wallet in a million years. He knows just how much I hate other people knowing my business.

An impotent anger boils in me that threatens to spill over the longer Alex stands there staring at me.

'I have done everything to prove my loyalty to you, Darcy. We're getting married, we're having a baby. When will it be enough for you to start trusting me?'

'Leave me alone!' I scream, hurling the condoms at him. They hit his chest and fall to the floor between us.

'I'm going now, Darcy. I'll let you know when I get to London.' He sighs, looking at me sadly before turning to go.

I'm breathing deeply, trying to compose myself, but I feel so attacked again for my trust issues. There always seems to be something making my insecurities mount, no matter how hard I try.

'You don't think I try and trust you, Alex? You think this is fun for me, being this way? Well, newsflash, it's not. It's awful,' I yell. 'If I could switch it all off, I would. I'd love nothing more than to be able to live each day knowing nothing is ever going to come along and rip everything away from me, but I just can't. It's bloody exhausting living every single day of my life in fear that all of this is going to be taken from me.' I look around our bedroom, at the life we've created together.

I've never been this open and honest with him about how I truly feel. I've always been too scared to upset him with these thoughts. It's always been easier to just let him think everything was fixed. Like a broken piece of pottery being put back together with gold, I'd let him think I wasn't shattered anymore. Of course, my insecurities would come out occasionally, like everyone's does, but I don't think he realized how bad it still is for me until now.

'Nothing is going to take this away from you. It's yours. You're safe now.' He looks at me sadly. 'I've got to go. For the record, I think you've never looked more beautiful. I just wish you'd believe it,' he says before walking away from me, leaving the condoms at my feet.

I text Lucy, thirsty for someone to understand me, to take my side. When my phone chimed with a message back from her, I couldn't be more grateful.

Meet at the beach in an hour?

I tell her I'll see her there and quickly escape the house.

***

'He didn't even acknowledge how I literally poured my entire heart out to him,' I say after filling Lucy in on my argument with Alex. I don't say that one of the biggest issues between us lately has in fact been my insecurities about *her*. She doesn't need to know that.

'Men!' she scoffs. 'Look, if it makes you feel any better, Art told me about the condom thing, so I know he's not making it up.'

'I thought Art wasn't there when they went to the pub?'

'He wasn't,' she says quickly.

'How did he know then?'

'He showed me pictures on the guys' group chat of them mucking around in the bathroom, Darcy. They were just drunk, guys being guys.'

I exhale, soothed by knowing it hadn't all been a lie but equally riddled with remorse for how I'd reacted to Alex. I dig my toes into the sand, staring out to sea and wishing I could call him to apologize.

'He probably hates me,' I groan, burying my head in my hands.

'He doesn't. I'm sure he understands. I mean if roles were reversed and he'd found something like that in your bag without knowing anything about it, I'm sure he'd be pretty upset too.'

'He'd go mental. But look at me, no one would want me right now anyway. I'm sure he's feeling pretty secure about where he stands with me,' I joke, but it doesn't land.

'You're beautiful, Darcy. Pregnancy looks good on you. Stop being silly.'

I don't tell her that the only time I make somewhat of an effort is when I'm leaving the house, that usually I'm drowned in Alex's clothes now that nothing of my own fits me anymore. I don't tell her that I know I should probably make more of an effort to look good, if not for Alex, then at least for myself. Some days I'm so embarrassed by my appearance that I don't even want to open the door for the Amazon delivery person. It makes me wonder what Lucy would look like if I just showed up unannounced, if she always looks so put together and smelling like duty free or if she is in fact human.

'Thanks for letting me talk to you about this. It means a lot,' I say.

'That's what friends are for, right?' She smiles, and we both look out to the waves crashing against the shoreline.

* * *

Alex still hasn't checked in, not even to make sure everything's okay with the baby. I wouldn't mind, but he promised he'd let me know when he arrived. Ever the worrier, I start to think something terrible has happened to him like an awful car crash. During the day it's easy to pass the time with Lucy. We make a trip to the shops and do some retail therapy, loading our trolleys up with a collection of baby clothes. I marvel at the excitement of it all. Gone are the days I'd be chucking in clothing I didn't need for me after a fight to cheer myself up. I don't leave the shops with a single item for myself and strangely enough, I don't even care. I'm just excited to go home and do the first load of baby laundry while the sun's still out.

Lucy comes back to the house with me and helps me remove all of the tags before I shove everything into the washing machine. While we wait for the cycle to finish, we sit out in the garden with one of her fancy bottles of Saicho she brought with her and look out at the horizon. It's nowhere near as impressive as the view from her own home, but she showers me with compliments on the house and garden regardless.

'Thanks. I've been so bad at maintaining it all to be honest. I need to get my hands stuck into those beds and pull out all the weeds. Alex hasn't mown the grass in weeks, either.'

'At least Alex mows the lawn himself. Art just hires someone to do ours,' Lucy says with a roll of her eyes. We both laugh.

I'm taking a sip of Saicho when it hits me that this exact moment is everything I'd been wanting in life, a real friendship. Someone to sit with and moan to about my partner, someone who would listen and be there for me when things got tough. I blink, unable to stop wondering why, if I have everything I'd wanted in life, do I suddenly feel so incredibly sad?

* * *

When the baby's clothes are all pegged up on the washing line, we sit and stare at them swaying in the warm summer breeze.

Henry slinks over, giving a deep meow. His amber eyes widen at the sight of Lucy, his hackles rising. He hisses, baring his teeth.

Lucy recoils, stumbling back.

'Sorry,' I say in disbelief, shooing Henry away. 'He's never liked strangers.' The lie slips out of me easily, and I silently wonder what's got into him. He stalks down into the garden, as far away from us as he can get.

'Not long to go now,' Lucy says, seeming to centre herself as her breathing evens out. She looks down at the swell of my belly. At that moment the baby presses their little bottom out. I feel their entire body stretch and curl up to one side, the side furthest away from Lucy. While I check my phone for messages from Alex, Lucy's own phone rings.

'I better take this. One sec,' she says, answering the call and walking off into the garden.

There's still no word from Alex. I look at the time, telling myself he's probably still on the road. Alex is the kind of guy that hates stopping when he has somewhere to go. Unless it's an emergency pitstop for more fuel or a bathroom break, he powers on through a drive until he reaches his destination.

I look up at the sudden sharpness to Lucy's voice carrying across the garden. She's by the dying rose bush, hissing into the phone.

'Fine, I'm coming back now. Give me ten minutes.' She hangs up the call, pocketing her phone, and sighs dramatically.

'You alright?' I ask her, bemused. Evidently, I'm not the only one with issues.

'Oh, yes. Art's just needing some help with his kids,' she says in a sugary sweet voice. She tries to hide her annoyance behind a big, bright smile. 'Let me know how you get on with Alex. I'm sure you guys will be just fine.'

I watch her drive away, then turn my gaze back towards the flutter of cream, white and beige baby clothes already drying in the afternoon sun.

* * *

By evening, when I still haven't heard from Alex, I dial Debbie's number to settle my nerves. It takes her an age to answer and when she does, I automatically know she's already knee deep in a bottle of whiskey. Alex is going to be thrilled about that.

'Didn't even know he was coming. I'll make up his old room for him,' she slurs. 'Stop worrying, he probably just went straight to the office if he had some work to catch up on. Long drive like that, I'm sure he's missed out a whole day's work.'

I know she's taking a dig at me about the distance between London and Cornwall. Over five hours on a good day with no traffic.

'It's such a pity, you know,' she says, her voice trailing off into the ether.

'What is?' I bite, wondering what sort of nonsense she's going to start talking about now in her drunken stupor.

'You and Alex. It's just a pity you're fighting like this, already. It really shouldn't be this way, you know. Not when you're at the most exciting and happiest time of your lives, starting a family and getting married.'

'We're absolutely fine,' I lie, unable to hide the denial in my words. I stop myself from saying more, running my tongue along my top teeth. If I carry on, I'm afraid I'll say something I regret.

'Have you thought about postponing the wedding a bit longer, Darcy? Until the two of you are in a bit of a better place together?'

My anger flares and I realize it's because I know there's actual sense to what she's saying; I just don't want to admit it. Alex and I are in no position to get married right now, not really. Things haven't been good between us for months; I'd just thought we were better at hiding it. Clearly not.

I hang up on her. She won't remember our conversation or the abrupt ending of it by morning anyway.

***

When Alex finally contacts me, his excuse is exactly as his mother had predicted it would be. He'd gone straight to the office and only got back to his mother's in time to find Debbie already passed out in her armchair, covered in her own urine and an empty bottle of whiskey beside her.

'I'm sorry you had to see that, Alex. I know how much you hate it,' I say down the phone, feeling terrible for him. I step cautiously over the scattered condoms, still strewn across our bedroom floor. The thought of picking them up revolts me, so I conclude it's better to leave them there for as long as possible, a constant reminder of our argument.

'I'm used to it. Anyway, it's late. We should both be getting some rest. I just wanted to let you know I'm alright.'

'Sure,' I say. I'm about to say good night, but he's already disconnected the call.

'Love you,' I whisper down the line as though he can still hear me.

I head into the bathroom, finally feeling able to get ready for bed without worrying about where Alex is. That worry has been replaced by something else, a question I've been asking myself all too often lately. Are we okay?

The house is quiet, too quiet without the familiar tapping of his keyboard coming from his office. When I've brushed my teeth, I rinse my mouth, splash water on my face and pat my skin dry. When I've finished moisturizing, I pull the string light down and the room turns black.

I'm about to turn back to the bedroom when one of the security lights outside floods the bathroom with a dim glow. Something has triggered it. I drop to my knees, so my silhouette is no longer visible from the window to people on the outside looking in. I'm frozen to the spot, even though logically I'm sure it must be a fox or some other kind of animal lurking around out there. My pulse is throbbing at the side of my head, my heart beating too quickly.

I'm reaching for my phone balanced on the sink when the eerie silence is broken by the sound of someone running outside. Feet stamping over dead rose petals and parched grass. I hear the handle to the back door getting tugged down. Thank God I remembered to lock it earlier when I'd brought in the washing. Angry whispers trail up through the cracked-open window. I grab my phone and dial 999, trying to control the shake in my hands.

'There's someone outside my house. They're trying to get in,' I whisper when I finally get through. They tell me they're dispatching someone right away and to stay where I am.

My knees are weak and wobbly as I force myself to look back outside. Two shadows hover by the back door, making me buckle to the floor again in terror.

Trembling, I open the security camera app on my phone, trying to get a better look at who is outside. None of the cameras are connecting. Someone's tampered with them. I scream inwardly, wishing Alex were here. My mind is racing with thoughts of being dragged into my kitchen and slaughtered like Arthur's wife. I clutch at my neck, digging my nails in deeply.

The people outside are disturbed by the blue flashing lights that sweep over the property. I watch as the two shadows quickly dart away, off into the bushes and out of sight.

'Thank God you're here,' I say when I open the door for the police.

'It's you.' The policewoman investigating my missing wedding dress looks me up and down.

I can tell she's judging me as she takes my statement, that she doesn't quite believe me.

'Ms Holloway,' she says. 'Do you think these two crimes are related?'

'I never said that. I have no idea. Why?' I frown.

'I just find it odd that first your wedding dress goes missing and then you claim there's someone outside your house late at night.'

'Two people. It was definitely two people,' I say.

'Right. Two people. To me, this sounds like the start of a harassment case, especially if it's causing you fear?' She looks me in the eyes, gauging my reaction.

I nod my head. 'I was scared tonight, but I don't know if the two things are related. They're totally different,' I say.

'I'd say it sounds like someone's toying with you.' She pockets her pen and considers me carefully.

Her partner steps inside, making me jump.

'I've checked out the entire area. Clear,' he says.

She nods. 'Make sure you lock up behind us. If anything else happens, you can call again.' She gets to her feet and starts walking towards the front door.

'Wait, that's it? You're leaving me here?' My heart rate spikes. I don't want to be left alone. Isn't it their duty to stay, to protect me and make me feel safe? I look at them desperately, silently pleading with them not to go.

'Ms Holloway, there's nothing more we can do at this stage. The area's secure. You're safe. If there were people outside earlier, they've had a scare and are long gone.'

I twist the key in the lock quickly as they leave, watching as their car slowly creeps down the driveway.

I stay up all night listening to every creak and groan the house makes as the wind rattles through the walls.

***

For two days I'm left on my own. The nights are the worst. Every tiny sound makes me jump, but nothing more happens. I don't tell anyone about it either. Telling the girls or Alex the police want to start a harassment case sounds too dramatic and ridiculous, and besides, I haven't even told Alex about the dress yet. So, I keep it to myself, like everything else. I'm starting to feel the weight of these things resting heavily on my shoulders.

I'm stuck in my own head, stewing not only on what Debbie said to me about postponing our wedding but on Alex's cold behaviour towards me too. Lucy's busy with Arthur's kids and the other girls seem preoccupied. For two days those condoms glare up at me whenever I enter the bedroom, pervading my thoughts. I try to keep busy, forcing myself out into the garden to prune the wilting rose bush, but I'm too irritated to bother much, giving up the second a thorn buries itself under my skin.

The wedding venues we'd visited are chasing us for a response, sugarcoating their emails with niceties in the hopes of securing an astronomical deposit from us. Copying and pasting the same email to them all, I tell them we've decided to go in a different direction and that their venue was lovely but just not the right fit for us. Hitting send to Roscarrock specifically is enough to break my heart.

Alex gets back late on a Friday evening. I find him sitting on the bed when I open the door from the bathroom, his dark and unexpected presence making me jump in fright. I'm wrapped in a crusty dry towel, my hair wet from the shower.

'I wasn't sure what time you'd be home,' I say shyly.

'I left a few hours earlier than expected. Wanted to surprise you. I see those haven't moved.' He motions towards the condoms.

I don't have to tell him they gross me out; my expression says it all. He gets up from the bed and bends down to pick them up, sighing as he bins them.

'It really isn't anything you need to worry about,' he says, his tall body so close to mine I can feel the heat radiating from him.

'I know,' I say, gingerly taking a step towards him.

He pulls me closer, and I feel myself thaw in his arms.

'I'm sorry everything's been so shit lately,' I speak into his chest, and he hugs me tighter.

'I just want you to be happy, Darcy. I've been feeling a lot of pressure lately that I haven't really wanted to bother you with, but it is difficult feeling like your happiness is completely dependent on me. It's tough enough feeling like you and the baby are my responsibility financially, especially with work being so rubbish at the moment.'

'I honestly didn't know you felt like this,' I say, sighing. Alex has never been someone to be open about his feelings, so I'd just taken it for granted and assumed he was fine. 'I feel awful for not realizing how hard things are for you right now.'

I raise my hand up and cup his face, kissing him gently. Those soft, warm, familiar lips kiss me back hungrily, his breath hot against my skin. His fingers climb under the towel, expertly unhooking it from around my chest. It drops, spilling at my ankles, and I stand there naked in front of him. His eyes roam over my body, so different from the supple, toned form I'd had this time last year.

I let his eyes feast on my swelling breasts until his hands can't control themselves anymore. He squeezes my sensitive, darkened nipples between the tips of his fingers and groans as my hand explores his throbbing erection. For the first time in months, I'm not self-conscious of my body with its new stretchmarks and curves. I take control, straddling him on the bed and guide him inside me. It's been so long that despite how wet I am it hurts as he pushes deeper, his thrusts becoming more eager. I take him fully into me, claiming him as mine. It's a carnal, possessive act as we reacquaint ourselves with each other. I let him watch me ride him, writhing on top of him until we both reach a magnificent climax.

Lying in his arms, both of us emanating the sweet scent of sex and sweat, I drift to sleep peacefully, comforted by his presence. The condoms and my insecurities are forgotten about for a few blissful hours.

At around midnight, I wake with a start. I'd been having a nightmare about Alex removing the towel from around my body, but when I turn to the mirror in the room, it isn't my face staring back at me; it's Lucy's. I can't escape the dream, trapped in a world I don't want any part of. The scene plays out in my head so vividly as Lucy mounts Alex, letting him inside her with a cry of pleasure. She tosses her head back, looking at herself in the mirror, her long blonde hair cascading down around them. It's an image I can't get out of my head. Alex reaches out for me drowsily, noticing my shallow breathing.

'Night terror?' he whispers, slowly sitting up in the darkness.

'The worst,' I grumble, thinking it best to lie rather than tell him the truth, especially when things between us are still so raw. Our recent wound hasn't even had a chance to scab over yet.

***

The next couple to have their baby is Cora and Jack. When I'm doing the maths, I realize in a moment of sheer panic that I'm next, or I should be anyway. Out of the remaining mothers-to-be, my due date's next on the list with Carmen due just a few days later and Lucy two weeks following that. It feels a bit like a race I have a head start in. I'm convinced Carmen will go into labour first though, making the wait even more painful for me. Either way, it's inevitable that we'll all have our babies at some point in the very near future and that fills me with trepidation.

Unlike the others, Cora and Jack take a while to invite everyone to meet their baby boy. Cora shares an update the day after the birth to say they're just enjoying their little bubble right now but tells us the baby's name is Sean. Even the picture she sends to us is vague, a faraway shot of a tiny bundle in her arms.

When they do slowly start extending the invites, they only want to invite one couple per visit. Once again Lucy and I become a couple, with Arthur away at a work conference and Alex back in London again, this time visiting his mum after a bad fall. I'm slightly hesitant about going, worried Lucy'll bring out her nasty streak again if Cora doesn't let her hold Sean, but at the same time, I'm eager to catch up with Cora and so we make the journey to meet Sean in my car.

Jack's right outside to greet us as we arrive and scoops us both up into a big hug. He ushers us inside and offers us both a drink, which he goes off to make while we settle in the lounge with Cora. She looks positively shattered but delighted all at once.

'I don't want to scare you at all, so if you want me to stop, then please say so,' Cora tells us after we've asked her to share her birth story. Lucy and I nod, holding onto our bumps fervently.

'Basically, I went into labour after a membrane sweep. Lost my mucus plug, started contracting, it all seemed pretty straightforward. But the hospital kept turning me away, telling me my contractions weren't close enough together yet and said I'd be more comfortable at home. I tried really hard to get through them, but I found it really painful. By the time my mum arrived at our house to help us, she took one look at me crippled over the sofa and rushed me to the hospital.'

'Cora's mum is the kind of person you just don't argue with, so when we got there, they admitted us straight away,' Jack says, handing us both a Le Creuset stoneware mug.

'Anyway, hours went by, but I wasn't progressing from four centimetres in dilation. They'd put the epidural in, so I couldn't feel any pain anymore, which was a relief, but while they were monitoring the baby they noticed his heart rate was really fast. They told us he was in distress and said I needed to get wheeled in for a caesarean.'

'The doctors said we could wait a while to see if things improved but said if they got worse, the alarm bells would all go off and it would be a lot more traumatizing for all of us, so I got scrubbed up while they wheeled Cora into surgery,' Jack says, finishing the story.

I'm starting to regret asking her to tell us the whole story, understanding now why people wait until after everyone has given birth to share their experience. What if my baby gets distressed? Will the midwife be able to monitor that from home? Will there be time to get to the hospital if there's an emergency? It worries me that I don't have the answers to all of these questions, and I start making a mental note of everything I need to ask the midwife at my next appointment. How can I be so close to my due date and be starting to doubt my decision for a home birth?

I try not to show how anxious she's making me, but even after they've finished telling us the story and Cora has picked Sean up from his moses basket, I'm on edge. I can't even enjoy looking at his pudgy little face. Lucy, on the other hand, is enamoured. She doesn't ask Cora if she can hold Sean, but she makes it so obvious that she wants to that eventually Cora tells us she isn't letting anyone but family hold him yet. I notice Lucy narrowing her eyes, and I brace myself for her irritation once we're alone together again.

It's only later, once our tea is finished, my nerves have simmered down and Sean has fallen asleep that I look at him properly. He's got a distinctive flat nose I'd somehow missed earlier and almond-shaped eyes.

'He's—' I start to say, but Cora interrupts me.

'He's perfect.' She smiles down at her little boy with the unquestionable features of Down syndrome.

* * *

'She annoys me so much,' Lucy mutters once we've waved goodbye and are walking down to my car.

'I really like her,' I mumble, not wanting to get involved in another one of Lucy's rants about one of the other girls.

'Oh, come on, Darcy. She's being ridiculous. Not letting anyone hold her baby? She needs to learn to loosen up a bit.'

'I wish you'd stop saying things like that,' I admit, looking at her awkwardly.

'Things like what? Like that baby's got a face only a mother could love?' She laughs.

I'm horrified by her words and feel a sickening twist in my gut. I almost stop the car and tell her to get out. When I'd seen Sean, I thought he was just as beautiful as any other newborn. I've never understood people who say babies are ugly. Granted they all come out in different shapes and sizes, haven't grown into their features and have uneven moulded heads from passing through the birth canal, but that's only to be expected.

'That's a horrid thing to say, Lucy: "Sean's got a face only a mother could love." Maybe Cora is being ridiculous and could do with loosening up a little in letting people hold her baby — but it's understandable, don't you think?'

Lucy simply sneers in response.

'At the end of the day, it's her decision, Lucy. I just don't think you saying things like that is right,' I protest.

'You're right, I'm sorry I said anything. I guess I'm still getting a bit triggered by the babies,' she says a little too quickly, flashing me a smile as fake as Rachel's Ibiza tan had been when we'd first met her.

I frown at her, not picking up any genuine remorse in her words. It feels as though she's just playing a pity card, the same one she'd used when she'd been nasty about Rachel.

'I kind of get Cora's decision, though. To be honest I'll probably be the same. It's a big thing to just hand your brand new tiny baby over to someone else,' I say, turning out of Cora and Jack's driveway and onto the main road.

Lucy snorts, shaking her head. 'You better not be that way with me, Darcy. Any of the other girls, fine. But we're different, aren't we?' She looks at me expectantly, badgering me for a response, but I don't know what to say. I can't believe she'd speak to me that way, as though she's entitled to hold my baby, as though it's her right. I swallow, unsure how to respond.

'It's a decision I'll make with Alex once we've given birth. I don't know what it's going to be like yet or how I'm going to feel,' I say truthfully.

She sighs, looking away from me. I hate feeling like I've upset her even though she's been appalling. She's making it abundantly clear I've upset her, too.

When I drop her off at her house, she gets out of the car and walks away without saying anything. For a while I just sit there on her driveway, blinking in surprise. Her mood swings throw me; they're so unexpected.

When I eventually start to drive away, I look back at the manor in my rearview mirror and shudder. I swear Lucy is peering down at my car through the curtains from one of the upstairs windows. They fall back into place before I round the corner.

CHAPTER 18

For June, the weather is miserable, the trek from spring to summer seemingly endless after a few days that had provided false hope. There hasn't been a day over sixteen degrees and the constant cloud cover and rain showers have been making my already gloomy state even worse.

Alex has noticed me moping around the house, getting progressively more irritated with me. I haven't told him about the falling out with Lucy, if you can even call it that. I'm not sure I know what it is; all I know is I've started to wonder if keeping a friendship going with her is the best thing for me. I don't like that my need for friendship is overshadowing my gut instincts that she's not the sort of person I want in my life. I just don't want to be alone anymore, and when she's not being spiteful and vindictive I actually really enjoy her company. I had enjoyed her company, anyway. We haven't spoken for days, something I don't tell Alex or anyone else for that matter.

I keep what happened between Lucy and me to myself, letting it fester until Alex eventually snaps and thrusts an umbrella into my hands. 'You need to get out of the house,' he says, ushering me to the front door on a drizzly Tuesday morning.

I've had nothing but the cat for company for days, with Alex's work keeping him locked away late into the night. I sigh, knowing he's right. The umbrella springs open, fat raindrops pelting down onto the nylon material.

As I walk away in no particular direction, I already feel like it's easier to breathe. The house has been suffocating me for days without me realizing it. With days having gone by since I heard from Lucy, each time my phone chimes with a notification I grab at it like a lovesick teenager, hoping it's from her. It never is.

She's made it obvious she's upset with me by giving me the cold shoulder. The worst part is I don't even really know what I did to upset her so much. Part of me thinks I should just swallow my pride and reach out to her, apologize for something I'm not even sure I've done. I can't bring myself to do it, though. I replay the conversation over again in my head, trying to remember the smallest fragments of it to see what could have caused such an issue. As hard as I try, I come up empty-handed. She can't blame me for being reserved about letting other people hold my baby. As someone about to become a mother herself I'd have thought she'd understand that feeling more than most.

While I walk through the empty puddled streets my heart longs to be back in London. As excited as I was to be here with the beach at my fingertips each day, I'm starting to realize that maybe I'm not cut out for this kind of lifestyle. It's too boring here, too quiet.

I can't even find a local book club or a pottery group to join here. It has me wondering what the locals do to fill their days besides eating fish and chips and having a glass of wine looking out at the harbour. Perhaps they're all functioning alcoholics with decrepit livers, guzzling bottle after bottle of fancy wine from their cellars. Maybe they're all slowly giving themselves skin cancer as they lounge by their private pools, wishing they hadn't moved here either. These thoughts, although ludicrous, amuse me. They must do something with their time, or are they all like me, skulking around at home, barely dressed and watching reruns of *Desperate Housewives*? Somehow, I doubt it.

Asking Alex if we can move back to the city would be like admitting defeat. I just don't like being left alone with my thoughts, to have the time and space to rummage through my tortured head. It's a dangerous place for me to be. When there's nothing to fill my time with, I end up letting those painful memories from my past resurface. I'm still walking aimlessly, my head cast down to my feet, when I bump into Carmen. I instantly paint on a smile, trying to mask my sadness. Her face remains expressionless beneath the hood of her dripping rain jacket.

'How are you?' I ask her, slowly letting the smile slip from my face.

'Good,' she says, looking through me.

I turn, glancing behind me. Something seems more interesting to her than I am, but I can't work out what it is. I shift from foot to foot, hating the awkward silence around us.

'Doing much today?' I ask eventually, very aware of her clipped response and the way she's not looking me in the eye.

'I'm in a rush, actually. See you later,' she says, brushing past me and hurrying down the road.

I stand shellshocked for a moment. Carmen's never been the friendliest of people to me, but that just seemed rude. I don't want it to get to me the way it does. Instead of shrugging it off I add it to my pile of building insecurities, feeling my chin weaken as tears spring to my eyes.

Clutching the umbrella a little tighter, I let out a huff and continue down to the shop where I pick up a loaf of bread and a box of coffee pods for Alex. While I peruse the shelves a strange feeling works its way into my bones. Why does it feel like everyone is angry at me? I realize while looking at the various flavours of Tony's chocolate bars that I haven't heard from any of the girls for a while. Not even Cora, and she usually checks in at least every couple of days.

Have I done something, or is it just an odd coincidence? It's easy enough to assume Carmen's just being Carmen, but Cora's always chatty and getting in touch to check in. I hadn't noticed until now how much I appreciated those messages from her. I've been taking them for granted, I think, guilt clawing at me.

My stomach growls hungrily as I pass by the deli bakery on my way back. I haven't eaten all day. My hand touches my stomach. I haven't been looking after myself or my baby. When was the last time I felt movement? I've been so consumed in my pathetic self-pity I've hardly thought about the baby at all. I head for the café, ready to drown my sorrows in a large chocolate milkshake to hopefully get the baby wriggling again.

When I get to the glass doors, I do a doubletake. Carmen is inside, sitting at a table with Rachel, Cora and Lucy. I hadn't seen anything on the group chat about everyone meeting up today, and Carmen definitely hadn't mentioned anything when I'd just seen her down the street.

Why would they exclude me like this? Hurt washes over me, the rejection like a rodent gnawing at my insides. I stand in the pouring rain, watching them all huddled closely together, deep in conversation. I'm keenly aware of the wait staff looking at me hovering in the window, probably wondering why I'm not coming inside. I must look a sight, like a deranged outsider watching other people from afar, and I guess, much to my horror, that's exactly what I am.

I think about going inside and pretending to accidentally bump into them, but the awkwardness of it has me pulling back. So instead, I gather what little pride I have left and walk away beneath the shelter of my umbrella, getting drenched not by the rain but by my own tears.

* * *

After another few hours I still haven't felt the baby move, and my unease starts inching closer to complete panic as my heart rate accelerates. If I hadn't seen the girls together at the café, I'd be reaching out to them now for some advice, but I can't do that. Glugging back a glass of ice-cold water, I wait to see if it does the trick, but I still don't feel a thing. Eventually I have no choice but to knock hesitantly on Alex's office door and tell him I haven't felt anything all day.

'Why didn't you tell me sooner?' he asks, alarm written all over his face.

'I–I knew you were busy. I didn't want to bother you, but it's been hours now and I'm getting really worried,' I stammer.

He slams his laptop shut and tells me to call the maternity triage team to let them know we're on our way. His anger towards me stings, and I have to use all of my strength to keep myself composed.

Even though I know he's angry at me, he holds my hand on the way to the hospital, the need for reassurance more important than anything else. I look up at him gratefully, but he keeps his eyes on the road. We don't speak, the strain between us tightening with every bend in the road.

It takes what feels like forever to be seen, so long that I start to think they've forgotten about us. Midwives and nurses continually shuffle by, ignoring us completely. There's nothing but the glug, glug, glug of the water dispenser across from us for company while we wait.

When they finally do get around to giving us some attention, they find our baby's galloping heartbeat instantly. I breathe out a sigh of relief and despite everything, I find myself starting to laugh. Both the midwife and Alex look at me, concerned.

'I'm sorry,' I say, but I can't stop. It's been such a rubbish day, so to be hearing the gentle rhythm of the heartbeat releases so much tension from me that I don't know what else to do.

Alex gives me a disgusted look while the midwife tidies up around us. I don't know how to explain myself to him. We're told the baby must just be having a sleepy day, but she reassures us we did the right thing by coming in. Somehow, I still leave feeling like I've wasted everyone's time.

Back in the car, Alex sits there with his seatbelt buckled but the engine off. 'Did you just need some attention or something, Darcy? Did you really have to use the baby like that?'

I recoil, looking at him in shock. 'What do you mean? I'd never lie about something like that!'

'I don't believe you. I bet you've been feeling movement all day; you'd just had enough of being by your bloody self once again.' He shakes his head at me, removing his keys from the ignition and chucking them into my lap. I stare down at them blankly.

'I'm walking home. You can take the car.' He slams the door shut behind him and storms out of the hospital car park on foot.

I sit there deserted in a soul-destroying silence, the loneliness tearing me apart. He's wrong, he has to be. I hadn't felt any movement all day, had I? I touch my tummy now and straight away a little limb jerks out at me. I rub it gently while I try to think back. I'd been miserable, sulking about my friendship with Lucy being in tatters. I'd had an argument with Alex and been forced to take a walk in the torrential rain. I'd bumped into Carmen, who was really standoffish, and then I'd caught most of the girls together at the café behind my back.

Had there been any movement at all during that time? I'm starting to doubt myself. Maybe Alex is right, maybe I did make it all up to get some attention. Whatever happened today, there's only one thing I'm certain of. I'm struggling to get a firm grasp on reality and it's really starting to scare me.

* * *

I'm surprised when Alex gets into bed beside me later that night. I'd been preparing myself for another night of him camping out downstairs. If I had any hope of him actually letting the anger go and talking to me though, it's shot down as he pulls the blankets over his head and goes straight to sleep. I squeeze my eyes shut, working hard not to say anything and make everything even worse. Eventually I fall asleep curled into my pregnancy pillow.

Another night terror shatters the peace at about three in the morning. It starts like it always does, tyres screeching and a deafening crash. This time though, I scream out loud, the noise ripping violently from my chest. Alex plays his role perfectly, holding me tightly and gently waking me up to calm me down slowly. When I stop shivering, he unfurls me from his arms and gets out of bed.

'I can't take this anymore,' he shouts, his voice breaking. He grabs his pillow and the glass of water from his nightstand and leaves the bedroom. I hear the slam of the door to the guest bedroom downstairs.

I lie awake for hours, too afraid to go back to sleep only to be greeted by another bad memory. By six o'clock the Rock Mummies group chat is awash with messages from the girls sharing photos of their babies. Cora had a morning that started with baby poo being projected across her bedroom, splattering up the walls and curtains. Rachel got peed on and Violet spent the evening in hospital with mastitis. I wonder if that explains why she wasn't out at the café with the other girls yesterday.

Instead of responding to everyone on the group chat like Carmen does, I decide to send Violet a private message.

Hey Violet, I hope you're okay and on the mend (mastitis!? Ouch!). Let me know if there's anything you need, I'm happy to help. I just wondered if you knew about the meetup at the café yesterday. I walked by and saw everyone else there — it made me feel a bit left out to be honest.
Darcy

I click send before I have a chance to reread it and back out. I see her come online and watch the two ticks turn blue. She stays online for a while, but eventually her status disappears from view.

She doesn't type a response back to me.

CHAPTER 19

No one, not even Cora, reaches out to me when my due date comes and goes. With the antenatal classes finished, I don't see them anymore either. Violet never texts me back, and if they are getting together, they never disclose that information to me or on the girls group chat, which seems to have ebbed away.

It's only when I log onto Facebook and click on Cora's profile at the top of my search bar that I see her updates. She's uploaded photos of all the babies together, mums with wine in hand at the sailing club. It would be fine if it weren't for Carmen and Lucy at either side of the group, still showing off their pregnant bellies. I've been totally excluded; it wasn't just a meetup for those who have already given birth. It's apparent that they're all upset with me, but I can't work out why. Paranoia works its way into my system, spreading through me like wildfire. Lucy must have said something to them at the café; it's the only thing I can think of, but why would she want to sabotage my friendships with them after the smallest of things? Surely she's not that petty. I log out of Facebook and delete the app from my phone before I start torturing myself by lurking over Cora's social media daily. I don't want to see updates from the girls all getting together behind my back and I certainly don't want to start obsessing over it while I'm trying to prepare for a baby.

Even though the last thing my body feels it can handle is a walk, Alex and I chuck a picnic in the car and head out for a light stroll. The midwife had told us walking would be good for my body, so even though every step I take makes me feel like this baby is going to fall straight out of me, I keep going.

We finally find a bank of sand to set up the blanket and picnic basket, which Alex does before I collapse in a heap. I wince in pain as another Braxton Hicks contraction seizes the muscles in my pelvis.

'Sorry,' I gasp, clutching at my stomach.

'Don't be sorry,' Alex says, looking at me worriedly. 'Maybe we walked too far.' He's spreading a thick layer of clotted cream onto a sliced scone, but his eyes don't leave mine.

'I'm fine. I've been getting these for days and looked it up,' I say, forcing a smile. 'They're not regular or getting worse, so I think it's just another delight from pregnancy.' My voice is laced with sarcasm.

He smears some jam onto the scone and hands it to me. 'There's a reason I wanted to come out here today, Darcy,' Alex says, lifting his sunglasses up from his eyes. He squints in the sun, busying himself by preparing another scone.

'What do you mean?' I ask, then jump in fright at a tap on my shoulder. I twist around and see Cora and Jack standing above us. They've both got stony expressions on their faces as they stare down at me. Sean is wrapped up tightly in a baby carrier, attached to Cora's body.

Alex stands and greets them both with a hug then helps me to my feet.

'I thought we could have a bit of a chat, Darcy. Let the boys go off for a bit to the brewery.' Cora nods at Jack, who leads Alex away.

I watch Alex and Jack head in the direction of the Bluntrock taproom. Alex hadn't even said goodbye to me.

Cora sits in his place and helps herself to one of the scones I'd baked earlier. I look vacantly at her, not sure what to say. Does she know I know she's upset with me? Does she know I know about the other girls all meeting up without me?

'The others should be here soon. Don't worry, Alex doesn't know what's really going on. He thinks we've arranged a bit of a celebration for you before you give birth,' she says, licking jam from her lip.

'Why? What's going on?'

'I think we all just need to clear the air, don't we?'

I still don't understand what she's implying, and I start to wonder why this feels like some sort of intervention that everyone knows about but me. Even Alex seems to have played a part in it. There I'd been naively thinking we were going to have a nice picnic on the beach.

An ageing Golden Retriever limps over to us to investigate, her fur matted and sandy. She takes a sniff at the picnic basket, her dirty paws treading over the blanket we're sitting on. Her owner runs up to us apologetically and Cora offers him a kind smile, patting the dog on the head before the owner leads her away. As I cast my eyes out to the sea, I wish Cora would offer me some of that kindness she seems to so easily give to others, but I've never seen her look so serious.

'Hi.' Rachel's voice comes up behind me.

I groan inwardly as I look in her direction. She's with Carmen, Violet and Lucy. I throw Lucy a churlish look, which she returns. Cora sighs, noticing our exchange. Everyone remains silent for a moment, the roar of the waves adding to the tension between us.

'I'm not really sure where to start,' Violet says, looking nervously at the other girls.

'How about starting with why you're all excluding me from everything you're doing?' I snap at her before I can stop myself. I wish I could take it back, knowing full well they'll wonder how I know. I can't tell them I've seen the posts on Cora's Facebook page when I'm not even connected with her on there. If they do wonder how I know though, they don't ask.

'Why would we want to hang out with you though, Darcy?' Rachel says, giving me a dirty look that makes me feel like we're back in school.

I glower at her, fighting back the emotions bubbling to the surface. I'm afraid if I speak, I'll crack.

'Oh, for God's sake. We know you've been saying things about us behind our backs,' Carmen says, folding her arms across her chest, staring me down.

'I don't know what you're talking about?' I clench my jaw, trying not to cry.

'Lucy?' Cora nods towards Lucy, who pulls out her phone. Over the sound of the waves, a recording starts to play.

'Rachel was being a bitch today. And Sean's got a face only a mother could love. Cora's being ridiculous and could do with loosening up a little in letting people hold her baby.' It's undoubtedly my voice. There's a lump in my throat as I listen to the recording in confusion. It goes on and on, small snippets of private conversations I'd had with Lucy playing back to me in one long, edited file. Tiny things I'd said in passing, that I hadn't meant in a bad way but now compiled with the rest of the clips, sound awful.

'That's not real!' I say, bewildered.

Carmen scoffs, looking at me like I'm pure filth. The blanket I'm sitting on flaps in the breeze, the chalky cliffs towering over us as confrontational as the conversation.

'Is that or is that not your voice on the recording?' Rachel demands.

'Yes, it is, but it's been completely edited and taken out of context!'

'You did say all of those things, then?' Carmen asks.

'I did, but it's not what you think.'

'That's all I need to hear.' Carmen shakes her head disappointedly and stalks away with Violet right behind her.

'Cora, please listen to me,' I beg, unable to hold back the tears anymore.

'I really want to understand this, Darcy, I do. But the things you've said have really hurt us.' She cradles Sean's tiny head, dipping him forward so she can check on him. The look on her face is enough to break my heart. *He's got a face only a mother could love.* She thinks I meant those words. She doesn't realize how twisted this all is.

'We came here today hoping you'd give us some kind of explanation and apologize. Instead, all you've done is deny everything and lie right to our faces,' she says.

'I'm not lying, Cora. I can't explain it, but I swear to you I never said those things about you or the others. I can't apologize for something I didn't do.'

She huffs, looking at me disappointedly before walking off, following Carmen's footsteps in the sand.

'And you called me the bitch? Take a good long look in the mirror, Darcy.' Rachel looks me up and down before turning to leave too. Her shadow stretches in the fading light of the sunset, traipsing along after her. The only person left standing in front of me is Lucy.

'You.' I snivel, pointing a quivering finger at her.

'Me,' she says, looking smug.

'Why would you do this to me? Those are the things you said about everyone and made me repeat! You tricked me.'

'I don't know what you're talking about. I think it's time you stop lying to everyone, including yourself.'

I flinch, so stunned I don't know what else to do or say.

'I think they'd have forgiven you, you know. If you'd just said sorry.' She shrugs, turning to walk away, then looks back to me, flicking something at my feet. 'Here, you might need this. Don't want Alex knowing about this, do we?'

I pick it from the sand, grains getting stuck beneath my bitten fingernails. It's a metalized plastic balloon with the words *We can Bearly wait* printed in gold italics across it. When

I look back up, she's already gone along with the sun that has dipped beneath the sea.

I sift through my memories, trying to recall every conversation I've had with Lucy. She is the one that started being nasty about the other girls, wasn't she? She did make me repeat those things, didn't she? How had she managed to record our conversations like that, when I thought we were so close too? I never once noticed her recording our conversations or even having her phone out while we spoke.

None of it makes any sense. I massage my temple, thinking back on the friendship we'd formed so quickly. It had been a friendship, hadn't it? I'd been so thrilled to have someone in my life like her, someone to confide in and share everything with. I'd been swept up in it all, loving that she'd chosen me out of all the girls to connect with. But now I'm starting to doubt myself and I hate it. I hate that I'm suddenly not sure if I can trust myself and what I thought was real.

I blow the balloon up while I sit pathetically on the sand by myself, not wanting Alex to know what's just happened. When he comes back from sampling craft beers with Jack at the converted container, he smiles, noticing the balloon dancing in the wind.

'Nice surprise?' He grins, the malty hum of beer clinging to his skin.

I wonder, not for the first time, if he's on a slippery slope, following in his mother's footsteps, getting closer to addiction.

If I tell Alex what's happened, I'm scared he'll make me book a doctor's appointment. He'll make me tell them I'm losing my grasp on reality, that I'm struggling to cope. They might think I'm unfit to care for my baby once I go into labour. I refuse to let that happen. This baby needs me, so even with the heartache weighing me down, I give him a tight smile and nod my head.

'I was definitely surprised,' I say.

**PART IV
JULY**

CHAPTER 20

Almost two weeks over my due date, I'm reaching the end of my tether. I wouldn't say I've hated being pregnant, far from it, but it's become too much now. My patience has worn thin. The midwife is pushing towards getting me induced if I don't go into natural labour soon, which I'm not keen on. So tonight, Alex is heading out to pick us up an Indian.

'Just get me the spiciest thing on the menu. A vindaloo or something,' I say as he's on his way out the front door. I'm taking a page from Carmen's book, not that spicy food worked for her either.

I never thought I'd be one of those girls to try all the different methods to bring on labour, but I've reached the stage of desperation. My palate is currently raw from the amount of pineapple I've eaten, my bowels empty from all the castor oil and my body aching all over from the seven-kilometre walk I did earlier in the day in the blistering July heat. This just isn't fun anymore, not in this weather.

It feels like the skin above my belly button is splitting, angry red stretch marks already climbing up from my pelvis. I've got no ankles left and currently resemble the Hulk as I shuffle around, knocking everything over with the enormity of my bump. Things I can't physically bend down to pick back up again just get left on the floor, forgotten about.

I've had two membrane sweeps, the last one earlier today, which was followed by the midwife retracting her hand from my insides and recommending Alex and I go home and get the 'love hormone' flowing by getting into the bedroom.

'What got that baby in there will get them out.' She'd smiled wickedly at us as I clambered back into my knickers in the hospital room.

I'd grimaced at her, not wanting to tell her that I could imagine nothing worse than sex right now after the level of violation I'd just endured. Plus, the idea of being intimate with Alex at all almost repulses me right now as I'm so annoyed with him. While we were at the hospital, he'd asked the midwife if he could ask a question. I was left open-mouthed.

'Can post-natal depression sometimes start before the baby is born?' he'd asked.

My stomach had dropped at his words. I felt exposed and betrayed. I wanted to yell in his face that I'm not depressed, but then part of me wondered if maybe he's right. I've been feeling so down lately, but I'd pinned the blame fully on Lucy and what she'd done to me.

The midwife had eyed me seriously before asking us what symptoms I have. I didn't even get a chance to speak before Alex started rattling them off to her.

'She's hardly been eating, barely sleeps, but when she does her night terrors are out of control. It's worse than I've ever seen them. She just seems so sad and agitated all the time, too. She's not interested in doing anything anymore either. All she does is sit at home with her face buried in a book with the cat. She's stopped seeing all her friends.'

'I've stopped seeing the girls from our antenatal class because there's been a bit of a misunderstanding!' I'd blurted out, desperately trying to defend myself.

'I know about the *misunderstanding*,' he'd said, using air quotes.

I'd stared at him for a moment, wondering how the hell he knows. I'd not said anything to him.

'Lucy told me.'

My insides had flamed in fury. *That bitch*. I'm sure she's trying to turn everyone in my life against me. The worst part is, it's working.

'Don't look at me like that, Darcy. Lucy was just trying to help. She's worried about you. Everyone is.' He'd turned his attention back to the midwife and wouldn't look back at me for the rest of the appointment. Hearing him talk about me like that, like I wasn't even there, was soul destroying. I've been mad at him since we left the appointment. The midwife'd told us I could have what they call peripartum depression and said while it's rare, I could be at risk of postpartum psychosis.

I'd hobbled painfully back to the car, mortified. A deep searing pain between my legs and a brown paper bag with a prescription for peripartum depression inside it clutched in my hand.

***

While I wait for Alex to get back with the takeaway, both of us needing some time apart, I think about everything that's been happening in my life lately. My stolen wedding dress, the people trying to break in, all of the girls getting turned against me. Could they all somehow be connected?

I'm exhausted from keeping quiet about everything when it feels like my life is completely falling apart. It's been getting into my head, making me lose my grasp on reality. My relationship is crumbling. My friendships are ruined. My dress is gone. I wonder if I should call the policewoman back and explain it all to her, tell her maybe there is a harassment case to look into here after all. It does suddenly feel like someone is out there trying to torment me at every turn, that someone being Lucy.

As plausible as it all sounds in my head, I know it would all come out wrong if I said it aloud to the policewoman. If I got the police involved to investigate Lucy, that would only damage things further with everyone in my life, anyway. Especially if she turns out to not have anything to do with any of it, but then I think of the way she recorded me and put that crazy edited clip together to turn all of the others against me. Why would she do that to me?

To try and take my mind off things, I plonk myself down in front of the television and put on an old episode of *Friends*. Coincidentally, it's the one where Rachel has a baby, and I spend the next twenty minutes in floods of tears. So much for oxytocin. My body feels like it's on fire with cortisol; I'm so anxious and fed up.

Now, not only am I more uncomfortable than I think I've ever been in my life, but for the first time in nine months my stomach is cramping like I've got the worst period pain in existence. I haven't missed this. Despite the humidity I'm curled up with a hot water bottle to try and ease the pain.

I wish I had the girls to talk to right now, but they've not spoken to me since the day at the beach with Lucy. I've never felt this isolated before. Instead of watching Jennifer Aniston in the throes of labour I stare numbly at the box of pills the midwife had given me. I already know I'm not going to take them.

By the time Alex gets home with our takeaway, the cramps have turned into toe-curling spasms so sharp they knock the breath from me.

'Do you think it's Braxton Hicks or the real thing?' Alex asks, spooning out some rice.

'This feels different.' I can hardly speak through the pain.

Everything we learnt at the antenatal classes is gone from my memory. I don't know what's supposed to happen next. I can't remember how far apart contractions are supposed to be or if this is actually a contraction or not. I can't remember what Emma told us about membrane sweeps, if they just caused severe cramps like this or if this could be the start of labour. The not knowing makes me want to cry.

'If you're in labour, we need to get the birthing pool here,' Alex says. 'We should have done this days ago!' He pulls at his hair in stress, but I'm not concentrating on anything he's saying. I'm scared and emotional; suddenly everything feels so out of my depth. I can't do this.

'We should call the labour ward. Go to hospital,' I say. We might not have time to get the birthing pool here, and now I'm not sure I want to. I just want to be around people who know what they're doing. I want to be in safe hands.

'You'll regret it, Darcy. You wanted a home waterbirth so badly. Let's just try it.' He looks at me, a mixture of nerves and excitement mottled together.

I know he's got my best interests at heart, but I hate that he isn't just doing what I'm telling him. Why did I ever say I wanted to stay home for this? It's already indescribably painful and the dread I feel inside is only building.

When another spasm ends, I look down at the plate of curry Alex dished up for me. I can't stomach it and push it away apologetically. Alex takes our uneaten food into the kitchen, leaving the strong smell of cumin behind. It makes me dry heave as I rock in agony on the sofa.

He comes back a little while later with a birthing ball he's blown up. I clamber onto it and start to bounce the way I've seen Cora do so many times before. If it helps or not, I'm not sure. I'm too panic-stricken to tell.

'You're doing great,' he says, his voice gentle and soothing, just the way Emma taught him during the classes.

I try to calm my breathing, focus on the sound of his voice. This is happening. I'm in labour. Considering this is the day I've been waiting on for so long, I'm struggling to believe it's real. I'm going to wake up any second now, I'm sure of it. I'll wake up back in my bed with my pregnancy pillow curled around me, amble into the bathroom on swollen legs and worry I'm about to break the toilet seat as I pee for the millionth time. I'll be right back to being unimaginably uncomfortable and feeling like this baby is never coming out.

My muscles contract, hurling me back into the present moment. I'm not dreaming. This is very, very real. I look out of the window, at the churning waves in the distance. Scorched leaves are being ripped from trees as they blow in the wind. It had been such a beautiful summer's day just moments ago. Where has this weather come from?

Alex is busy massaging my lower back when Lucy barges in, walking right past me juggling a bunch of equipment in her arms.

'What's she doing here?' I say through gritted teeth.

'I told her you were in labour,' Alex admits.

'Alex, the birthing pool is in the car. Can you get that for me?' Lucy orders, sifting through the items she's brought over.

'I don't want her here.' I gasp as a contraction ripples through my body, squeezing my stomach muscles tightly.

'Darcy, now isn't the time for your childishness!' Alex snaps, throwing open the front door and heading to Lucy's car.

I suddenly wish I'd told him everything, about how she'd ruined everything here for us, taking away any friendship I'd just started forming. Now it's too late and I know even if I do tell him, he won't be interested in listening, not when it's apparent that at some point within the next twenty-four hours we're going to become parents.

'Have you started timing the contractions yet?' she asks me.

I shoot daggers at her, refusing to answer. How can she just breeze in here like nothing happened between us? Why would she even want to help me, anyway?

'They're not that close together yet,' Alex huffs, staggering under the weight of the rest of the birthing equipment Lucy brought with her.

'Start timing them,' she orders, motioning to the clock hanging from the wall.

'Where's my phone? I have an app.' I look around but can't see it anywhere. They're both too busy setting up the birthing pool to take notice of my question. I'm left with my birthing ball, trying to bounce away the pressure mounting up in my body.

'Just keep bouncing. It'll help you dilate faster,' Lucy says, glancing over at me.

I have no choice but to follow her instructions, holding onto my hips as a pain shoots down my back. I want my phone, to call the midwife, but I'm too afraid to get up. Everything hurts too much.

'Alex,' I pant through another contraction, desperate for him to stop what he's doing and help me the way Emma had told him to once labour started. Why has he stopped helping me? I need him back here, sitting behind me, massaging my back again. I need him here with me, but he's over by the birthing pool with *her*.

'I've changed my mind,' I say, making both of their heads shoot up. 'I want to go to hospital.'

CHAPTER 21

'Lucy, please call my midwife,' I gasp as another crippling contraction seizes my insides.

'That one was less than five minutes apart from the last one,' Alex says, looking at the contraction timer app we'd downloaded on his phone just days ago. I grip the sides of the birthing pool, waiting for the contraction to end. It's the longest thirty seconds of my life.

'Breathe, Darcy. Like we practised. In through your nose, out through your mouth,' Lucy schools me. When my muscles have finally relaxed, I start to traverse back and forth across the living room, no longer able to keep bouncing on the birthing ball. I can't keep still; there's so much adrenaline coursing through my body.

'Maybe it's time to get into the birthing pool?' Alex suggests.

'Maybe it's time for Lucy to call the midwife,' I snap back, letting Lucy dab my face with a dampened cloth.

'I'll go,' he says, leaving the room with his phone in hand.

When he's gone, Lucy hands me a glass of water and I take a big gulp.

'Not long to go now. You're doing great,' she says.

'Why are you helping me?'

She doesn't answer me. Her head twists over her shoulder, looking for Alex.

* * *

'I'm going to go find him, see if he's been able to get through to the midwife,' she says when there's no sign of him.

As soon as she's left the room, it feels like the baby gives an almighty kick. There's a pop, and a gush from between my legs. Fluid runs down my thighs, wetting my clothing. I know instantly my waters have broken. I want to call out to Lucy and Alex to tell them, but the adrenaline is making me shake uncontrollably.

Alex is right, I need to start getting into the water, anything to help ease the pain of the contractions. I start to strip, but I stop dead at the sight of Alex and Lucy reflected in the mirror. They're in the kitchen, standing incredibly close. I can see them talking, their heads pressed closely together, but I can't hear what they're saying. Why aren't they calling the midwife? I gape as Alex's hand reaches up and touches Lucy's face. They're smiling. Lucy's big grey eyes look up at him and she smiles shyly. He smiles back.

I don't understand what's going on. I'm about to storm over to them when another contraction debilitates me completely. More fluid gushes from between my legs, leaving me feeling like something from *The Exorcist*.

I let out a roar of both pain and confusion, which reaches a crescendo as I stumble away from the mirror. I need to get into the birthing pool. I need the midwife to arrive with the gas and air. I can feel my body starting to panic. The doubt is creeping in. *I can't do this*, I repeat over and over in my head, all the positive affirmations Lucy had taught me entirely disintegrating. They re-enter the room as I'm stepping into the water.

'What did the midwife say?' That question is the one that's most important right now. My need to know she's on the way obliterates anything else going on. I can't stop the tears from falling. I'm frightened and every muscle in my body is aching in ways they have never ached before.

'She's on the way. Darcy, it's okay. Everything is going to be okay. You're strong, you can do this,' Lucy soothes, crouching down beside me.

'What the hell were you two doing in there?' I manage to rasp.

'What do you mean? We were calling the midwife.' They both look at me in confusion.

'I saw you,' I cry.

'Saw what?'

I point at Alex with a trembling hand as I submerge myself under the water. 'I saw you touching her.'

He shakes his head at me, baffled. 'Darcy, you know I would never do that to you.'

I don't tell him I don't know that, that he has in fact done that to me before and that it has been something that has thoroughly crushed my confidence. Instead, I start to doubt myself. Maybe the pain is getting to my head. I can't concentrate or focus, and soon another contraction takes hold. More fluid spurts from between my legs, and I notice Alex's wide-eyed look of horror.

'How far apart are they now, Darcy?' Lucy asks, gripping hold of my arm.

'I don't know. I'm not counting anymore.'

She sighs, then notices my clothing I'd chucked onto the floor by the pool. She holds up my white leggings and looks at me panic-stricken. 'Why are your leggings stained like this?'

'I think my waters broke.'

'Oh my God, Darcy. They're green! Alex, I think the baby's passed meconium in the womb.' She looks visibly distressed.

'Is that bad?' I ask, my heart racing.

Alex's face falls into his hands and he makes a disconcerting cry. 'I can't do this,' he says.

'You said the midwife is on her way. She'll be here soon! She can monitor the baby and make sure everything is okay, right?' I look between them, unable to read the expressions on their faces.

'Shut up, Darcy! Just let me think!' Lucy snaps and I'm so bewildered by her response that I do as she says. I stay quiet, even as yet another contraction ripples through my abdomen.

After a while, Lucy seems to have composed herself and thrusts a mirror at me. 'Take this. I need you to check to see if the baby is crowning yet. Can you feel anything if you put your hand down there?'

'Where is the midwife?' I demand, ignoring her question. Neither of them answers me. They leave the room and start a heated discussion away from me, but I can still see them in the mirror. Alex looks like he's about to pull his hair out, but instead I watch in horror as his fist connects with the wall in front of him. It makes Lucy flinch. They're arguing about something, but I can't hear it over the birthing music Alex and I had spent hours meticulously putting together.

Jack Johnson is currently singing about memories looking so pretty. I've never seen Alex look so angry or act so violently before. I know now that something is going on that they aren't telling me. I feel a primal sense of protection towards my unborn child, giving me the strength to pull myself up and out of the birthing pool. I need to go and call the midwife and make sure she's on her way.

Grabbing a towel from the sofa, I wrap it around myself and search the room for my phone, but I can't find it anywhere. I'd asked Alex specifically to keep it close to the pool so that when the time came, we could get photographs of the birth of our baby.

They haven't noticed I've left the pool yet, so I sneak up the staircase towards Alex's office where I know there's a landline. If I can't call the midwife, I have no choice but to call for an ambulance. As I drag myself up the staircase, I notice a trail of blood following me. I'm bleeding, badly. Every part of me wants to break down and cry, but I force myself forwards, lurching into the office and grabbing the phone with my quivering hands.

The emergency number has just started to ring when I hear Lucy's voice behind me. 'What the hell are you doing out of the pool?'

A woman answers the call, but I'm so terrified that I'm unable to speak. Alex appears behind Lucy and looks at me wide-eyed.

'Why is she bleeding like that?' he asks, staring down at the blood dripping down from between my legs.

'I don't know!' Lucy barks, marching towards me and pulling the telephone from its socket. The line goes dead.

'Alex?' I whisper desperately, my eyes searching his for some kind of sign as to what is going on.

'Baby, you need to get back into the pool,' he tells me, his eyes pleading with me.

'I don't understand what's going on.' I'm blubbering now, unable to hold in my emotions anymore. A contraction comes hard and fast, bringing me to my knees. Alex crawls over to me and I collapse into him involuntarily. He smells so familiar, so safe and yet so unequivocally foreign to me all of a sudden. When the contraction finally releases, giving me a moment of respite, I push away from him.

'Lucy's just trying to help us have our baby. Come on, Darcy. I need you to come with me and get back into the pool.' He holds his hand out for me to take, but I just stare at it, unsure if I can trust him. Nothing is making any sense to me. Why did she disconnect the phone line? Where is the midwife? What is happening with Lucy and Alex?

'I need something for the pain,' I beg, my body quaking in agony. Alex looks over at Lucy miserably, but she just shrugs.

'She's not following the techniques I taught her. That's her fault.'

When another contraction arrives, I feel the overwhelming need to push. The towel falls away from me, leaving me lying naked on the office floorboards as I bear down.

'Is that—' Alex doesn't get to finish his question. He turns away from me and throws up all over the floor.

'The baby's crowning,' Lucy breathes, a crazed smile spreading over her face.

I start shaking my head aggressively, trying to stop my body from doing what seems to be coming so naturally. This isn't how it's supposed to happen. I need to keep this baby in, safe.

'Please, take me down to the pool. It hurts so much,' I mewl.

Lucy looks over at Alex, who has started to collect himself. He nods slowly and makes his way over to me. I drape myself over him, the vomit foul on his skin. We make our way slowly back down the stairs, covered in my blood.

He lowers me back into the pool and I feel an excruciating sting as my perineal hits the water.

'Alex, please. Call the midwife. I need help.' I grab at his wrist.

Blood is spreading like ink into the water, clumps of dark red bobbing to the surface. I can see the fear in his eyes. He subtly nods his head, grabbing his phone from his jeans pocket. He unlocks the screen, and I watch as he pulls up the midwife's number. He's just about to press the call button when Lucy charges up behind him.

'You are not ruining this for me!' she screams, swinging something heavy down onto his skull. I hear the crack of bone as Alex crumples to the floor, blood draining onto the tiles.

'No!' I howl, months of loving him eliminating all else as I see him sprawled face down on the ground.

Every part of my body starts to tremor, rippling the water in the pool. Is he dead? Was I imagining everything I thought was going on between him and Lucy? I must have been; she wouldn't have done this to him otherwise. I hate myself for the paranoia that made me doubt him, because now I might have lost him forever.

Lucy drops the bronze lamp in her hand, which clatters noisily to the floor. She huffs, looking up at me with those large grey eyes that have never seemed more unhinged. They bulge out of their sockets so much it nauseates me.

'It's time for you to start pushing that baby out, Darcy,' she says through gritted teeth.

I shake my head no, yelping as yet another contraction works its way down my uterus. I writhe, falling onto my hands and knees in the water, arching my back. My body is doing things I can't seem to fight against; I just have to follow its lead. Jarring noises that sound like they're coming from a wounded animal escape my lips.

'I can't do it,' I cry once the pain has subsided.

'Women used to give birth without any pain relief all the time, Darcy. Our bodies were built to do this.' There's no sympathy in her tone as she looks down at me in revulsion. The way she stares at me makes the hair stand up on the back of my neck. She's looking at me like I'm half-dead roadkill, weak and meaningless. I feel like she's standing over me, trying to decide whether she should just put me out of my misery or not.

I'm suddenly all too aware of how isolated we are. The neighbours' houses are too far away for anyone to be able to hear me scream. Alex hasn't moved, his stiff body lifeless on the ground, making me wonder if he's dead.

'What do you want?' I ask her, biting my lips so hard I draw blood.

'What you took from me, Darcy.'

I don't understand what she's saying. I want to tell her I've taken nothing from her, but I can't stop looking down at Alex's body. His fingers have started to twitch. He's alive.

'Alex!' I gasp in relief.

Lucy snaps her head up; she looks over to him and starts to laugh. 'If you really think he can help you, then you're honestly more stupid than I'd realized.'

I don't understand what she's saying, but I don't care. Alex, the only person who could possibly save me right now, is trying to pick himself up. His palms slip in the thick puddle of blood around him. I want to help him, but I know that this baby is coming whether I want it to or not. I can't hold on any longer. A burning sensation blazes through me as my body stretches in ways I never imagined it could.

There's a flood of relief as the baby's body slips free from between my legs, an immense feeling of euphoria. I feel exhilarated as I pull the baby out of the water and up towards my chest. Everything going on around me fades into the distance.

'Why isn't she crying? She's blue! Darcy, give her to me,' Lucy demands.

My hold on the baby tightens, but Lucy claws at my arms, urging me to let her check the baby is okay. I don't let go, but I tilt the baby so that we can examine it. It's a girl, beautiful and perfect, with a shock of dark hair and deep blue eyes that are wide open, but she isn't moving. Dread ties my stomach into knots. Lucy picks up the umbilical cord, holding it between her fingers.

'I can feel a pulse,' she says and despite it all, her words bring me comfort. She keeps the cord in her hands, monitoring the pulse closely. Eventually I feel a gentle, tiny breath against my neck, and we watch as her skin tone starts to change. I'm so lost in the moment that I don't notice Lucy cutting the cord, severing the connection with my baby with a pair of kitchen scissors. It's only when she prises the baby out of my arms and a heart-stopping angry wail erupts from the tiny newborn that I register what is going on. She's taking my baby.

'Please, stop,' I beg, but she's bundling the baby up and placing her into the palm leaf moses basket, paying no attention to me. I can hear muffled cries from my daughter coming from beneath the blankets.

My daughter. I have a daughter, and she's being taken away from me. I look over at Alex. He's slowly coming around.

He's picked himself up from the floor and is leaning against the wall, holding his head in his hands. Words I can't decipher mumble from between his blood-soaked lips.

I feel faint, teetering on the edge of collapse, but I summon up the energy to lift myself out of the birthing pool. Ignoring the utter agony and trauma my body has just endured, I try to get to my baby girl. Lucy registers my progress, dropping the bag she's packing to the floor. Milk bottles and formula topple out, scattering all over the room.

Before I can get to my daughter, Lucy grabs me by the arm and hauls me in the other direction. My battered body slams into the oak dining table, the pain paralyzing me. Thick, dark red blood runs down my inner thigh. I wipe at it with my fingertips, only causing it to spread. I don't know if bleeding like this is normal after giving birth, but I feel off-balance.

I stagger from the table and fall to the floor beside Alex. The blood on his head is starting to coagulate. There's so much of it that I can't see how bad the wound is. He's incoherent, feverishly muttering under his breath. As Lucy steps over me, I lunge for her ankle, making her stumble forwards. She growls furiously, trying to kick free from my grasp. As we're wrestling on the ground, the heel of her boot connects with my nose, making a crackling crunch. I jerk back, screaming as I cover my face with my hands.

'I didn't want to have to do this,' Lucy says, scraping herself up from the floor. She rifles through the bag she'd dropped, pulling out a packet of cable ties. Wrenching my hands away from my face, she binds my wrists together behind my back and tightens the cable tie until it bites right into my skin. She does the same to my ankles.

I watch, restrained and motionless as she starts jamming bottles back into the backpack. Fury rages through me like a hurricane. The cable ties are so tight my bones cry in torment. She scoops my baby up into her arms and gives me one last lingering look.

'Why?' I cry, naked and broken, curled into a ball on the cold tiles. Alex is doing nothing to help me; he doesn't seem to have a clue what's going on. I'm worried he's got a serious head injury, but there's nothing I can do while I'm like this.

'Do you honestly still not know who I am?' she asks me.

I stare at her, my brain working in overdrive. I don't understand what she's asking me. She laughs, an awful cackle, pulling up her shirt. I blink in surprise as she tugs off what looks like a padded inflatable belly strapped around her. She was never pregnant. It's been a lie all along. My jaw drops open in horror.

'A long time ago you took something from me, Darcy.'

I want to tell her that she's wrong, that she's mixed me up with someone else, but I can't speak. There's too much going on to digest; my brain physically hurts. It feels like it's about to implode.

'Look at me, Darcy. I need you to recognize me,' she orders, gripping my chin in her hands. She forces me to look her in the eyes. I try to do as she says. I look at those dove-grey eyes, the coarse blonde hair, her milky skin. I search for anything that could possibly trigger some sort of memory, but I come up short.

'You really have no remorse, do you?' she says, looking repulsed.

The baby cries, making us both turn our attention to the tiny bundle squirming around in her arms.

'Lucy, please. She needs me. Give her to me. Then we can talk this whole thing through,' I beg. 'If you give her to me now, I'll let you walk away. I won't call the police. Please, just give me my baby.'

'*Your* baby?' She laughs. 'Darcy, this is my baby. It has always been my baby. You were nothing more than a surrogate. It's the least you can do after what you did to me.'

When she sees the confusion on my face, she rolls her eyes at me. 'The accident, Darcy. Remember? The car accident you caused in Australia?'

How does she know about the accident? No one knows. It's the first time someone has ever brought the accident up to me. An overwhelming dizziness wraps itself around me, strangulating me. This cannot be happening. She can't possibly know about the accident, about the day I made a decision I've regretted every single moment of my life ever since.

CHAPTER 22

I'm transported, flashing back into the alps of New South Wales. I was trapped in the middle of an Antarctic blast, barely able to see two metres in front of me. Despite the weather warnings, I'd stupidly thought I could make it back home from the ski resort I'd been working at over the winter months. My manager had told me not to leave, but I'd been desperate to be back in the comforts of my tiny rented apartment.

My car, a cheap find from some shady Facebook marketplace ad, was slipping and sliding all over the roads. The blizzard was beating down ferociously. I'd been drinking. Not a lot, not enough to be drunk, but enough to push me just over the limit. It was just sherry. Something to warm the bones. I didn't think anyone else would be out in those conditions. Who would be as crazy as me to brave a storm like this?

The radio crackled as it attempted to find a signal, a man's voice coming in and out. I kept hearing snippets of sentences, 'bitter cold,' 'polar outbreak' and 'incredibly dangerous, stay indoors'.

As aggressively as my windscreen wipers worked, they were no match for the constant flurries of snow. I tried to listen. I tried to turn my car back around and head back to the ski resort, admitting defeat. I didn't see the headlights up ahead until it was too late. Our cars collided and I remember my arms vibrating from the impact. Our tyres skidded over black ice, spinning both vehicles wildly around, hurtling us both towards a sheer alpine drop. We would have plummeted to our deaths had it not been for the pearly white snow gum tree with its warped branches.

My car hissed, piled on top of the other, now nothing more than a deformed crumple of aluminium. When I woke up, I'd looked into the rearview mirror and noticed a deep gash in my eyebrow where my head had hit the steering wheel. The airbag hadn't deployed.

Deliriously, I tried to open the car door, but it wouldn't budge. The window had shattered, glass covering my legs. I'd tried to brush as much of it off as I could before unbuckling my seatbelt. Climbing through the window, the glass had sunk into my thighs, but I'd tried to ignore the pain as it lacerated my skin. I had to check on the other driver, I had to know if they were okay. Thick, gummy sap coated my hands as I pulled myself out of the car, using one of the tree's amber-streaked branches as leverage.

She was not okay. A woman lay unconscious, crushed almost entirely by her car. I didn't know what to do. There was no possible way to get her out, but what would that have achieved anyway? She was undoubtedly dead. Horror had descended in a tidal wave over me. I'd killed her. This was my fault.

I was about to stumble away when I saw the woman's eyes flicker open. Her thick blonde hair was matted with so much blood. Bloodshot dove-grey eyes surveyed me; her pupils had been huge. I remember gasping then, rushing over to her. Her hand was freezing in my own, her delicate fingers twitching ever so slightly. I'd lied, telling her that everything was going to be okay. I told her I was going to find help, and at the time I'd meant that. But then she'd drawn in a bone-chilling breath and closed her eyes. They didn't reopen. I'd waited, but there was no rise and fall of her chest. She was gone. The snow pelted sharply down on me; it was already starting to cover the wreckage.

I realized then I had two choices, fight my way through the blizzard on foot and find help for a woman who was most certainly dead, or I could run. I'd killed her. I'd go to jail for an awful, tragic mistake. A misjudgement. It didn't seem fair. I couldn't be held responsible for manslaughter, and that's what it would be classed as surely. I had no idea how the law worked in situations like this, but I knew that this wasn't how I wanted to find out. Terrified, I'd dropped the woman's limp hand and fled the scene.

By the time the storm had subsided I'd already managed to flee the country, returning to England alone harbouring the vilest, most soul-destroying secret I knew would haunt me forever. But it was too late to hand myself in; that would only make my sentence worse. I had to keep silent about what I'd done forever. I had forced myself to never google the accident, petrified it would trace the police back to me. My mutilated legs would be the only constant reminder of what I had done.

***

'It's you,' I whisper, in shock. I look at her features and connect them with the woman I'd seen mangled in the car on the edge of the snow-covered mountains in Australia. You'd think I'd never have forgotten her face, but the truth is I'd worked so hard to forget the accident had ever happened that eventually her face had been erased from my memory. Until now.

'Yes. It's me. The woman you left to die, Darcy.' Her lip is curled up in disgust. She hoists my baby up as she walks over to me.

'How did you—' I start to say, but she interrupts me.

'How did I *find* you? You sicken me, you know that?'

I look down at the ground, shamefaced.

'Well, the police did nothing. They couldn't trace you back to your shitty little car and had given up. About a year after the accident, once my husband and I had recovered physically, we went back there. Let's say we were looking for closure.' She stands over me, watching me struggle against the cable ties.

'We stayed up at that ski resort for several days and one day I just happened to look through their wall of photographs showing their employees helping out guests on the slopes. I recognized you instantly. Told the woman behind the bar you were an old school friend but for the life of me I couldn't remember your name. She gave it to me so easily. Darcy Holloway. The woman that ripped my entire life away from me.'

'But... you survived? You and your husband were okay!' I don't know whether to laugh or cry. I hadn't even known there had been another passenger in the car, but that didn't matter now. I hadn't killed anyone.

'We did, yes, but our child didn't.'

My eyes grow wide. I hadn't noticed a child in the car. I'd been certain it had only been one person. How had I missed her husband and child? Had they been that badly crushed?

'No,' I whimper brokenly.

'Yes, Darcy. You see, I was finally pregnant when you caused that accident. We'd been trying for years to conceive. It took even longer to start fertility treatment and get the help we needed. Everything I said in my message to the Rock Mummies group was true.'

I thrash my head around violently; I don't want to hear this. I don't want to hear how much I've destroyed someone's life, even though I know it's the least I can do.

'I lost the baby, Darcy. You killed my unborn child.' Her words hit me hard and fast. I throw up, convulsing on the floor at her feet. I beg her to stop talking, but she doesn't listen to me.

'The accident caused such severe injuries that the doctors told me I'm infertile. Infertile, Darcy. My one and only dream in life, to be a mum, gone.'

I can feel the cable ties starting to loosen slightly at my wrists as I continue to work my way free. I keep twisting and pulling my wrists in every direction behind my back, undeterred by the throb from the nylon cutting into my bones.

'I could have told the police I'd found you, but what good would that have done? I needed you to experience the kind of heartbreak that you made me go through. You took the chance of being a mum away from me, so now I'm taking it away from you, too.' With that Lucy turns on her heels and leaves me writhing on the floor next to Alex's body.

She strides into the kitchen, and I hear a knife blade ring sharply as it's pulled from a metal stand. I struggle and pull as much as I can, my heart drumming quickly as I watch her walk towards me with Alex's chef's knife in hand.

'This is for everything you've done to me,' she says, plunging the knife down into my neck. The knife hits my collarbone, pain radiating throughout my entire body as I scream. She withdraws the knife, raising it high above her head before bringing it back down again. This time the knife sinks deeply into my shoulder blade. She does this again and again and each time the knife hits me, I feel a searing agony like being punched. I've only ever felt this kind of pain once before in my life, when the glass tore my legs to shreds.

I watch her bring the knife down again and although I know what's happening, it's like I'm suddenly not in my body. I'm a stranger looking at the attack from above, disassociated. *I have to survive this*, I tell myself. *I have to be okay for my daughter.* When she finally stops, she drops the knife to the floor and howls with laughter.

'You're lucky I don't slit your throat, but I'd rather you bleed out slowly.' She smiles coolly.

I look from the knife to Lucy; she's covered in my blood and in that moment, I see her as the woman from my dream who murdered Arthur's wife all those years ago. Subconsciously I guess a part of me had always known what a lunatic she is, and now it seems it's too late. The damage has been done.

I've lost count of how many times she's stabbed me. My body convulses as I throw up all over myself. My baby starts to cry, a piercing sound that pulls at every heartstring I have, but I can't help her. I can do nothing but watch helplessly as Lucy carries my baby away from me.

When I hear the sound of a car engine starting, I bellow, overcome by a hysterical strength. The cable ties snap, freeing my wrists. Breathing heavily, I drag myself over to the birthing pool where the scissors that had cut the umbilical cord lie discarded. I snip the bindings at my ankles and with every ounce of willpower my body has left in it, I lurch towards the front door. By the time I make it there, Lucy has sped away. The shriek that rips my vocal cords to shreds travels after her.

For a moment I don't know what to do. Standing stunned in the doorway, fresh blood trickles down my legs and onto the carpet. Shakily, I make my way back into the house. I need to check Alex's pockets for a phone. I need to call the police.

As I pass the kitchen where our uneaten curries solidify, I catch sight of a phone on the countertop. I hurry over to it, but it needs a passcode. I try a few dates, but nothing unlocks the screen. I growl in frustration, squeezing the phone between my hands. Suddenly, the screen lights up with a few different options. There's a bright red SOS sign next to an option for Emergency Call. I slide the SOS sign to the right and the phone starts to ring.

When the operator answers I whisper something I can't even begin to comprehend.

'My baby's been taken, please hurry.'

* * *

At the sight of us, Alex with his head wound and me with my pallid skin and stab wounds, the police arrange an ambulance. While we wait for it to arrive, they pepper us apologetically with questions. The younger of the two officers keeps pressure applied to my injuries, soaking towel after towel with blood. They're asking us for Lucy's full name, which I give them. They ask for her date of birth, but both of us look at them blankly, unable to answer.

'Do you have her address?' one of the officers asks.

I nod my head vigorously, grimacing in pain, and give them the directions to the Harolds' manor house, noticing how their eyebrows raise in surprise as I tell them where she lives.

'Isn't that the house that woman was murdered in?' I hear the younger police officer mutter to the other.

'What?' Alex reels back in shock.

I keep quiet, not letting anyone know I know about the home invasion that happened there years ago. The police don't acknowledge Alex; instead they keep pummelling the questions directly at me. I'm starting to get dizzy from them, the adrenaline surging through my body the only thing keeping me going.

They ask what car she was driving. I give them all the information I have. A pearly white Mini Cooper with a sunroof and personalized licence plate, I somehow remember. When they've gathered as much from us as they can, the older officer makes a call and gets Lucy's car details on an ANPR list.

'If her car pings a camera, we'll know where she is now she's on that list. I've arranged for an area search to start immediately and Rob's on his way to the Harold house now to check the premises,' he says, nodding to his colleague.

I want them to listen to me, to cordon off every possible exit Rock has before it's too late. I'm terrified it already is. When I try to speak to them though, my head starts spinning. My vision blurs and I grab onto the officer, about to beg for help, but before I can say anything the floor falls away from beneath my feet.

CHAPTER 23

A monotonous beeping of monitors stirs me. I wake in a bright white room. It takes a while for my eyes to adjust, to work out where I am. There's a tube in my mouth, a drip in my hand. My chest tightens as I realize I'm in hospital. My eyes dart wildly around, my mind racing. I can sense movement from the corner of my eye, but I can't seem to turn my head to look.

A nurse eventually scoots around the bed, her eyes growing huge when she sees me staring at her. 'You're awake! One moment, let me call the doctor,' she says, scampering from the room.

I move my hands to my stomach, shocked to feel the usual hard, tight bulge isn't there anymore. Instead, my skin feels loose and squishy beneath the hospital gown. *I've had my baby*, I think excitedly. Once again, I try to turn my head, to find my baby, but the movement sends a shockwave coursing through my entire body. Everything hurts.

A doctor comes in and peers down at me from behind a pair of spectacles. He's an older man, grey and balding. He has that sort of no-nonsense look about him. He starts talking to me, explaining to me what procedures I've had done, but I'm hardly listening. I'm drowsy, my memory of what's happened foggy. He's telling me something about life-saving surgery, but I can't compute it. I just want my baby. I want Alex. Where are they? Why isn't he telling me those things? He removes the tube from my mouth, making me cough and splutter.

'Where's my baby?' I croak, my throat raw.

He looks down at me in the hospital bed, and the look he gives me chills me to the bone. He opens his mouth then closes it again, shuffling from one foot to the other.

'I'll be back in just a moment,' he says.

I watch him scurry from the room just like the nurse had done. Dread rinses me of any composure I have. Is my baby dead? Why won't he tell me what's going on? I see him out in the hallway; he's talking to a policeman.

There's a clipboard at the foot of my bed the doctor must have forgotten to take away with him. I wince in pain as I shuffle down to get it. It's filled with pages of notes, most of which I can't understand. There's a list of medications that have been administered to me, the list trailing on and on. I glance over at the drip currently taped to my hand, making me feel nauseated. A few pages in there's a detailed section about what I'm here for. I read the words 'severe blood loss', 'fourth-degree perineal tear' and 'multiple stab wounds'.

Stab wounds? I drop the clipboard and start touching my body all over. Bandages cover my shoulders and neck. My fingers shakily explore them as I try to remember what happened to me, but the last thing I remember is having contractions, begging for the midwife.

The doctor comes back into the room with a policeman at his side. I know it's bad news just from looking at them.

***

They tell me it's been three days. I've been unconscious for three whole days. My baby is gone. Alex was treated with a serious head injury, but he's on the mend and has been discharged already. He can't seem to recall anything that happened either though, which is little help to me.

'We've wasted no time. I can assure you of that, Darcy,' the policeman tells me while I sob. He says his name is Robert, and it's a name I cling to. This is the man who is going to help find our baby.

He's young, probably in his mid-thirties. A face full of freckles with kind sky-blue eyes, coppery hair and ginger stubble. In any other circumstance I'd have liked him instantly, but instead filled with a mother's grief, all I can do is doubt him. How is this kind, boyish officer going to fix this? How can I depend on him? And how do you even start searching for a baby when you don't even know what they look like? We have no photograph to go on, nothing. Yet despite my lack of certainty, he is all I have, the only person who can give me answers right now.

'We had your entire house fingerprinted and found prints matching to a Claire Harold. We went to her home, but it appears she disappeared around the same time as your incident. We've made the necessary arrangements to have everyone looking for her as the prime suspect. This is her; do you recognize her at all?' He slides a photograph across to me that makes my jaw drop open.

'Her name isn't Claire. That's Lucy, Lucy Harold. She's one of the girls in our antenatal class,' I say, looking fixedly at the grainy picture of Lucy. She's hardly recognizable, her straw-like hair hacked into a strange asymmetrical bob, her grey eyes vacant. She is skin and bone, scowling at the camera. She looks far from the placid, somewhat shy girl I've come to know, but it's definitely her.

'This woman is Claire Harold. Lucy may have been the name she chose to give you. The evidence we have suggests that she's the person responsible for taking your baby,' Rob says patiently.

Lucy? I want to tell them it can't be Lucy or Claire, whatever her name is. I want to tell them that until very recently, we were friends. But I don't say anything. I don't think I can for a while.

'We searched her room, found an old phone she'd been using, pretending to be Arthur on some group chats. There were tons of recordings of your conversations with her on there, too.'

I don't know what to say or do. I don't know how to feel. The confusion is so intense I'm numb to everything and the police officer's words drift away from me while I try to make sense of this.

'I need to see Alex,' I say, desperate to have him close to me. The doctor nods, leaving the room.

'Claire's brother has been more than willing to comply with everything we've asked,' Officer Rob says. 'We will find her, Darcy. It's just a matter of time.'

'Claire's brother?' I ask, confused. Nothing is making any sense.

'Arthur Harold. She's been staying with him for a while.'

'I'm sorry, what? Arthur Harold is Lucy, sorry, Claire's husband,' I correct him, frowning.

He sighs, his blue eyes brimming with sympathy. 'Is that what she told you?'

At that moment Alex arrives and the second I see him, I get a flashback of Lucy and Alex in the kitchen, Alex's hand caressing Lucy's face. It's so vivid that I reel back.

'I'm so glad you're okay,' he says, rushing to my side.

I try to move away from him, to look at him more closely, but the pain is stifling. I thought the moment I saw Alex, I'd feel like everything was going to be okay, but I don't. In contrast, I feel worse having him around; I just can't figure out why.

'We'll get her back,' he's promising me, picking my hand up and bringing it to his lips. I rip my hand away, unsure if I should say anything to the officer.

'She's suffering from memory loss. It's common after the anaesthesia she's had,' the doctor reassures him.

Alex nods, his eyebrows knitted together as I glare at him. He carries on trying to comfort me, his familiar hand running up and down my arm just the way he knows I like it, but I don't like it now. Now, it feels like he's invading my personal space. It's making my skin crawl.

'Please stop,' I say. I need time to be able to process this new information, that Lucy is in fact Claire.

He looks wounded but retracts his hand, tucking it away between his thighs. Both the doctor and Officer Rob look away awkwardly. While I try and work out why I have this fragmented memory of Claire and Alex, Rob tells us Claire's been staying at her brother's manor for weeks now, looking after his children for him until he finds a nanny.

'Can I see him?' I ask. 'Arthur, I mean.' I can't wrap my head around the fact that Lucy, or Claire as I must learn to call her now, is not Arthur's wife. I don't think I quite believe him. How can everything she told us be a lie?

'I'll see what I can do,' Rob says, looking confident as he puffs his chest out. He reminds me of a male peacock spreading his feathers and it makes me wonder just how new he is to his role.

A nurse arrives to change the dressings on my neck and shoulders, making me wince as she peels back the wet bandages. 'You're lucky to be alive, you know,' she says softly, sponging my wounds with clean water.

'I'm lucky you're alive. I don't know what I'd do without you, Darcy,' Alex says from the corner of the room. I look over to him, blinking rapidly. I don't know if I believe him.

When he gets taken away for a check-up with another team of doctors, the room feels lighter somehow. I need time alone to sift through my hazy memory. Unattended in the hospital bed, I lie there trying to work out if I've fabricated something between Alex and Claire from some sort of horrible nightmare or if there's something concrete behind it.

I don't have long to root around for information as I make the mistake of turning on my phone. It blows up with three days' worth of frantic messages. All of the girls are in absolute shock, sending me condolences like my baby is already dead. I can't bring myself to read through all of them individually. They want to visit me, but I don't respond. I can't see them now; I can't look at them with their babies in their arms or at Carmen's pregnant belly. It would break me. Claire's face is plastered all over every available news platform, the world looking for her and a tiny, faceless newborn.

* * *

'It's you,' Arthur says when he walks into the hospital room later in the day.

'You two know each other?' Rob asks, his eyebrow cocking up in surprise.

'She's been to my house before, to one of the parties my sister threw for some of her mates. Then I saw her again at that café by the estuary when I was on a date,' he says. 'I thought she was a journalist looking for a story on me after everything that happened with Jessica. You know how reporters like to dig up stories like that.' He's squeezing the ridge of his nose, trying to process who I am and what Claire has done.

'Lucy . . . Claire told us you were her husband. She always said you were too busy with work to come to the classes.'

'What classes?'

'Our antenatal classes.'

'Antenatal classes? Claire isn't pregnant, she can't be. She can't have children,' he says, bewildered.

'Oh my God,' I whisper, suddenly remembering her ripping off some sort of fake pregnancy belly and after that, it all comes flooding back.

The world is spinning on its axis, dizzying me. More memories hurtle to the forefront of my mind, memories of the crash, of seeing Claire in the driver's seat, being sure she was dead. The birth, the stabbing, the truth.

I collapse back onto the lumpy hospital pillows, bile rising in my throat. 'I don't understand. She lied about everything,' I mumble, my brain physically aching.

'That's what Claire does. She lives in a fantasy world. I was trying to help her feel somewhat normal again when I said she could stay with me after the institute released her,' Arthur says.

'Institute?' Officer Rob and I say in unison, making me flick my gaze in Rob's direction. Shouldn't he know this information already?

Arthur exhales, running a hand through his peppery hair. 'Claire's been extremely unwell, staying at a psychiatric hospital for years. She needed a lot of help after an accident overseas, a hit and run. She and some guy she'd been seeing had basically been left to die,' he says, and my stomach churns. 'She'd been pregnant, lost the baby and to make matters worse her injuries were so extensive she found out she could never conceive again. It broke her. She only just got discharged a few months ago. She should never have left in my opinion. It's pretty apparent she wasn't ready.'

I fight against the scream clawing its way up my throat, the effort it takes making my body shudder. I caused this. It's all my fault. Claire has been suffering for years because of me. My baby is missing because of what I did. My eyes start to water, and I break out into a cold sweat.

'She's going to throw up,' I hear Alex say. I start convulsing, trying not to throw up all over everyone in the room. The doctor quickly grabs me a cardboard bowl and holds it beneath my chin. I miss the bowl, spewing all over myself and the doctor, the sour stench coating us both.

'She needs to rest. This is too much for her,' the doctor says hurriedly, checking the monitor screens nervously.

A nurse bustles into the room and starts cleaning us both up. I can't speak or look at anyone. I can hardly hear what anyone's saying around me. My eyes stare at a dent in the hospital room's wall; it's the only thing I seem to be able to focus on.

Arthur and Rob both leave, Rob promising me he'll be back soon. Alex stays a while, but he doesn't touch me or speak; we just sit there in a haunting silence until the daylight is stolen by a blanket of evening cloud. When visiting hours are over, he leaves without a word.

I feel so disconnected from him suddenly, this man I'm supposedly engaged to. I look at my left hand, but my ring is missing. The only thing that seems to be binding us together now is our daughter, a tiny defenceless newborn out there somewhere. A little girl we haven't even met yet. As soon as I'm alone in the hospital room I allow myself to cry, loud racking sobs escaping me.

***

I can't tell them the truth. I can't tell them Claire's taken my baby from me out of revenge for what I did to her all those years ago. I can't say I caused the accident she was in. They'll put me in jail, surely. I was involved in a hit and run; what sort of consequences would that have? How long would I be locked away for? And if I'm locked away, how can I help to find my daughter? I need to be able to get out of this hospital and search for her myself. I don't care how many reporters are sharing Claire's photo with the world right now, asking people to come forward if they see her anywhere. It's been three days; she could be anywhere by now.

I have to keep quiet to be able to get my baby back, but if I don't tell them everything, I know it might ruin any chance we have of getting her back at all. I always knew I wouldn't be able to run from my past forever; I just never thought it would come back to bite me like this.

I don't know how it's possible, but at some point I must have drifted off to sleep because when I next open my eyes, the sun is just starting to rise. The guilt I feel for having slept while my baby is out there somewhere is insurmountable.

I feel wet and sticky. At first I think my stab wounds have opened up and started to leak, but then I look down at my chest and see two big wet patches over my breast. My milk has come in. I hold onto my full, aching breasts and cry all over again.

CHAPTER 24

The doctors tell me I have to stay in hospital for a few more days at least. All I want is to be out there, searching for my baby, but I know my body wouldn't be able to handle it right now. I can hardly walk to the bathroom, let alone down the endless corridors.

I have to put complete faith in the police, that they're doing everything they possibly can to get her back safely. I used to believe in the phrase 'No news is good news' until now. Now, with every hour that ticks by without any progress on my baby's whereabouts, the likelihood of us ever finding her fades.

I'm at my most vulnerable, hormones and emotions at an all-time high, when Officer Rob knocks on my door during visiting hours. 'Ah, you're alone,' he says, stepping inside.

I don't tell him that Alex hasn't visited today, that I have no idea where he is. We haven't spoken since I pushed him away from me when all he was trying to do was be there for me. I try to tell myself he's grieving just as much as I am. I try to block out the insecurities and suspicions, telling myself I have no hard evidence that he's done anything wrong. With countless hours alone in this hospital bed,

I've almost managed to drill into my head that everything I thought I saw wasn't real. Every time doubt resurfaces, I remind myself Alex has done nothing but try to be there for me all along. I'd been hoping the knock at the door would be him so I could apologize to him and slowly rebuild our fractured life, but it's not.

Instead of fixing my relationship, I spend the afternoon with Rob, who fills me in on any updates in the case. There isn't much he tells me that I don't already know, but I still listen intently.

'I'm sorry, I need the loo,' I say when he's finished. I'm desperate for a moment alone. Hearing about Claire and going through the details of the birth again has left me overwhelmed and exhausted.

While he sits on the chair at the corner of my bed, I hide behind the four white walls of the bathroom. I try to pee, a task I've come to hate with the excruciating sting that swiftly follows since my tear.

On my way back to the bed, I wobble unsteadily on my feet. The stitches between my legs feel so tight that putting one foot in front of the other is almost insufferable. I buckle, grabbing hold of the wall at the same time Rob shoots up, catching me in his arms.

'I'm so sorry,' I mumble in embarrassment.

'It's okay, Darcy. You've been through so much.' There's so much kindness and warmth in his bright blue eyes it's enough to make me cry. I fall into his chest and weep.

'Ssh,' he soothes, rocking me gently until I've calmed down. A passing nurse notices us, surprise flickering across her face as she quickly averts her eyes.

Rob helps ease me back into the hospital bed before taking a step backwards, creating a yawning chasm between us. At that moment, Alex walks into the room, bristling at the sight of Rob. The space between Rob and me grows substantially.

'Hello. Sorry, wasn't expecting company,' he says, placing a hesitant kiss on the top of my head.

I don't pull away from him this time, and his relief is apparent. He takes it as his cue to be as affectionate as possible, stroking my hair and touching my legs whenever he can. Usually I'd love his attentiveness, but in front of Rob I can't help but feel like it's all for show. Yet how else should he be towards his fiancée, lying in a hospital bed with multiple stab wounds?

For the next hour Rob goes through what's going to happen when I get discharged from hospital. He tells us we need to prepare statements for the public.

'The more information out there, the better our chances are of finding Claire and your baby,' he says.

He helps us start a list of things he recommends including and by the end of it, I'm shattered. The list is extensive and from the looks of things, it's overloaded Alex, too. His eyes are swollen from lack of sleep, his shoulders sagging. Throughout Rob's visit he's kept a hand resting steadily on mine. It's somewhat territorial, possessive even.

'Right, I'll let you get some rest. I've got to get back to work anyway,' Alex says, brushing his thumb across my cheek as he says goodbye. Once again, I'm sure there's tobacco and alcohol lingering on his breath.

On his way out he looks back over his shoulder at us before walking away, leaving behind a residual awkward energy.

'I should be off myself.' Rob checks his watch, his knees cracking as he stands.

'Can I ask you something?' I ask, not ready to be left alone with nothing but my thoughts for the rest of the day.

'Anything,' he says, smiling. It's a smile that opens his entire face like a book.

I look at him, taking in every part of him. As lovely and as kind as he is, I need to know he understands what it's like to be in my shoes right now. To be so helpless and lost while the baby I came to know over nine long months through every wriggle, kick, hiccup, punch and somersault is missing. I need someone who gets it, who gets the ache and the drive of a parent with a missing child. I know that person should be Alex, and from seeing him today I know he's as distressed as I am, so I can't really blame him for taking up smoking or anything else he's doing right now to cope. Yet still I find myself pulling back from him emotionally and physically. It's as though I won't allow myself to reconnect with him until our daughter is home to complete us as a family unit. Never again will it be just Alex and me, and without our daughter with us, we can never again be whole.

I may have only held my daughter for a few minutes when she was born, but those nine months of protecting her in my womb bonded us more than anyone bar another mother and child can understand. Even if Claire has taken her, no one can ever take away me being her mother and I need someone who understands just how much I'm willing to do to get her back, someone that isn't Alex. So, while Rob is looking down at me, I grapple for a question that will tell me if he's the person I can truly rely on. Eventually, I clear my throat.

'Do you have kids, Rob?' I need something solid to grab onto to humanize him. I need to be putting my trust and faith into more than just another police officer doing his duty.

He studies me closely before giving me a subtle nod of his head. 'I do. A boy and a girl. They're only little, five and three,' he says.

'And if they were missing, you'd do anything to get them back?'

'Of course I would. Off the record, there's nothing I wouldn't do.' We stare at each other for a moment, a deep understanding forming between us.

'They stay with me on my rest days,' he says. It's information he didn't need to provide, clues dropped in about his life and who he is outside of being a police officer.

I give him a small smile filled with gratitude before he gathers his things and walks away.

'Rob,' I call after him, his name strange on my tongue.

He turns back towards me and stands in the doorway, the baton on his belt swaying slightly.

'Please help me get my daughter back.'

A look passes between us, assuring me that he knows what I mean without needing to say more. *Do everything you can.* He bows his head, his eyes never leaving mine.

'I promise you I'll do everything in my power to get her back for you, like if she were mine.' It's as though he's read my mind. Everything shifts knowing I can count on him as a father himself to do what he can to find my baby. I watch him walk away down the long stretch of the corridor.

I find myself wishing he didn't have to leave me here but at the same time knowing he can't find her if he's here with me.

'She doesn't even have a name,' I rasp after him, but he's already gone.

***

Being someone who has wanted a baby my whole life, I'd have thought a name would come easily to me. I used to have lists on my phone with loads of names, especially for girls. I always felt like it was so much easier to name a girl; there seemed to be more options out there. You could be quirkier. I remember loving the names Blue, Phoenix, Dahlia and Story, but every time I'd share them with someone, they batted them down. Then Gwyneth Paltrow went and named her baby 'Apple', and I didn't feel so weird anymore.

I'm sure if I scrolled down the notes saved on my phone, I'd find a list of names tucked away somewhere, but I can't bring myself to do it. Seeing a list of names now, when my daughter is missing, would be the start of a downward spiral for me. I'm not strong enough to handle it.

I always said to Alex we'd name our baby after meeting them, making sure we pick a name that really suits them rather than one we'd decided on before getting some sort of sense of who they are.

As I'm lying in the hospital bed by myself, I let my thoughts roam. What is my daughter like? Does she cry a lot? Does she have a good appetite? Is she inquisitive? My heart breaks knowing I'll never get this precious time with her back. Will she even want to be held by me when we're eventually reunited, if we ever are? Will she instinctively know who I am through some sort of special bond, or will she think I'm a stranger and cry until I put her down? It's been days, so I couldn't even blame her for not wanting me.

It horrifies me that I wouldn't be able to pick her out in a room full of babies myself. In the little time I'd had with her, I didn't get to look at her properly, and what little I did see of her is already shamefully fading from my memory.

For the past nine months, one of the things I'd daydream about the most is what our baby would look like, and now I'm wondering if I'll ever know.

How can I give a name to a baby I don't even know? No name will feel right until I have her back in my arms.

CHAPTER 25

After a week, I'm discharged from the hospital, although walking is a slow process that requires a lot of help. I have no choice but to lean on Alex for support. Each time I see him the stench of tobacco and whiskey on his skin gets stronger.

When we arrive home, the house I'd come to love feels eerily empty and sinister. Alex has made every effort to clean the place up. The birthing pool is gone, the bloodied tiles have all been scrubbed clean. As I limp from room to room, I notice it would be like nothing had ever happened here at all if it weren't for the echo of horrifying memories.

I stand brokenly where the birthing pool once stood. A week ago, my baby was right here, in this room. It doesn't feel real. I reach out into thin air, as though trying to grab hold of the only memory I have of holding her.

* * *

The guest room is set up, so I don't have to climb the staircase. It's a room I've never used before, making it feel cold and alien.

'Can I get you anything?' Alex asks, sitting down on the edge of the bed with me.

I shake my head, biting my lip, trying to suppress the tears threatening to spill. I want to ask him why we're here, why aren't we out there now, looking for her? But what good will it do? For days the police have been getting calls from people claiming to have seen Claire at various locations, some as far as five hours away in Milton Keynes. Every mother now out alone with a newborn gets reported and the worst part is not one of those calls can be ignored because what if they ignore that one reported sighting that is actually Claire?

Rob has been pulled in every direction, but if he's fed up with it, he hasn't let it show. Every time I see him, he treats me exactly the same, with a deep understanding and tenderness. It isn't a friendship between us exactly; it's more professional than that, but then again it doesn't feel professional at all. Thinking of Rob now while sitting on the bed with Alex feels wrong, indecent, even though none of the thoughts are bad. It makes me wonder if that's how it felt for Alex with Claire. Then I remember the bizarre image I have in my head of Alex touching her. It's so lucid and detailed that it has to be real. It isn't like a dream that eventually falls away from you in its entirety.

'Alex, why do I keep feeling like something went on between you and Lucy? Sorry, not Lucy. Claire.' I have to ask. I feel like if I don't, I'm going to go mad.

'Darcy, please. Not this again. Not now.'

'But I remember it, Alex. I saw you touching her face in the kitchen. I know I did!' I cry, ashamed that I'm accusing him of this with everything else we're going through. What if I'm wrong? Could he ever forgive me for doubting him during a time when we need each other the most? I know I've been awful to him, keeping him at arm's length. As much as I keep telling myself I'm going to let go of these insecurities and trust him, I'm powerless against the paranoia eating me alive.

He looks at me in disappointment, breathing out steadily as he gets to his feet and leaves me alone.

***

I feel like I'm living in some sort of parallel universe when we're called down to the police station and asked to make the press appeal. I feel imprisoned by the hoard of camera crew around us, lenses forced right into our faces. There's no escape. The flashing lights and people shouting questions at us is unbearable. We can't provide a description of our daughter or attempt to humanize her in any way when we have no information to provide the public with. So instead, we focus on a plea for her safe return. Alex urges anyone with any information to come forward even though the police have already done that themselves.

I can hardly speak. If I do, I'm afraid I'll speak directly to Claire through the cameras and scream at her. Yet what right do I have to accuse her when I ripped her child away from her? I stare at the cameras, trying to hold myself together while I listen to Alex provide all of the relevant information we have. That's when I realize, I know what I need to do. I need to tell the world everything. All of the awful secrets I've kept squirrelled away for so many years need to come out. I have to communicate directly with Claire, no matter how much it scares me. I can't see any other way of doing that than through the media. I take a deep breath, readying myself for the impact this is going to have.

'I have something I need to say,' I whisper, interrupting Alex.

He, and what feels like the rest of the world, look at me expectantly. I'm incredibly aware this is going to be broadcast live and that once I've said what I need to say, there's no taking it back.

'Claire Harold has taken my daughter from us out of revenge. I know this because many years ago, I caused an accident she was involved in. She'd been pregnant and she lost the baby.' I swallow hard, trying to work out how to say everything I need to say. For the first time since we arrived, there's nothing but silence around us.

'I—I thought she was dead. I panicked.' I start to cry.

Alex has turned to face me now, his expression the picture of shock and horror.

'I ran away. I left her there in the car and I ran away. I didn't know what to do. I didn't know she was still alive.' I look up at the news crew, remorse written all over my face.

'I just want to tell Claire, if she's out there somewhere listening to this, that I'm sorry. I'm so, so sorry for everything I caused. I've regretted it every single day of my life ever since and I know there's nothing I can do or say to make you forgive me. But for what it's worth, I'm sorry. I'm asking you now, mother to mother, to please bring our baby back home. I will pay for everything I've done; I'll go to jail if I have to. I just need to know our baby is okay, please.' I stare right into the cameras as I speak, hoping Claire is out there, watching me.

Chaos erupts around us, every reporter from every different news company thrusting a microphone in my face, shouting questions at me. Rob steps in, herding Alex and me away from everyone and back into the austerity of the police station.

Alex looks dumbfounded, gaping silently after me as I'm ushered into a private room with two officers. They ask me if I want a lawyer, but I realize I don't want one. I've never had a need for one. My chances of being able to afford one would be very slim without Alex's help, anyway.

I'm about to tell them to proceed without a lawyer present when there's a knock at the door. 'There's an Arthur Harold here for Darcy Holloway. He's said he will be acting as her solicitor,' a uniformed officer tells us.

'I can't afford him,' I say instantly.

'We'll sort it out later.' Arthur nods in my direction, entering the room in a striped herringbone suit.

At first, I'm unsure whether I can trust him or not. He's Claire's brother, but I realize very quickly that he is all I have, and I have no idea what I'm doing without him.

'Why are you doing this for me?' I ask him flatly.

'What you did to my sister is inexcusable and there will be consequences; that much is inevitable. However, you're a mother and your baby's missing. Without me, the media and the justice system will eat you alive. I can't just sit idly by and let that happen, especially when the person who clearly has your daughter is my sister, who frankly should never have left the psychiatric care she was under.'

We speak for what feels like hours, me sharing every intricate detail I can recall from the accident all those years ago. He helps me to prepare a statement that we share with the police. The next day, a police press conference is held, and they share the story, my story, the one I'd kept hidden for so long, with the world.

Upon Arthur's recommendation, I stay far away from televisions and phones, terrified to know what everyone is saying about me. Perhaps they all think I got what I deserved, this awful woman from a hit and run accident who could have killed people. Who did kill someone. A baby. Unborn, but still, a life, nonetheless. A life that was taken by her own hands. Even though the accident hadn't killed Claire or the guy she was with, it had caused her to lose her child. She'd been in her first trimester, so the baby had still been classed as an embryo. Arthur told me this like it was supposed to provide me with some level of comfort, but I assured him it didn't. Nothing could ever take that guilt away from me.

While we wait for an outcome on what's going to happen to me, the search for Claire has intensified. All of Rock seem to be involved, covering all of the walking trails and coves. Every hotel in the area is searched, every campground, bed and breakfast, guesthouse and hostel turned upside down in the hunt for Claire. She's disappeared without a trace. I try to remain optimistic, try to tell myself it's only a matter of time until she slips up and gets caught, but as each day passes my positivity wanes and Alex has been so detached that's he's been offering little in the way of comfort. I keep reminding myself that everyone grieves differently, and I'm trying my best not to push him when he must be just as fragile as I am right now. Yet, my heart hurts. I've lost my fiancé. He's here, but he's not. His eyes are clouded with the judgement I'd always feared, and it makes me physically ache in the deepest parts of me. Things have been different since I'd told the world what I'd done; he's barely looked at me since. He thinks differently of me now, just like I always knew he would.

I'm profoundly aware that I have a daughter out there somewhere, a tiny little girl I don't know and who I wouldn't know if I passed her in the streets. As a mother I'm devastated, consumed with despair.

Each night I fall asleep, I hate myself for it, wondering how I could possibly rest at a time like this. I can't forgive myself for needing to reset and close my eyes when I should be doing something, anything to help, but there's nothing I can do. Not really. I said everything I possibly could say when I spoke to Claire through the media, but it's been days, and she hasn't reached out or come forward.

I just want to know my baby is alive. Surely I'd feel it if she wasn't, but then again, I feel nothing but a ginormous, hopeless void. My body knows it's supposed to be a mother right now, it knows the grief of that motherhood having been ripped away from me, and it knows it's yearning for a baby. But I feel like my body is starting to lose hope along with me. My milk has already started to dry up, my breasts rock hard and tender. The purple and red stretchmarks across my stomach, sides and inner thighs are the only trace left that I'd ever been pregnant.

* * *

It's a Tuesday afternoon when a bouquet of flowers arrives. Muted hues of cream freesias, peach snapdragons and pale-yellow chrysanthemums wrapped in a hessian sack are placed into my hands by a delivery man whose eyes widen at the sight of me. Clearly my face is still all over the news. I guess I would shock the public now that I'm not being held by the police. Does anything ever prepare you for coming face-to-face with someone whose story has taken the world by storm? I pick the card from between the stems and read slowly.

Darcy, we're all so sorry for everything that's going on. We're sorry about what happened between us, too. We understand now that Lucy was trying to sabotage you.

We wanted to let you know that we are here for you, we are your friends, and nothing will ever change that now. Whenever you're ready, you have us to support you.

Cora, Rachel, Carmen and Violet

I well up in appreciation, not having realized how worried I was that the world now viewed me as some monster from a hit and run. I'd stopped opening the messages on my phone, denial feeling like the better option than having to confront everything going on, so I had no idea how they all felt about me until now. It's a new, strange sensation to feel like I have four women out there who genuinely care about me.

I breathe the flowers in, the sweet berry scent from the freesias tingling my nose. The slightest of smiles creeps up on me. It's a sad smile, the first emotion I've shown other than crying all week. I walk into the kitchen and put the bouquet into a vase, these flowers symbolizing the first true friendships I have had in many, many years.

Traipsing up the staircase, I go into the bedroom to retrieve my phone and send the girls a quick message to say thank you. I tell them I'm still not ready to see anyone. The idea of someone putting their arms around me right now and hugging me is enough to make me want to lose hold of any kind of strength I have left in me.

Cora messages me back almost instantly.

Like we said, whenever you're ready we will be there for you.

It's the first time in my life I think I actually believe those words being said to me.

On the way back downstairs, I hear Alex attacking the keyboard with his fingertips. The sound is violent and loud. I nudge the door to the office open gently and slide into the room, wanting to tell him about the flowers. When he notices me, he slams the laptop screen down, staring at me with bloodshot eyes.

'What're you doing?' I ask, suspicion leaking through my every pore, even now.

'Nothing. You don't want to see it.'

'See what?' I demand, stepping towards him.

He shoots out of the chair and scoops the laptop up under his arm. 'I was reading the news, Darcy. It isn't good, the things they're saying about you. I don't want you to see it.'

'Oh.' I sigh, my lip trembling. So, people do hate me.

'I'm going out for a bit to get some air. You stay here and rest up, okay?' he tells me, squeezing past me without so much as a kiss on the cheek.

I stand in the office alone, abandoned and shattered. I hear the scrape of his keys as he picks them up out of the bowl by the front door and listen as he starts the engine and drives away.

* * *

By ten o'clock Alex still isn't home. It's finally starting to turn dark, the stars dotting the sky. The house feels even quieter than usual, leaving me with a sense of unease. I brush my teeth and get ready for bed, but when I pull my pyjama set out of our wardrobe, I notice something strange. There's a big gap on the top shelf where Alex usually keeps his travel bag.

My heart drops. I rip open his drawers and find them mostly emptied, his boxers, socks and t-shirts all gone. The jeans he usually keeps hanging from the rail have disappeared too.

Alex is gone.

CHAPTER 26

I call the police, quoting Rob's force identification number, and wait to be connected. He sounds tired when he answers the phone, but as soon as I tell him Alex and all of his belongings have vanished, he tells me he'll be right over.

***

'Almost everything's gone. His clothes, his passport, even his toothbrush,' I say, letting Rob into the house. He's in his police uniform, the radio at his belt crackling loudly as an announcement we both ignore comes through. He looks down at my floral kimono robe I wrapped half-heartedly around myself, and we both turn crimson.

'He didn't tell you he was going somewhere overnight before he left?' he asks me, stepping inside. The leather of his thick, sturdy boots squeaks against the tiled floor.

'No. If he had, I wouldn't have called you. Obviously,' I say.

My bluntness makes him redden even more. In another world I'd apologize, but I'm so drained that I can't. I just need him to stop asking stupid questions and help me. He promised me a week ago he'd find my daughter and so far, there's been little if any progress. I still feel bad though. He's the sort of man you could never really say a bad word about. From the little time I've spent with him, he's been consistently warm, radiating compassion.

'I've tried calling him. His phone goes straight to voicemail. I've tried his mum, Debbie, too. She told me he isn't there right now, but he might be on his way. She said maybe that's why his phone's off, no signal or something.'

'What's Debbie's details? We'll need to do a check.'

I rush to get my phone and give him all the information I have. While Rob makes some calls to get local officers to search Debbie's house, I boil the kettle, surprising myself with how normal mundane tasks like this feel when there's so much happening in my life that isn't normal.

'I hate to have to ask you this, Darcy, but was everything okay between you and Alex?' Rob asks me when I come back into the room carrying a tray with our drinks on it. He takes a sip of tea, leaning back in the chair, and waits for me to respond.

'I don't really know how to answer that.'

He looks at me questioningly.

'I mean, I thought we were, but I get a bit paranoid,' I admit, wincing at my choice of words.

'Paranoid?' he repeats, his interest piqued.

I close my eyes, wishing I hadn't said anything. He's going to think I'm a crazy woman with insecurity issues. I decide to tell him the truth. He already knows the worst part of me anyway. His opinion of me can't possibly get any worse.

'Alex cheated on me back in London. I tried to get over it, but the whole thing caused some self-confidence problems, I guess.'

'I'm sorry to hear that,' Rob says, his kind eyes never leaving mine.

'It's fine. He never did anything again as far as I know, but after we met Lucy — Claire, I mean — I started feeling really threatened by her.' I look down, embarrassed. Despite everything, I don't want Rob to see me as weak.

I notice my robe has ridden up my legs, the silky satin bunching up at my thighs, only just hiding my scars. Rob notices, his eyes lingering on my legs a moment too long. I pull at the material, feeling exposed. I'm suddenly severely aware of how attractive he is. In the last week his ginger stubble has thickened into the start of a beard that tickles at his plump lips. For the first time I find myself noticing his forearms, muscular and covered in tattoos. I berate myself for being so selfish. How can I be thinking about him this way at a time like this, when my daughter is missing with a lunatic and my fiancé has vanished?

'Was there something in particular that caused you to feel that way?' he asks and for a moment I forget that he's asking me about feeling threatened by Lucy.

A blush warms my cheeks. 'She'd flirt with him. She'd flirt with all the guys in our antenatal class, but especially Alex,' I say once I've managed to compose myself.

'And did Alex ever flirt back?'

'No. Yes. I don't know.'

Rob gives me a puzzled look.

'I didn't think he did. I always thought he was just being friendly. But when I was in labour, I have this really vivid memory of him touching her cheek. It seemed really intimate. I asked him about it, but he denied the whole thing. So I honestly don't know if I've just made that up in my head or maybe I dreamt it.'

The radio hisses and cracks again, a voice coming through and filling the silence. Rob turns the volume up, and I catch hold of the words 'Possible sighting of Claire Harold near the Rock Sailing and Waterski Club.'

Rob and I both look up at each other in surprise. I'm so exhilarated that when he helps me to my feet, I fling my arms around his neck. It's only a fleeting moment, but I inhale his spicy cologne and feel a magnetic pull towards him. His body armour presses hard against my body. We're both smiling, his hands holding onto my hips, when I lean forward and press my lips against his. For just a moment I feel his mouth opening, inviting me in, but then he pushes away from me gently.

'Darcy.' He shakes his head, removing his hands from my body and stepping further back.

'I'm so sorry,' I say, horrified.

'It's okay. We need to go. You can drive with me.' He pulls his car keys from his pocket and strides away from me. If I had more time, I'd be stewing over what just happened, picking myself apart over it, but instead I pull out my phone and call Arthur while I follow behind Rob.

Arthur answers on the second ring, telling me he'll meet us at the club and hangs up the phone. In the car Rob and I remain silent, the tension building as we near the club. I wonder briefly if this kind of thing happens to police officers often, women forming emotional attachments to them after spending so much time around them during a time of crisis, or if it's just me. Am I just that desperate that I fling myself at the first man to offer me support?

I'm ashamed, wondering what Alex would make of it. While I've been so untrusting towards him for simply talking to Claire, I've just gone and done something far worse. I've kissed another man while Alex is out there somewhere, needing space from me perhaps but undoubtedly looking for our missing baby. How could I have done that to him? I loathe myself, thinking about how broken he'd been when his ex-wife had cheated on him.

I'm a bad person, I realize in a painful moment of self-awareness. I left Claire to die after I'd crashed into her, and now I've cheated on my fiancé. I suddenly hope after all of this is over that they put me away. I deserve to rot in jail for everything I've done.

We keep the sirens off as we drive, not wanting to startle Claire if it is her at the club. It's an intolerable few minutes that seem to last a lifetime, every second that passes potentially inching me closer to my daughter.

When we step out into the humid, salty night air that smells of burnt wood, my nerves quickly turn to hysteria. My baby might be here, somewhere beneath the ominous grey clouds. Another police officer approaches us and speaks quietly to Rob, but I don't listen. I'm too busy scanning the area. It's chillingly quiet. The cacophony of the day has vaporized, leaving nothing more than the sound of the water lapping up against the old brick building and boats anchored offshore. I'm about to start searching when two figures step out of the shadows. Cora and Jack head towards us. Their usually smiling faces are serious.

'Cora!' I cry, running up to her. I fall into her pillowy soft body, noticing for the first time how comforting she really is and how much I used to take that for granted.

'Hey. Carmen's here somewhere. The others are on their way,' she tells me while Jack speaks with the policemen.

'What's happening? Why are you here?' I ask her.

'Jack and I were here for the sailing club's barbecue night. His mother's visiting, so she's with Sean.'

I nod my head, waiting for her to continue.

'Carmen was here too with Grayson. After dinner we thought we'd stay out a bit longer to have a bit of time to ourselves. Carmen swears she saw Lucy down by the water,' she says.

'Claire,' I correct her.

'I saw her too, clear as day. It was definitely her,' Jack says confidently.

Another car pulls into the car park, a white Tesla I recognize instantly. Violet and Rachel step out and hurry over to us. Each of them wraps me in a hug I don't want to be let go from.

'Ladies, I need you all to remain quiet. We can't risk her getting spooked and fleeing if it is her,' Rob tells us. Everyone falls silent.

Carmen points the officers in the direction she thinks she saw Claire while more police vehicles pull up soundlessly around us, their headlights switched off.

Suddenly a gut-wrenching cry rings through the night, chilling me to my core. At first, I'm sure it's a bark from a fox it sounds so savage, but then the distinctive mewl of a baby echoes across the water. I instantly know it's my daughter. There's something primal and instinctive pulling me towards the noise. I start to run, refusing to be controlled by Rob or anybody else as I race down to the water's edge.

I study the water closely until I see a ripple coming from a resting sailing boat just visible in the inky darkness of the night. I can just make out the figure of a woman cradling a bundle in her arms as she steps onto the weathered vessel.

I'm about to barrel towards them when something stops me dead in my tracks. The silhouette of a man illuminated in the moonlight, taking stilt-like strides across the gentle waves rolling onto the shore. It's a gait I've come to know so well. I'm immediately overcome with emotion. I don't know how he knew to find Claire here with our baby, but he did it. He found them. Alex is trying to save our daughter.

'Alex!' I shout before I can stop myself, unsettling the stillness of the night. I see both Alex and Claire startle.

Racing over to them, my bare feet sink into the cold sand as the delicate fabric of my robe billows in the breeze. At first, I'm sure Alex is trying to coax her from the barnacle-ridden boat, a neglected craft with splintered wood and flaking paint. But then I hear the rumble of an engine and see him chucking a bag on board, grappling frantically with a line.

A sharp glint of the anchor catches the moonlight as it's released from the seabed and the old, tattered sails are hoisted up in a flurry of movement. As the engine of the boat is killed, I hear heavy footsteps battering the sand behind me. Sirens blare and glaringly bright lights flood the perimeter of the beach.

I hear the sound of my baby crying once again, drifting off into the distance with the sailing boat that is well underway.

I don't stop running towards them. My feet carry me into the depths of the shockingly, bitterly cold water. I wouldn't stop if it weren't for Rob, who has waded in after me. His strong arms wrap around me, preventing me from completely submerging myself into the depths of the sea.

'Alex,' I say again, mystified. I don't understand what's happening. Why is Alex leaving with her? Why is he taking my baby away from me? She was so close to me, just metres apart. How had I let her slip through my fingers once again? I feel the loss like a vital organ having been taken away from me, leaving my heart spasming in my chest. This cannot be real. I'm dreaming again, a horrible nightmare I need to wake up from.

'We'll get them, Darcy. Come back to shore,' Rob whispers into my ear. I let him pull me numbly out of the water, a rumble of thunder reverberating around us. No storm had been on the forecast, but it seems like one is rolling in very quickly.

Carmen comes up behind me and wraps a stiff towel around my shoulders. I'm vaguely aware of the abundance of police swarming the area, but the only thing I keep repeating is Alex's name again and again. I can't make any sense of what's going on.

Arthur's Lexus purrs into the car park and he steps out with his two children in tow.

'Didn't have time to find a sitter,' he tells me. It's the first time I've seen him out of a suit. In his grey tracksuit bottoms and a baggy hoodie with his usual sleek hair standing up at all angles, he looks so different from the uptight businessman I've become so used to.

'Where's Lucy, Daddy?' the little girl says, looking at us with sleepy eyes, her hand firmly clasped in his.

'I don't know how many times I need to tell you this, Olivia. Her name's Claire,' he says sternly, making her eyelashes flutter with emotion.

'But she told us we had to call her Lucy. She made us write her new name over and over again in our notepads until we remembered it. She said if we didn't call her Lucy, you'd be really upset with us.' Olivia's eyes are huge with fear, tugging at my heartstrings.

'She's there,' the little boy says, his finger pointing out towards the sailing boat colliding with waves sweeping over them. For a terrifying moment I think they're going to capsize, but Alex somehow manages to right the boat. I never knew he could sail. They're gaining speed now, heading off into the distance.

'She won't get very far. Those waves are too big and there's a strong current, see?' the boy says softly, sounding much older and wiser than his years.

'Little sailor, my Finn. He's been doing it since he was five,' Arthur explains, his son nuzzling shyly into him.

'The Marine Policing Unit have already prepared their watercrafts. They aren't going to get far at all,' Rob reassures me. He shrugs off his police jacket and drapes it over my shoulders in place of my drenched robe. I gaze at him gratefully.

'Is Aunty Claire in trouble again, Daddy?' Olivia asks.

'Yes, pet. She is. She's been very bad.'

I find myself wishing I could take away all of the trauma Olivia and Finn have gone through. They've experienced too much for such a tender age. They shouldn't need to be watching this unfold. As if reading my thoughts, a policewoman appears between us and asks Arthur if she can help with the children. He nods appreciatively, watching as she shuffles his children off, into the warmth of the sailing club.

'You're finally going to meet your baby girl, Darcy,' Cora says. As scared as I am to put trust into her words, my anticipation mounts. She puts an arm over my shoulder, making me grimace, my body still hurting as it heals from the stabbing.

The only thing I still can't figure out is what Alex is doing. I don't know if he's trying to help me in some warped way. Maybe he's just trying to keep our baby safe. He is her father after all, but then why would he be sailing the boat further and further away from us? Do they even have life jackets on? It's impossible to tell. Whatever Alex is doing, my fury is rising like the storm around us.

Rachel removes the cap from a flask of hot tea, offering it to me. My hands tremble as I bring the flask to my lips, my body slowly warming with each sugary sip I take. A tawny owl swoops down low, hunting food. A deep macabre hoot adding to the eerie atmosphere of the night.

With all the girls huddled around me, we watch in awe as the launched police boats inundate the water. The searchlight from a hovering helicopter blinds us, its blades cutting through the air as it methodically circles the area. Fighting with the swell of the waves, the police trail after Claire and Alex. As each wave attacks the deck of the sailing boat, I fear for the safety of my baby, finding myself praying that Claire holds onto her tightly before I lose her forever.

The boat is being flung around relentlessly, a policeman demanding them to stop through a megaphone barely audible above the scream of the wind. My baby's cry has all but vanished into the darkness.

I can't take it anymore; I need to do something. I twist to find Rob standing close by. He's watching the boat intensely. It's as though he feels my eyes on him when his gaze flickers in my direction. His mouth is set into a grim thin line.

Do something, I beg silently. He looks back out to the water for a few moments before breaking into a run. My stomach turns at an ear-splitting crash. I whip around just in time to see the sailing boat veer dangerously on its side. Rob is already ripping off his uniform, revealing more tattoos snaking their way across his broad shoulder blades. He dives into the water, immediately lost in the unrelenting waves.

Cora grabs my hand, holding on tightly. As much as I want to make sure Rob is okay, I can't take my eyes off the boat carrying my daughter on board. The fight against the rough sea is a losing battle.

'Oh my God,' I shriek as the boat is engulfed by yet another wave.

CHAPTER 27

Rain lashes down, beating our faces with the strong winds and spray of the ocean. It's impossible to see what's going on through the dense fog shrouding the shoreline.

'There's Rob, there!' Rachel cries over the howling wind, pointing out towards the water. I see him then, making huge powerful strokes towards what's left of the boat. The water is weighing it down, swallowing it beneath the surface, and besides Rob I can't see any signs of life amongst the debris.

I fall to the sand, overcome with grief. I don't know how much time passes; nothing seems to matter to me anymore.

'Darcy, look!' Carmen, who at some point must have knelt down beside me, says. I follow her finger back out to the water and there stepping out of the sea is Rob. He's holding something tiny in his arms. My breath catches in my throat. Paramedics are rushing over to him. I stagger to my feet, lurching towards him, powered by some invisible force. With the help of Carmen, Rachel, Violet and Cora, I battle through the wind, making my way to my baby.

Every cell in my body wants to rip her away from everyone and hold her close, but I know I need to let the paramedics do their jobs. They assess her, checking her breathing and pulse. I almost scream when they immediately start performing CPR.

'Don't look, Darcy.' Rob, still dripping wet, stands in front of me. I sag into him, burying my face deep into his freezing cold chest.

'Is she alive?' My words come out trembling. He doesn't respond.

Out of the corner of my eye I catch a glimpse of a group of police officers approaching one of their watercrafts. I see two figures, unmistakably Claire and Alex, being removed and handcuffed. Why are they handcuffing him? I want to tell them to stop, that he's my fiancé, my baby's father.

'What are they doing to Alex? Tell them they've got it all wrong, Rob. He was trying to help!' I look up at him, his blue eyes glistening in the darkness.

He shakes his head at me slowly. 'I'll fill you in later,' he says, pulling me back into his chest. I watch, bewildered, as Alex and Claire are put in the back of a police car.

I can't wait, needing answers now. I push away from Rob and start marching to the police car. Rob chases behind me and grabs at my arm.

'Don't stop me right now,' I growl at him, outrage pouring out of me. I'm all power and determination, a mother seeking vengeance. I've never felt anything quite like it. Our eyes lock, an intense understanding shared between two people with children to care for. He drops my arm and lets me go.

I want to scream at them for taking my little girl on that boat, to make them see what they've done to her. They're soaking wet, sitting glumly in the backseat with their arms behind their backs when I get to them.

Claire sneers at me as I get closer. Alex refuses to meet my gaze.

'What the hell is going on?' I spit, baring my teeth at both of them like a lioness on a warpath.

'Do you want to tell her, darling, or should I?' Claire rolls her head onto Alex's shoulder, smiling at me disparagingly.

'Darling?' I repeat, looking to Alex for any kind of explanation.

'Oh Darcy, you simple-minded little idiot,' Claire says, chuckling. It's a goading noise, and my knee-jerk reaction would be to hit her if we were alone. Instead, I stand over them, disconcerted.

'Alex?' I urge, desperate for him to say something, but he keeps his head hanging low.

'Alex has never been yours, Darcy. Not once in all these months. In fact, you can take that ridiculous ring off your finger now. It's a fake, anyway.'

My eyes drop to the ring on my left hand, sparkling dubiously. I'd always known it was a cheap ring; that much was obvious. I'd always wondered why he'd never bought me something a bit nicer, more extravagant, when I knew he could afford it. I'd always put it down to him having been married before and not wanting to spend a crazy amount of money on a ring again. I always told myself he showed me love in other ways, so the ring never really mattered. Now, I twizzle the band around my finger hesitantly, unsure what to do.

'Oh, for God's sake, he's mine, Darcy. He's been mine all along. It was him with me in the passenger seat of the car in Australia. It was him you left to die with me out there.'

I start to shake uncontrollably. I never saw the man she'd been with in the accident. I hadn't even known there'd been another passenger in the car until recently.

'You're lying,' I say, not taking my eyes from Alex. He isn't denying it. He isn't doing anything.

'You didn't just take my chance of being a mother away from me that day. You took Alex's chance away of being a father. So, we planned this entire thing.' She's laughing now, a feverish giggle growing louder and louder. Her unhinged smile shows just how much she's relishing this moment.

I shake my head violently, refusing to believe it.

'Alex never loved you, Darcy. He got you pregnant for me. You carried that baby for us. That baby is his flesh and blood, his! She is everything that you took away from us. You owe her to us after everything you did.'

Her words are hitting me too fast; I can't comprehend them. How can months of my life have been a lie? What about every moment we shared together, every laugh and cuddle and smile? What about every time we made love and kissed each other tenderly? Was it all really an act? I feel sick to my stomach as I try to grasp at reality, but Alex remains impassive.

'Remember Evie, Darcy? That girl you thought Alex cheated on you with. That was me. He changed my name on his phone every few months to avoid suspicion. Alex has been in on this the entire time. He's been mine all along.' She's laughing between sentences. 'Oh, and your wedding dress? That awful thing you'd picked from the bridal shop. I took it. You really thought you were going to marry him? You fool.'

I look at her with her tousled blonde hair, those immense grey eyes and that hair-raising smile she gives me as she tells me things that break my world apart. Everything I thought I knew isn't real. It's all fake, invented. What kind of psychopath would go to these lengths?

I look at Alex, horrifying myself with my ache to ask him if any of it was real. Needing to believe that some part of him had actually loved me, that it wasn't all put on. I open my mouth to speak, but no words come out.

'Darcy, the paramedics are asking for you,' Rob says gently from behind me. I don't know how long he's been standing there or what he's heard, but I feel the humiliation creeping up my spine.

How have I been so naive? How did I let someone like Alex into my life like that? I don't have the time to think about it now though. Rob is pulling me away from them, the incessant ring of Claire's laughter following after us.

I'm scared to death as we make our way back across the sand to the paramedics with my baby. I don't want to see her frail, lifeless body. That will tip me over the edge. I can't handle it. I'm so close to falling apart already.

When I can eventually bring myself to look over to my baby, the paramedics are removing the sodden clothes she's in. She's wrapped in a foil blanket, a bag valve mask placed securely over her face. Hope sparks inside me. They wouldn't be doing this if she was dead.

'Is she okay?' I whisper so quietly I don't think anyone can hear me.

One of the paramedics carries my baby over to where Rob and I are standing. I can hardly see her over the layers of blankets she's curled up in.

'Do you want to meet your daughter, Darcy?' she says, lowering her arms so that I can see her properly.

Water droplets cling to her hair, falling down her precious little face. She's fast asleep, her wet eyelashes sticking to her cherubic red cheeks. I can see the rapid rise and fall of her chest and in that moment, that's all that matters. She's alive.

Before I clamber into the back of the ambulance, I look back out to sea. It's only a matter of time before the sailing boat disappears completely. This eerie doomed harbour the locals have dubbed the 'graveyard' for ships has claimed another vessel. If I believed in folklore, I'd almost say the mermaid who cursed these shores before she died brewed the storm tonight to help me get my daughter back. I'm so convinced by it I swear I hear the sweet sound of her singing through the whistling winds.

En route to the hospital, my baby's fingers wrap tightly around mine and I make a silent promise to her that I will never let any harm come to her ever again.

CHAPTER 28

Lily. I decide to call her Lily, after the July birth flower. Not because of how she emerged from the water that night but because in Buddhism, water lilies symbolize rebirth. The petals close at night and reopen come morning. In a strange way I feel like that's exactly what's happened to my relationship with Lily. It was closed for a dark, awful period of time, but as soon as she was back in my arms, it opened up again and flourished beautifully.

Lily and I were given the opportunity to meet each other again, to start anew. Mother and daughter reconnecting. She was horrifyingly unwell when she got to the hospital and started immediate treatment for malnutrition. Her body was weak and floppy; she couldn't feed and had terrible stomach issues. It took us some time and a lot of help from midwives and nurses, but eventually we got her latching onto me. Once she started feeding consistently and my milk started producing again, the change in her was breathtaking. She was like a different baby. Each day her dainty, featherlight body gained a little more weight, the doctors monitoring her progress closely.

I try my best to never leave her side, petrified that if I do, something terrible will happen to her again. Cora visits daily and I take that time to wash the grime of each day away beneath the lukewarm dribble of the hospital shower. It's an unsatisfying race, leaving a soapy residue on my skin each time. The other girls visit too, bringing in food and books. Anything to keep me occupied while Lily sleeps, though I never tell them I can't take my eyes from her. I could stare at her all day long.

I'm still waiting to hear an outcome on my penalty for the hit and run in Australia. It's like a heavy cloud hanging over my head, constantly threatening to rupture over everything so fragile and new. Arthur seems to think he'll be able to get me off lightly considering what happened in Australia. He says the statute of limitations has passed, though I can't bring myself to believe him yet. I can see why he's so good at his job now, though. He's been working day and night to help me, keeping me under his wing at all times.

Alex and Claire haven't been so lucky. They're both in jail, and there's talk of a seven-year sentence for both of them, but only time will tell. Right now, the only thing that matters to me is being there for my daughter while she grows stronger. I'm painfully aware that it can be snatched away from me at any given moment, so I take nothing for granted.

I didn't think I'd hear from Rob again once the case was closed. I'd assumed he'd done his job and that he'd be off on the next big adventure in his budding career, but he visits me every week. He's never late. Besides Cora, he's the most dependable person in my life. We haven't brought up what happened between us the night we found Lily, how our lips had grazed, and we'd felt a passion so intense it could have stopped my heart. There's nothing to say about it, but it's always there, lingering in the back of my mind. Maybe one day there will be time to give whatever it is between us some attention, but right now all I have time and space for in my heart is my daughter.

EPILOGUE

Claire

A seven-year sentence isn't that long.

She'd expected far worse, if she were being honest. Alex isn't thrilled, but he'll get over it, and it won't be that hard for them to find Darcy again once they get out. Not with Cora there, watching Darcy's every move.

Poor, naïve little Darcy. Still letting the wrong people into her life.

Claire marvels at the carelessness of the police force. How had they not been able to connect Cora to them yet? The way she's seamlessly slotted her way into Darcy's life as her new best friend makes her laugh. She is the best sister-in-law Claire could ever ask for.

She also wonders how, after all this time, she hasn't been linked to the murders of her parents or Jessica. She can't stop the insatiable need to kill, and it's even more thrilling getting away with it. She should have murdered Darcy when she had the chance. Next time.

* * *

They'll be back. They have seven years to come up with a better plan. Who knows, she may even be able to escape before the seven years is up. She's been put in a psych ward, which, she thinks with a twisted smile playing at her lips, is much easier to escape from than a prison.

THE END

ACKNOWLEDGEMENTS

G.D. Wright — not only are you a fabulous sounding board, but my book also wouldn't be here without you. Had you not sent through Joffe's link for thriller submissions, my novel wouldn't be where it is today. I'm eternally grateful.

Secondly to Kate Lyall Grant, Joffe's publishing director, for seeing the potential in my novel and fighting its corner, sailing it through to where it is today. I appreciate you more than you'll ever know. To Kate Ballard and Tara Loder too, for your fine attention to detail, helping chisel this book into what it is today. To subagent Lorella, who fell in love with my book enough to take it to London Book Fair.

I'd also like to thank my husband, my very own Gardening Geek, who has been more than patient with me for slinking off every night after the boys have gone to sleep so I could carry on writing. I promise you a fabulous date night after this book has been released and at least a week of uninterrupted cuddles before I dive into the next writing project!

Thank you to my sons, Felix and Chester, too young to know it now, but they make my world unequivocally better in every single way. Everything I do is for you.

And Dad. Two weeks before you passed away, two weeks before my youngest son was born, I thought to myself: I should send this manuscript to my dad.

I don't know why I never did. Busy, I guess, rolling around nine months pregnant in the blistering sun that gave me cankles.

You used to read everything I wrote. You were my biggest cheerleader and always believed in me. That's why this book is dedicated to you. I just wish I could turn back time and send these pages to you. I wish you could've read even a snippet of the book that finally made my lifelong dream become reality. I wish you could've met your grandsons and son-in-law, and I wish you could've walked me down the aisle in May 2025. It was the one thing that always, always meant the world to me. So when that was no longer possible, dedicating this book to you became my way of eternalizing you. You passed too soon and there will be a constant chasm in my heart because of it.

Thank you to everyone who follows and supports me on my bookstagram page @boho_bookworm. You know who you are. I see you. And I appreciate you.

For everyone who buys my book, you're making a lifelong dream come true. So thank you to you, reader. I'm filled with gratitude.

THE JOFFE BOOKS STORY

We began in 2014 when Jasper agreed to publish his mum's much-rejected romance novel and it became a bestseller.

Since then we've grown into the largest independent publisher in the UK. We're extremely proud to publish some of the very best writers in the world, including Joy Ellis, Faith Martin, Caro Ramsay, Helen Forrester, Simon Brett and Robert Goddard. Everyone at Joffe Books loves reading and we never forget that it all begins with the magic of an author telling a story.

We are proud to publish talented first-time authors, as well as established writers whose books we love introducing to a new generation of readers.

We won Trade Publisher of the Year at the Independent Publishing Awards in 2023 and Best Publisher Award in 2024 at the People's Book Prize. We have been shortlisted for Independent Publisher of the Year at the British Book Awards for the last five years and were shortlisted for the Diversity and Inclusivity Award at the 2022 Independent Publishing Awards. In 2023 we were shortlisted for Publisher of the Year at the RNA Industry Awards, and in 2024 we were shortlisted at the CWA Daggers for the Best Crime and Mystery Publisher.

We built this company with your help, and we love to hear from you, so please email us about absolutely anything bookish at feedback@joffebooks.com.

If you want to receive free books every Friday and hear about all our new releases, join our mailing list here: www.joffebooks.com/freebooks.

And when you tell your friends about us, just remember: it's pronounced Joffe as in coffee or toffee!